THE WONDERFUL GARDEN

The Nesbit Books

And through it, in trailing velvet, came a lady.—P. 392.

THE WONDERFUL GARDEN

By
E. NESBIT

Illustrated by
H. R. MILLAR

ERNEST BENN LIMITED
LONDON

COWARD – McCANN INC
NEW YORK

First re-issued in this edition 1959
Published by Ernest Benn Limited
Bouverie House · Fleet Street · London · EC4
and Coward-McCann Inc
210 Madison Avenue · New York 16 · NY

Printed in Great Britain

TO
CECILY · KATHLEEN AND
MAVIS CARTER
WITH LOVE FROM
E · NESBIT

Crowlink · Sussex · 1911

CONTENTS

CONTENTS

LIST OF ILLUSTRATIONS

CHAPTER I

THE BEGINNING

IT was Caroline's birthday, and she had had some very pleasant presents. There was a blotting-book of blue leather (at least, it looked like leather), with pink and purple roses painted on it, from her younger sister Charlotte; and a paint-box — from her brother Charles—as good as new.

'I've hardly used it at all,' he said, 'and it's much nicer than anything I could have bought you with my own money, and I've wiped all the paints clean.'

'It's lovely,' said Caroline; 'and the beautiful brushes, too!"

'Real fitch,' said Charles proudly. 'They've got points like needles.'

'Just like,' said Caroline, putting them one after the other into her mouth, and then holding them up to the light.

Besides the paint-box and the blotting-book,

a tin-lined case had come from India, with a set of carved chess-men from father, and from mother some red and blue scarves, and, most glorious of imaginable gifts, a leopard-skin.

'They will brighten the play-room a little,' said mother in her letter.   And they did.

Aunt Emmeline had given a copy of *Sesame and Lilies*, which is supposed to be good for girls, though a little difficult when you are only twelve; and Uncle Percival had presented a grey leather pocket-book and an olive-wood paper-knife with 'Sorrento' on the handle. The cook and housemaid had given needle-book and pin-cushion; and Miss Peckitt, the little dressmaker who came to the house to make the girls' dresses, brought a small, thin book bound in red, with little hard raised spots like pin-heads all over it, and hoped Miss Caroline would be kind enough to accept.

'The book,' said Miss Peckitt, 'was mine when a child, and my dear mother also, as a young girl, was partial to it.   Please accept it, Miss, with my humble best wishes.'

'Thanks most awfully,' said Caroline, embracing her.

'Thank you,' said Miss Peckitt, straightening her collar after the sudden kiss.   'Quite welcome, though unexpected; I *had* a bit of southernwood given to me this morning,

which, you will find in the book, means a
surprise.'

And it did, for the book was *The Language
of Flowers*. And really that book was the beginning of this story, or, at least, if it wasn't that
book, it was the other book. But that comes
later.

'It's ripping,' said Caroline. 'I do like it
being red.'

The last present was a very large bunch of
marigolds and a halfpenny birthday-card, with
a gold anchor and pink clasped hands on it,
from the boy who did the boots and knives.

'We'll decorate our room,' said Charlotte,
'in honour of your birthday, Caro. We've
got lots of coloured things, and I'll borrow
cook's Sunday scarf. It's pink and purple
shot silk—a perfect dream! I'll fly!'

She flew; and on her return they decorated
their room.

You will perhaps wonder why they were so
anxious to decorate their room with coloured
things. It was because the house they lived
in had so little colour in it that it was more
like a print of a house in a book—all black and
white and grey, you know—than like a house
for real people to live in. It was a pale, neat,
chilly house. There was, for instance, white
straw matting on the floors instead of warm,

coloured carpets; and on the stairs a sort of pale grey cocoa-nut matting. The window curtains were of soft cotton, and were palely lavender; they had no damask richness, no gay flowery patterns. The walls were not papered, but distempered in clean pale tints, and the general effect was rather like that of a very superior private hospital. The fact that the floors were washed every week with Sanitas gave a pleasing wood-yard scent. There were no coloured pictures in the house—only brown copies of great paintings by Raphael and Velazquez and people like that.

The Stanmore children lived here because their father and mother were in India and their other relations in New Zealand — all except old Uncle Charles, who was their mother's uncle and who had quarrelled with, or been quarrelled with by, their father and mother in bygone years.

The owners of the house, whose name was Sandal, were relations of some sort—cousins, perhaps. Though they were called Uncle Percival and Aunt Emmeline they were not really those relations.

There was one thing about this so-called aunt and uncle—they were never cross and seldom unjust. Their natures seemed to be pale and calm like the colours of their house;

and though the children had meat every day
for dinner, Mr. and Miss Sandal never had
anything but vegetables, and vegetables are
said to be calming.

Now India is a highly-coloured country, as
you may have noticed in pictures, and the
Stanmore children felt faded in that grey
house. And that is why they loved colour so
much, and made so much fuss about the
leopard-skin and the Indian embroideries and
the marigold flowers and the little old red
book and the wreath of gold forget-me-nots
outside it encircling the words *Language of
Flowers*.

'When Aunt Emmeline sees how beautiful
it is she'll want to have the whole house
scarved and leoparded, I shouldn't wonder,'
said Charlotte, hanging the pink scarf over a
picture of a blind girl sitting on an orange,
which is called 'Hope.'

'I don't suppose so,' said Caroline. 'I
asked her once what old Uncle Charles's house
was like, that mother said was so beautiful,
and she said it was far too full of things, and
somewhat imperfectly ventilated.'

'It's a pity Uncle Charles was quarrelled
with, *I* think,' said Charlotte. 'I shouldn't at
all have minded going to stay with him. I
expect really he likes nice little girls. I

wonder what the row was all about, and why
they didn't all kiss and be friends before the
sun went down upon—like *we're* told to?'

I cannot tell you what the row was about,
for I know no more than you do, or than
Charlotte did. And you must have noticed
that grown-up people's quarrels are very large
and most mysterious. When you quarrel with
your brothers or sisters it is always about some
simple thing—as, for instance, who left your
paint-brushes in the water, or who forgot your
Water Babies out in the hayfield, or whether
it was you who upset the gum over your
brother's map, or walked on the doll's house
sofa that day when you all upset it scrapping,
and the furniture was put back in a hurry.
Anyhow, your quarrels are soon over, because
quarrelling is so uncomfortable, and, besides,
you have most likely been taught, as Charlotte
had, that you must not let the sun go down
upon your wrath. But with grown-up people
it is different. They seem sometimes to have
forgotten about the sun not going down, and
their quarrels last on and on and on for weeks
and months and years, till you would think that
they must have forgotten what the fuss was all
about. But they don't, and when Aunt Jane
comes to tea you will still hear fragments about
how Uncle William behaved, and what a pity

it was about Edward acting as he did. If the grown-ups notice you, they will tell you to run away and play. You will never hear what the quarrel was about, and if you did you wouldn't understand, and if you understood you'd probably think it was a silly fuss about nothing, and wonder how they could have kept it up all these years—for it is as likely as not that Uncle William did that unfortunate behaving of his many many years ago, and that Edward acted in that extraordinary way long before you were born. The only thing you can find out for certain about these grown-up quarrels is that they seem to be always about money, or about people having married people that their relations didn't want them to marry.

No doubt you will have noticed all this, and you will perhaps have noticed as well that if you suddenly speak of a person, that person very often turns up almost at once. So that when Charlotte said, ' I wish Uncle Charles had not been quarrelled with,' it would have occasioned you no surprise if Uncle Charles had suddenly walked up to the front door.

But this did not happen. But some one walked up to the front door. It was the postman.

Caroline rushed out to see if there were any more birthday-cards for her. It was now the beginning of the summer holidays, but some of the girls at the High School might possibly have remembered her birthday. So she rushed out, and rushed into Aunt Emmeline, who must have been hurt, because afterwards Caroline's head was quite sore where it had banged against Aunt Emmeline's mother-of-pearl waist-buckle. But Aunt Emmeline only said :

'Gently, my child, gently,' which, as Caroline said later, was worse than being scolded, and made you feel as if you were elephants. And there weren't any birthday-cards for her, either.

All the letters were for Miss Sandal. And just as the leopard-skin had been spread on the floor she came to the door of the children's room with one of the letters in her hand.

' I have a surprise for you,' she said.

' Do come in and sit down,' said Caroline. That was another nice thing about Aunt Emmeline. She always treated the children's room as though it really was the children's room, and expected to be treated as a visitor when she came into it. She never sat down without being asked.

' Thank you,' she now said, and sat down. ' The surprise is that you are going into the country for your holidays.'

There was a silence, only broken by Charles, and he only said :

'We needn't have bothered about decorating the room.'

'Oh, is this decoration? Miss Sandal asked, as though she thought pink scarves might get on to picture-frames and leopard-skins on to floors, or marigolds on to mantel-pieces, just by accident or untidiness.

'I may say that I have known for some time that this was likely to happen—but the letter which has just come makes everything settled. You are to go the day after to-morrow.'

'But *where*?' Caroline asked. And Miss Sandal then uttered the memorable and unusual words, 'Did you ever hear of your Great-Uncle Charles?'

'The one that was quarrelled with?' said Charles.

'I did not know you knew of that. Yes. The quarrel is now at an end, and he has invited you to spend your holidays at the Manor House.'

There was a deep silence, due to the children's wanting to shout 'Hooray!' and feeling that it would not be manners.

'I thought you'd be pleased,' said Miss Sandal. 'It is considered a very beautiful house, and stands in a park.'

'Are you going, Aunt Emmeline?' Caroline asked.

'No, dear. Only you children are invited. You will be quiet and gentle, won't you, and try to remember that your Great-Uncle Charles is a quiet student, and not used to children. You will have a great deal of liberty, and I hope you will use it well. You have never been on a visit before without—without some one to remind you of—to tell you——'

'Oh, that's all right, Aunt Emmie,' said Charlotte. 'But who'll sew on our buttons and mend our stockings?'

'There is a housekeeper, of course,' said Miss Sandal. 'I shall pack your things to-morrow; and if you will decide what toys you would like to take with you, I will pack them too.'

'Yes,' said Caroline, still feeling it polite not to look pleased. 'Thank you, Aunt Emmeline.'

'I hope he'll like us,' said Charles. 'He ought to when we're all named after him. I say, couldn't we all pretend to be called something else? It's bad enough now; but it'll be awful when there's an Uncle Charles in the house as well as all us. I say, Aunt Emmie, are we to call him "Great"?'

'He means Great-Uncle Charles,' Caroline explained. 'I expect we'd better call him plain "Uncle," hadn't we?'

'He wouldn't like being called "plain,"' said Charles.

'Don't be silly,' said Caroline, still a prey to politeness. 'He won't mind what little boys call him.'

'I bet he would if I called him the sort of things you call me. Silly yourself!'

'Children! children!' said Miss Sandal. 'I thought you'd be so pleased.'

'We *are*,' said Caroline. 'Only won't you be rather dull without us? That's why we don't seem so glad as you seem to think we ought to seem.'

Miss Sandal smiled, which made her long, whitey-brown-paper-coloured face look much prettier.

'Thank you, Caroline. Your Uncle Percival and I are also about to take a holiday. We are going to Switzerland, the Italian Lakes, and to Venice. You may be as happy as you like without worrying about us.'

And it was then that the three children felt that politeness and sincerity might meet in a heartfelt shout of 'Hooray!'

'I shall take the leopard-skin and all my other presents,' said Caroline.

'And I shall take the draughts and the spilikins,' said Charlotte.

'Mother said there were draughts made of

ebony and ivory with lions' heads and mother-of-pearl spilikins in the drawing-room when she was a little girl,' Caroline reminded her.

'I shall take every single thing I've got, and my cricket set as well,' said Charles.

12   THE WONDERFUL GARDEN   CH.

and Aunt Emmeline most likely wondered
what it was all about. Perhaps she didn't.
She was very kind. Anyway she must have
known when, as the cab drew up in front of
the door, the three children presented themselves before her with bouquets in their hands.
They all three began at once.

Then Charlotte, Caroline, and Charles
with a hasty, breathless presentation—

It means literally,' she said, 'to cause

CHAPTER II

THE MANOR HOUSE

You can imagine the packing, the running up
and down stairs, the difficulty of choosing what
to leave behind—for that is, after all, what it
comes to when you are going away, much
more than the difficulty of choosing what you
will take with you. Miss Sandal, surrounded
by heaps of toys and books—far too large to
have been got into the trunks, even if all the
clothes had been left out—at last settled the
question by promising to send on, by post or
by carrier, any little thing which had been left
behind and which the children should all agree
was necessary to their happiness. 'And the
leopard-skin takes so much room,' she said,
'and I believe there are wild-beast-skins as
well as stuffed animals at your uncle's house.'
So they left the leopard-skin behind too.
There was a good deal of whispered talk and
mystery and consulting of books that morning,

13

and Aunt Emmeline most likely wondered what it was all about. But perhaps she didn't. She was very calm. Anyway, she must have known when, as the cab drew up in front of the door, the three children presented themselves before her with bouquets in their hands.

'They are for you,' said all three at once.

Then Charlotte presented Aunt Emmeline with a bunch of balm from the garden.

'It means sympathy,' she said; 'because, of course; it's nice of you to say so, but we know that those geography places you're going to can't be *really* as nice as Uncle Charles's.'

Charles's bouquet was of convolvulus. 'It means dead hope,' he explained; 'but it's very pretty, too. And here's this.' He suddenly presented a tiny cactus in a red pot. 'I bought it for you,' he said; 'it means, "Thou leavest not."'

'How charming of you!' said Aunt Emmeline, and turned to Caroline, who was almost hidden behind a huge bunch of ivy and marigolds.

'The ivy means friendship,' said Caroline, 'and the marigolds don't count. I only put them because they are so goldy-bright. But if they *must* count, then they mean cruelty— Fate's, you know, because you're not coming. And there's a purple pansy in among it somewhere, because that means, "I think of you."'

There was a good deal of whispered talk and mystery.

'Thank you very, very much,' said Aunt Emmeline. 'I can't tell you how pleased I am. It is very sweet of you all.'

This floral presentation gave a glow and glory to their departure. At the very last moment Caroline leaned out of the window to say:

'Oh, Aunt Emmeline, when Miss Peckitt comes to finish those muslin frocks that you're going to send us, *would* you try to manage to give her a Canterbury bell from me? She'll know what it means. But in case she doesn't, it's gratitude—in the book. And we'll put flowers in our letters expressing our feelings. Good-bye.'

Uncle Percival took them to the station and——

But why should I describe a railway journey? You know exactly what it is like. I will only say that it was very dusty, and so sunny that the children wanted the blinds down, only a very tailor-made lady with a cross little grey dog said 'No.' And you know how black your hands get in the train, and how gritty the cushions are, and how your faces get black too, though you are quite certain you haven't touched them with your hands. The one who got the little bit of the engine in its eye was Charles that time. But some one always gets it, because some one always puts its head out of the carriage window, no matter what the printed notices may say. You know all this. What you don't know is what happened at the junction where, carefully attended by the guard, they changed trains. They had to wait for some time, and when they had looked at the bookstall—which was small and dull, and almost entirely newspapers—they looked at the other people who had to wait too. Most of them were of dull appearance; but there was one tall gentleman who looked, they all agreed, exactly like Mr. Murdstone in *David Copperfield.*

'And he's got David with him, too,' said Charlotte. 'Look!'

The Murdstone gentleman, having bought the *Athenæum*, the *Spectator*, and a sevenpenny reprint of the works of Marcus Aurelius, had gone to a bench on which sat a sulky-looking boy. He spoke to the boy, and the boy answered. And the gentleman walked off.

'He's gone to have a bun all by himself,' said Charles. 'Selfish pig!'

'I say, let's sit down on the bench. You sit next him, Charles. Perhaps he'd talk to us.' This was Caroline's idea.

They did; and 'he,' who was, of course, the sulky boy, did speak to them. But not till

'You sit next him, Charles.'

they'd spoken to him. It was Charles who did it.

'Are you going on in this next train?' he said, 'because, if you are, we can get into your carriage. We shall be company for you.'

'What's the good?' said the boy, unexpectedly; 'it'll only make it worse afterwards.'

'What worse?'

'The being alone.'

'Well, anyhow,' said Caroline, coming round to sit on the other side of him, 'you're not alone now. What's up? Who is *he*?'

'He's a schoolmaster. I should have thought you could have seen that.'

'We thought he was like Mr. Murdstone.'

'He is,' said the strange boy; 'exactly.'

'Oh,' said Charlotte joyously, 'then you've read *David*. I say!'

They were all delighted. There is no bond like the bond of having read and liked the same books. A tide of friendliness swept over the party, and when they found that he had also read *Alice in Wonderland*, *Wild Animals I Have Known*, and *Hereward the Wake*, as well as E. Nesbit's stories for children in the *Strand Magazine*, they all felt that they had been friends for years.

'But tell us all about it, quick, before *he* comes back,' urged Charles. 'Perhaps we

B

could help you — bring you jam tarts and apples with a rope ladder or something. We are yours to the death—you won't forget that, will you? And what's your name? And where do you live? And where are you going? Tell us all about it, quick!' he urged.

Then out it all came. The strange boy's name was Rupert Wix, and he was at a school —not half bad the school was—and old Filon —he was the classical chap—was going to take Rupert and two other chaps to Wales for the holidays—and now the other chaps had got measles, and so had old Filon. And old Mug's brother—his name wasn't really Mug, of course, but Macpherson, and the brother was the Rev. William Macpherson—yes, that was him, the Murdstone chap—he was going to take Rupert to his beastly school in the country.

'And there won't be any other chaps,' said Rupert, 'because, of course, it's vac—just old Mug's beastly brother and me, for days and weeks and years—until the rest of the school comes back. I wish I was dead!'

'Oh, don't!' said Caroline; 'how dreadful! They've got scarlet fever at *our* school, that's why our holidays have begun so early. Do cheer up! Have some nut-chocolate.' A brief struggle with her pocket ended in the appearance of a packet—rather worn at the edges —the parting gift of Aunt Emmeline.

'Is old Mug's brother as great a pig as he looks?' Charles asked, through Rupert's 'Thank-yous.

'*Much* greater,' said Rupert cordially.

'Then I know what I'd do,' said Charlotte. 'I'd run away from school, like a hero in a book, and have some adventures, and then go home to my people.'

'That's just it,' said Rupert. 'I haven't got anywhere to run to. My people are in India. That's why I have to have my hols at a beastly school. I'd rather be a dog in a kennel—much.'

'Oh, so would I,' said Charlotte. 'But then I'd almost rather be a dog than anything. They're such dears. I do hope there'll be dogs where we're going to.'

'Where's that?' Rupert asked, more out of politeness than because he wanted to know.

'I'll write it down for you,' said Caroline, and did, on a page of the new grey leather pocket-book Uncle Percival had given her. 'Here, put it in your pocket, and you write and tell us what happens. Perhaps it won't be so bad. Here he comes—quick!'

She stuffed the paper into Rupert's jacket pocket as the tall Murdstone - like figure advanced towards them. The three children left Rupert and walked up the platform.

'I'm glad we gave him the chock,' said Charles, and the word was hardly out of his mouth before a cold, hard hand touched his shoulder (and his cheek as he turned quickly) and a cold, hard voice said:

'Little boy, I do not allow those under my charge to accept sweetmeats from strange children, especially dirty ones.'

And with that the Murdstone gentleman pushed the chocolate into Charles's hand and went back to his prey.

'Beast! Brute! Beast!' said Charles.

After this it was mere forlorn-hopishness and die-on-the-barricade courage, as Charlotte said later, that made the children get into the same carriage with Rupert and his captor. They might as well have saved themselves the trouble. The Murdstone gentleman put Rupert in a corner and sat in front of him with a newspaper very widely opened. And at the next station he changed carriages, taking Rupert by the hand as though he had been, as Charles put it, 'any old baby-girl.'

But as Rupert went out Caroline whispered to him:

'You get some borage and eat it,' and Rupert looked 'Why?'

'Borage gives courage, you know,' she said, too late, for he was whisked away before he could hear her, and they saw him no more.

They talked about him, though, till the train stopped at East Farleigh, which was their station.

There was a waggonette to meet them and a cart for their luggage, and the coachman said he would have known Caroline anywhere, because she was so like her mother, whom he remembered when he was only gardener's boy; and this made every one feel pleasantly as though they were going home.

It was a jolly drive, across the beautiful bridge and up the hill and through the village and along a mile or more of road, where the green hedges were powdered with dust, and tufts of hay hung, caught by the brambles from the tops of passing waggons. These bits of hay made one feel that one really was in the country—not just the bare field-country of the suburb where Aunt Emmeline and Uncle Percival lived, where one could never get away from the sight of red and yellow brick villas.

And then the boy who was driving the luggage cart got down and opened a gate, and they drove through and along a woodland road where ferns and blossoming brambles grew under trees very green and not dusty at all.

From the wood they came to a smooth, green, grassy park dotted with trees, and in the middle of it, standing in a half-circle of chestnuts and sycamores, was the house.

It was a white, bow-windowed house, with a balcony at one end, and a porch, with white pillars and two broad steps; and the grass grew right up to the very doorsteps, which is unusual and very pretty. There was not a flower to be seen—only grass. The waggonette, of course, kept to the drive, which ran round to a side door—half glass.

And here Mrs. Wilmington the housekeeper received them. She was a pale, thin person—quite kind, but not at all friendly.

'I don't think she has time to think of anything but being ladylike,' said Charlotte. 'She ought to wear mittens.'

This was while they were washing their hands for tea.

'I suppose if you're a housekeeper you have to be careful people don't think you're a servant,' said Caroline. 'What drivel it is! I say, isn't this something like?'

She was looking out of the bow window of the big room spread with a blue rose-patterned carpet, at the green glory of the park, lying in the sun like another and much more beautiful carpet with a pattern of trees on it.

Then they went down to tea. Such a house —full of beautiful things! But the children hadn't time to look at them then, and I haven't time to tell you about them now.

I will only say that the dining-room was perfect in its Turkey-carpet-and-mahogany comfort, and that it had red curtains.

'Will you please pour the tea, Miss Caroline?' said Mrs. Wilmington, and went away.

'I'm glad we haven't got to have tea with *her*, anyway,' said Charles.

And then Uncle Charles came in. He was not at all what they expected. He could not have been what anybody expected. He was more shadowy than you would think anybody could be. He was more like a lightly printed photograph from an insufficiently exposed and imperfectly developed negative than anything else I can think of. He was as thin and pale as Mrs. Wilmington, but there was nothing hard or bony about him. He was soft as a shadow—his voice, his hand, his eyes.

'And what are your names?' he said, when he had shaken hands all round.

Caroline told him, and Charles added:

'How funny of you not to know, uncle, when we're all named after you!

'Caroline, Charles, Charlotte,' he repeated. 'Yes, I suppose you are.   I like my tea very weak, please, with plenty of milk and no sugar.'

Caroline nervously clattered among the silver and china.   She was not used to pouring out real tea for long-estranged uncles.

'I hope you will enjoy yourselves here,' said Uncle Charles, taking his cup; 'and excuse me if I do not always join you at meals.   I am engaged on a work—I mean I am writing a book,' he told them.

'What fun!' said every one but Caroline, who had just burnt herself with the urn; and Charles added:

'What's it about?'

'Magic,' said the Uncle, 'or, rather, a branch of magic.   I thought of calling it "A Brief Consideration of the Psychological and Physiological Part played by Suggestion in So-called Magic."'

'It sounds interesting; at least I know it would if I knew anything about it,' said Caroline, trying to be both truthful and polite.

'It's very long,' said Charles.   'How would you get all that printed on the book's back?'

'And don't say "so-called,"' said Charlotte. 'It looks as if you didn't believe in magic.'

'If people thought I believed in magic they wouldn't read my books,' said Uncle Charles. 'They'd think I was mad, you know.'

'But why?' Charlotte asked. '*We* aren't mad, and we believe in it. Do you know any spells, uncle? We want awfully to try a spell. It's the dream of our life. It is, really.'

The ghost of a smile moved the oyster-shell-coloured face of Uncle Charles.

'So you take an interest in magic?' he said. 'We shall have at least that in common.'

'Of course we do. Every one does, only they're afraid to say so. Even servants do. They tell fortunes and dreams. Did you ever read about the Amulet, or the Phœnix, or the Words of Power? Bread and butter, please,' said Charles.

'You have evidently got up the subject,' said Uncle Charles. 'Who told you about Words of Power?'

'It's in *The Amulet*,' said Charlotte. 'I say, uncle, do tell us some spells.'

'Ah!' Uncle Charles sighed. 'I am afraid the day of spells has gone by—except, perhaps, for people of your age. *She* could have told you spells enough—if all the stories of her are true.'

He pointed to a picture over the mantelpiece—a fair-haired, dark-eyed lady in a ruff.

'She was an ancestress of ours,' he said; 'she was wonderfully learned.'

'What became of her?' Charlotte asked.

'They burned her for a witch. It is sometimes a mistake to know too much,' said the Uncle.

This contrasted agreeably with remembered remarks of Uncle Percival and Aunt Emmeline, such as 'Knowledge is power' and 'There is no darkness but ignorance.'

The children looked at the lady in the white ruff and black velvet dress, and they liked her face.

'What a shame!' they said.

'Yes,' said the Uncle. 'You see she's resting her hand on two books. There's a tradition that those books contain her magic secret. I used to look for the books when I was young, but I never found them—I never found them.' He sighed again.

'*We'll* look, uncle,' said Charlotte eagerly. 'We *may* look, mayn't we? Young heads are better than old shoulders, aren't they? At least, that sounds rude, but you know I mean two heads are better than yours—— No, that's not it. Too many cooks spoil the—— No, that's not it either. We wouldn't spoil anything. Too many hands make light work. *That's* what I meant.'

'They burned her for a witch.'

'Your meaning was plain from the first,' said the Uncle, finishing his tea and setting down his cup—a beautiful red and blue and gold one—very different from Aunt Emmeline's white crockery. 'Certainly you may look. But you'll respect the field of your search.'

'Uncle,' said Caroline, from behind the silver tea-tray, 'your house is the most lovely, splendid, glorious, beautiful house we've ever seen, and——'

'We wouldn't hurt a hair of its head,' said Charles.

Again the Uncle smiled. 'Well, well,' he said, and faded away like a shadow.

'We'll find those books or perish,' said Charlotte firmly.

'Ra-*ther*,' said Charles.

'We'll look for them, anyway,' said Caroline. 'Now let's go and pick an ivy leaf and put it in a letter for poor dear Aunt Emmeline. I'll tell you something.'

'Well?' said the others.

'This is the sort of house I've always dreamed of when it said luxury—in books, you know.'

'Me too,' said Charlotte.

'*And* me,' said Charles.

CHAPTER III

THE WONDERFUL GARDEN

It was very glorious to wake up the next morning in enormous soft beds—four-posted, with many-folded silk hangings, and shiny furniture that reflected the sunlight as dark mirrors might do. And breakfast was nice, with different sorts of things to eat, in silver dishes with spirit-lamps under them,—bacon and sausages and scrambled eggs, and as much toast and marmalade as you wanted; not just porridge and apples, as at Aunt Emmeline's. There were tea and coffee and hot milk. They all chose hot milk.

'I feel,' said Caroline, pouring it out of a big silver jug with little bits of ivory between the handle and the jug to keep the handle from getting too hot, 'I feel that we're going to enjoy every second of the time we're here.'

'Rather,' said Charles, through sausage. 'Isn't Uncle Charles a dear,' he added more

34

distinctly. ' I dreamed about him last night
—that he painted his face out of the paint-box
I gave Caro, and then we blew him out with
the bellows to make him fatter."

' And did it ? ' Caroline asked.

' He burst,' said Charles briefly, ' and turned
into showers of dead leaves.'

There was an interval of contented silence.
Then—

' What shall we do first ? ' said Charles.
And his sisters with one voice answered,
' Explore, of course.'

And they finished their breakfast to dreams
of exploring every hole and corner of the
wonderful house.

But when they rang to have breakfast
taken away it was Mrs. Wilmington who
appeared.

' Your uncle desired me to say that he
thinks it's healthy for you to spend some hours
in the hopen—open air,' she said, speaking in
a small distinct voice. ' He himself takes the
air of an afternoon. So will you please all go
out at once,' she ended in a burst of naturalness,
' and not come 'ome, home, till one o'clock.'

' Where are we to go ? ' asked Charlotte,
not pleased.

' Not beyond the park and grounds,' said the
housekeeper. ' And,' she added reluctantly,

'Mr. Charles said if there was any pudding you liked to mention——'

A brief consultation ended in, 'Treacle hat, please'; and when Mrs. Wilmington had minced off, they turned to each other and said :

'The brick!'

'The old duck!' and

'Something like an uncle.'

Then they went out, as they had been told to do.   And they took off their shoes and stockings, which they had not been told to do —but, on the other hand, had not been told *not* to—and walked barefooted in the grass still cool and dewy under the trees.   And they put on their boots again and explored the park, and explored the stable-yard, where a groom was rubbing bright the silver buckles of the harness and whistling as he rubbed.   They explored the stables and the harness-room and the straw-loft and the hay-loft.   And then they went back to the park and climbed trees—a little way, because though they had always known that they would climb trees if ever they had half a chance, they had not, till now, had any chance at all.

And all the while they were doing all this they were looking—at the back of their minds, even when they weren't doing it with the part you think with—for the garden.

And there wasn't any garden!

That was the plain fact that they had to face after two hours of sunshine and green out-of-doors.

'And I'm certain mother said there was a garden,' Caroline said, sitting down suddenly on the grass; 'a beautiful garden and a terrace.'

'Perhaps the Uncle didn't like it, and he's had it made not garden again—"Going back to Nature" that would be, like Aunt Emmeline talks about,' Charles suggested.

'And it's dreadful if there's no garden,' said Caroline, 'because of the flowers we were going to send in letters. Wild flowers don't have such deep meanings, I'm certain.'

'And besides we haven't seen any wild flowers,' said Caroline. 'Oh, bother!'

'Never mind,' Charles said, 'think of exploring the house—and finding the book, perhaps. We'll ask the Elegant One, when we go in, why there isn't a garden.'

'We won't wait till then,' said Charlotte; 'let's go and ask that jolly man who's polishing the harness. He looked as if he wouldn't mind us talking to him.'

'It was him drove us yesterday,' Charles pointed out.

So they went as to an old friend. And

when they asked William why there wasn't a
garden he answered surprisingly and rather
indignantly :

'Ain't they shown you, Miss?   Not a
garden?   There ain't a garden to beat it here-
abouts.   Come on, I'll show you.'

And, still more surprisingly, he led the way
to the back door.

'We aren't to go indoors till dinner-time,'
said Caroline ; 'and besides, we *should* like to
see the garden—if there really is one.'

'Of course there is one, Miss,' said William.
'She'll never see you if you're quick.   She'll
be in her room by now—at her accounts and
things.   And the Master's never about in these
back parts in the morning.'

'I suppose it's a lock-up garden and he's
going to get the key,' said Charles in a
whisper.   But William wasn't.

He led them into a whitewashed passage
that had cupboards and larders opening out
of it and ended in a green baize door.   He
opened this, and there they were in the hall.

'Quick,' he said, and crossed it, unlatched
another door and held it open.   'Come in
quiet,' he said, and closed the door again.   And
there they all were in a little square room with
a stone staircase going down the very middle
of it, like a well.   There was a wooden railing

round three sides of the stairway, and nothing else in the room at all, except William and the children.

'A secret staircase,' said Charlotte. 'Oh, it can't be, really. How *lovely*!'

'I daresay it was a secret once,' said William, striking a match and lighting a candle that stood at the top of the stairs in a brass candlestick. 'You see there wasn't always these banisters, and you can see that ridge along the wall. My grandfather says it used to be boarded over and that's where the joists went. They'd have a trap-door or something over the stairway, I shouldn't be surprised.'

'But what's the stair for?—Where does it *go*? Are we going down?' the children asked.

'Yes, and sharp too. Nobody's supposed to go this way except the Master. But you'll not tell on me. I'll go first. Mind the steps, Miss. They're a bit wore at the edges, like.'

They minded the steps, going carefully down, following the blinking, winking, blue and yellow gleam of the candle.

There were not many steps.

'Straight ahead now,' said William, holding the candle up to show the groined roof of a long straight passage, built of stone, and with stone flags for the floor of it.

'How perfectly ripping!' said Charlotte

breathlessly. 'It *is* brickish of you to bring
us here. Where does it go to?'

'You wait a bit,' said William, and went on.
The passage ended in another flight of steps—
up this time,—and the steps ended in a door,
and when William had opened this every one
blinked and shut their eyes, for the doorway
framed green leaves with blue sky showing
through them, and——

''Ere's the garden,' said William; and here,
indeed, it was.

'There's another door the other end what
the gardeners go in and out of,' said William.
'I'll get you a key sometime.'

The door had opened into a sort of arch—
an arbour, for its entrance was almost veiled
by thick-growing shrubs.

'Oh, thank you,' said Caroline; 'but when
did they make this passage, and what for?'

'They made that passage when the folks in
the house was too grand to go through the
stable - yard and too lazy to go round,' said
William. 'There's no stable-yard way now,'
he added. 'So long! I must be getting back,
Miss. Don't you let on as I brought you
through.'

'Of course not,' every one said. Charles
added, 'But I didn't know the house was as
old as secret passages in history times.'

'It's any age you please,' said William;
'the back parts is.'

He went back through the door, and the
children went out through the leafy screen in
front, into the most beautiful garden that could
be, with a wall. I like unwalled gardens
myself, with views from the terraces. From
this garden you could see nothing but tall trees
and—the garden itself.

The lower half was a vegetable garden
arranged in squares with dwarf fruit-trees and
flower-borders round them, like the borders
round old-fashioned pocket-handkerchiefs.
Then about half-way up the garden came steps
—stone balustrades, a terrace, and beyond that
a flower garden with smooth green turf paths,
box-edged, a sundial in the middle, and in the
flower-beds flowers—more flowers than I could
give names to.

'How perfectly perfect!' Charlotte said.

'I do wish I'd brought out my *Language
Of*!' said Caroline.

'How awfully tidy everything is!' said
Charles in awe-struck tones.

It was.

There was nowhere an imperfect leaf, a
deformed bud, or a misshapen flower. Every
plant grew straight and strong, and with an
extraordinary evenness.

'They look like pictures of plants more than like real ones,' said Caroline quite truly.

An old gardener was sweeping the terrace steps, and gave the children 'Good morning.'

They gave it back, and stayed to watch him. It seemed polite to say something before turning away. So Caroline said :

'How beautifully everything grows here.'

'Ay,' said the old man, 'it do. Say perfect and you won't be far out.'

'It's very clever of you,' said Charlotte. 'Ill weeds don't grow in a single place in *your* garden.'

'I don't say as I don't do something,' said the old man, 'but seems as if there was a blessing on the place—everything thrives and grows just-so. It's the soil or the aspick, p'raps. I dunno. An' I've noticed things.'

'What things?' was the natural question.

'Oh, just things,' the gardener answered shortly, and swept away to the end of the long steps.

'I say'—Caroline went after him to do it—'I say, may we pick the flowers?'

'In moderation,' said the gardener, and went away.

'I wonder what he'd call moderation,' said Charles ; and they discussed this question so

'How beautifully everything grows here.'

earnestly that the dinner-bell rang before they had picked any flowers at all.

The gate at the end of the garden was open, and they went out that way. Over the gate was a stone with words and a date. They stopped to spell out the carved letters :

HERE BE DREAMES
1589
RESPICE FINEM.

Caroline copied the last two words in the grey-covered pocket-book; and when Mrs. Wilmington came in to carve the mutton, Caroline asked what the words meant.

'I never inquired,' said the housekeeper. 'It must be quite out of date now, whatever it meant once. But you must have been in the garden to see that. How did you get in?'

An awkward question. There was nothing for it but to say :

'By the secret passage.' And Charles said it.

'No one uses that but your uncle,' said Mrs. Wilmington, 'and you were requested to keep out of doors till dinner-time.'

She shut her mouth with a snap and went on carving.

'Sorry,' said Caroline.

'Granted,' said Mrs. Wilmington, but not

cordially; and having placed two slices of mutton on each plate went away.

'It *is* jolly having meals by ourselves,' said Charlotte; 'only I wish she wasn't cross.'

'We ought to be extra manner-y, I expect, when we're by ourselves,' said Caroline. 'May I pass you the salt, Charles?'

'No, you mayn't,' said Charles. 'Thank you, I mean; but there's one at each corner. That's one each for us, and one over for——'

'For *her.*' Charlotte pointed to the picture of the dark-eyed, fair-haired lady.

'Let's put a chair for her,' said Charlotte, 'and pretend she's come to dinner. Then we shall have to behave like grown-up people.'

'I never can remember about behaving,' said Charles wearily; 'such a lot of things— and none of them seem to matter. Why shouldn't you drink with your mouth full? It's your own mouth.'

'And eating peas with your knife. I think it would be as good as conjuring, doing it without cutting yourself'—Charlotte tried to lift the peas from her plate with her knife— 'let alone the balancing,' she added, as they rolled off among the mutton.

'Don't,' said Caroline. 'She's looking at you. Charles, you're the only gentleman,

worse luck—I wish I was a boy—put a chair
for her.'

And a large green-seated chair, whose
mahogany back was inlaid with a brass scroll
pattern, was wheeled to the empty space on
the fourth side of the table.

'Now we must none of us look at her—in the
picture, I mean. And then we can't be sure
that she isn't sitting in that chair,' said Caroline.

After dinner Caroline looked up 'Remorse's
regret' in *The Language of Flowers*. It was
agreed that Mrs. Wilmington had better have
a bouquet.

'Brambles,' Caroline said, her finger in the
book, 'they're Remorse—but they wouldn't
make a very comfortable nosegay. And Regret's verbena, and I don't even know what
it is.'

'Put pansies with the brambles,' said
Charlotte; 'that'll be thoughts of remorse.'

So the housekeeper, coming down very neat
in her afternoon dress of shiny black alpaca,
was met by a bunch of pansies.

'To show we think we're remorsish about
the secret stairs,' said Charlotte; 'and look out,
because the brambles are the remorse and
they prick like Billy-o!'

Mrs. Wilmington smiled, and looked quite
nice-looking.

'Thank you,' she said.   'I am sure you will remember not to repeat the fault.'

Which wasn't the nicest way of receiving a remorse bouquet ; but, then as Charlotte said, perhaps she couldn't help not knowing the nice ways.   And anyhow, she seemed pleased, and that was the great thing, as Charlotte pointed out.

Then, having done something to please Mrs. Wilmington, they longed to do something to please some one else, and the Uncle was the only person they could think of doing anything to please.

'Suppose we arranged all the books in the dining-room bookcase, in colours,—all the reds together and all the greens, and the ugly ones all on a shelf by themselves,' Charlotte suggested.   And the others agreed.   So that the afternoon flew by like any old bird, as Caroline put it ; and when tea came, and the floor and sofa and chairs were covered with books, and one shelf was gay with red books and half a shelf demure in green—

'Your uncle isn't coming in to-day,' said Mrs. Wilmington, 'and I'm sure it's just as well.   *What* a mess !   Here, let me put them back, and go and wash your hands.'

'We'll put them back,' the children said, but in vain.   They had to go to wash their

hands, and Mrs. Wilmington continued to put
the books back all the time they were having
tea. Patiently and carefully she did it, not
regarding the colours at all, and her care and
her patience seemed to say, more loudly than
any words she could have spoken, 'Yes; there
you sit, having your nice tea, and I cannot
have *my* tea, because I have to clear up after
you. But I do not complain. No.'

They would have much rather she had
complained, of course. But they couldn't
say so.

CHAPTER IV

IN THESSALONIANS

Now you may say it was Chance, or you
may say it was Fate; or you may say it was
Destiny, or Fortune; in fact, you may say
exactly what you choose. But the fact remains
unaltered by your remarks.

When Mrs. Wilmington placed a fat brown
volume of sermons on the shelf and said,
'There, that's the last,' she, quite without
meaning it, said what was not true. For
when tea was over the children found that the
fat sermon-book had *not* been the last. The
last was *Shadoxhurst on Thessalonians*, a dull,
large book, and Mrs. Wilmington had not put
it back in its place because she had not seen it.
It was, in fact, lying on the floor, hidden by
the table-cloth. If Charles had not happened
to want his handkerchief, and gone down to
look for it on the floor—its usual situation
when it was needed—they would not have
seen the book either.

Charles picked up *Thessalonians*, and the cover 'came off in his hand,' as the handles of cups do in the hands of washing-up maids.

What was inside the cover fell on the floor with a thump, and Caroline picked *that* up.

'*Shadoxhurst on Thessalonians*,' Charles read from the cover.

'This isn't,' said Caroline, looking at what had been inside. 'It's—I say! Suppose it was the book—'

She looked up at the picture.

It was certainly *like* the painted book.

'Only it hasn't any brass clasps,' said Caroline; 'but look—it *used* to have clasps. You can see the marks where they used to go.'

You could.

'Glory!' cried Charlotte. 'Fancy finding it the very first day! Let's take it to Uncle Charles.'

'Perhaps it isn't it,' suggested Charlotte. 'Then he'd be furious perhaps.'

'We'll soon see.' Charles reached out a hand. 'Let's have a squint. It ought to be all magic and Abracadabra and crossed triangles like in *Ingoldsby Legends*.'

'I'll have first look any way,' said Caroline. 'I found it.'

'I found it,' said Charles. 'You only picked it up.'

'You only dropped it. Oh, *bother*——' she had opened the book, and now let her hands fall, still holding it.

'Bother what?' asked the others.

'It isn't English. It's French or Latin or something. Isn't that *just* like things! Here, you can look.'

Charles took the book. 'It's Latin,' he said. 'I could read it if I knew a little more Latin. I can read some of it as it is. I know *quam*, or *apud*, and *rara*. Let's take it to the Uncle.'

'Oh *no*,' said Caroline. 'Let's find out what it is, first.'

It was not easy to find out. The title-page was missing, and *quam*, *apud*, and *rara*, though quite all right in their way, gave but little clue to what the book was about.

'I wish we'd some one we could ask,' said Charles. 'I don't suppose the Wilmington knows any Latin. I don't suppose she knows even *apud* and *quam* and *rara*. If we had the Murdstone chap handy he could tell us, I suppose.'

'I'm glad we haven't,' Charlotte said. 'I don't suppose he'd tell us. And he'd take it away. I say. I suppose there's a church somewhere near. And a clergyman. *He'd* know.'

'Of course he would,' Caroline said with returning brightness. 'Let's go and ask him.'

Half an hour later the children, coming down a deep banked lane, saw before them the grey tower of the church, with elm-trees round it, standing among old gravestones and long grass.

A white faced house stood on the other side of the churchyard.

'I suppose the clergyman lives there,' said Caroline. 'Please,' she said to a pleasant-looking hook-nosed man who was mending the churchyard wall, and whistling 'Blow away the morning dew' as he slapped on the mortar and trimmed off the edges with a diamond-shaped trowel, 'please, does the clergyman live in that house?'

'He does,' said the man with the trowel. 'Do you want him?'

'Yes, please,' said Caroline.

'Well, here he is,' said the man with the trowel. 'What can I do for you?'

'Do you mean to say that you're *It*?—the clergyman, I mean,—I beg your pardon,' said Caroline; and the man with the trowel said, 'At your service.'

'I beg your pardon,' said Caroline again, very red as to her ears. 'I thought you were a working man.'

'So I am, thank God,' said the man with the trowel. 'You see we haven't much money to spare. The parish is so poor. So we do any little repairs ourselves. Did you ever set a stone? It's awfully jolly. The mortar goes on so nicely, and squeezes out pleasantly. Like to try?' he asked Charles.

Of course they all liked to try. And it was not till each had laid a stone and patted it into place, and scraped off the mortar, and got thoroughly dusty and dirty and comfortable, that any one remembered why they had come.

'Oh, this?' said the clergyman—for so I must call him, though anything less clergyman-like than he looked in his mortar-stained flannels and blue blazer you can't imagine. 'It looks interesting. Latin,' he said, opening it carefully, for his hands were very dirty.

'Yes,' said Charles with modest pride. 'I told them it was. I saw *rara* and *quam* and *apud*.'

'Quite so,' said the clergyman; '*rara*, *quam*, and *apud*. Words of Power.'

'Oh, do *you* know about Words of Power?'

'Rather! Do you?'

'Rather!' they said. And if anything had been needed to cement this new friendship well, there it was.

'Look here,' said the clergyman. 'If you'll just wait while I wash my hands I'll walk up

Of course they all liked to try.

with you.   And I'll look through the book and
report to you to-morrow.'

' But what's it about ? '

' About ? ' said he, turning the leaves
delicately with the least mortared of his fingers.
' Oh, it's about spells and charms and things.'

' How perfectly too lovely,' said Charlotte.
' Oh, do read us *one*—just only *one*.'

' Right O,' was the response of this unusual
clergyman, and he read : ' " The seed of the fern
if pulverised "—pounded—smashed, you know,
—"and laid upon the eyes at the twelfth hour"—
midnight, you know—at least I think that's it—
" last before the feast of St. John"—that's to-
morrow by the way—" shall give to the eyes thus
doctored "—treated—dealt with, you know,—
" the power to see that which is not to be seen."
It means you'll see invisible things. I say I *must*
wash.   I feel the dirt soaking into my bones.
Will you wait ? '

The children looked at each other.   Then
Charlotte said :

' Look here.   Don't think we don't like you.
We do—awfully.   But if you walk up with us
will you feel bound to tell uncle about the book ?
Because it's a secret.   He's looking for a book,
and we think perhaps this is it.   But we don't
want to tell him till we're quite sure.'

' I found it inside Somebody-or-other-quite-dull on Thessalonians, you know,' said Charles, 'and I saw it was Latin because of *quam* and——'

' My dear sir—and ladies,' said the agreeable clergyman, ' I am the soul of honour.   I would perish at the stake before I would reveal a centimetre of your least secret.   Trust me to the death.'

And off he went.

' What a different clergyman,' said Charles ; ' he is just like anybody else—only nicer.'

' He said thank God,' Caroline reminded him ; ' he said it like being in church too, not like cabmen and people in the street.'

' He said "Thank God he was a working man,"' said Charlotte.   ' I wonder what he meant.'

' I shall ask him some day,' said Caroline, ' when we know him better.'

But any one who had met the party as they went talking and laughing up the hill would have thought they had known each other for long enough, and could hardly know each other any better than they did.

.   .   .   .   .   .

Charles was dreaming of mortaring the Murdstone man securely into a first-class railway carriage, and tapping him on the head with a brass trowel which was also a candlestick, when he was awakened by a pinch given gently. At the same moment a hand was laid on his mouth, and a whisper said :

'Hist !—not a word.'

'Shut up,' said Charles, recognising at once the voice of his sister Charlotte. 'I'm asleep. Don't be a duffer. Go to bed.'

'No, but,' said Charlotte in the dark, 'Caroline and I have been talking about the fern-seed. And we're going to try it—putting it on our eyes, I mean. To see whether we can see invisible things.'

'Silly,' said Charles briefly.

'All right. Only don't say we didn't ask you to join in.'

'There isn't any fern-seed,' objected Charles.

'Yes, there is. Mrs. Wilmington's got some in the room they call the housekeeper's room. Under a bell-glass. Stupid little ferns ; but I expect the seed's all right. Caro saw them when she went in to ask the Wilmington if we might get up at seven instead of half-past because of everything being so new and lovely. She meant because of the charm-book, of course. And she saw the ferns then.'

'Are you *really* going to?' asked Charles, warm in bed.

'*Yes*,' said Charlotte in a take-it-or-leave-it tone.

'Oh, very well,' said Charles; 'only don't forget I told you it was silly rot. And of course nothing will happen. I was right about the Latin, you know.'

'Here's your dressing-gown,' said Charlotte, who had been feeling for it in the mahogany wardrobe. 'You can scrabble for your shoes with your feet; I suppose they're beside the bed. Hurry up.'

Charles got up, grumbling gently. It was not to be expected that he would feel the same about this wild fern-seed idea as his sisters, who had thought and talked of nothing else for more than three hours, and had had to pinch each other to keep awake. Still, he got up, and they all went down to Mrs. Wilmington's room, which was warm and seemed full of antimacassars, china ornaments, and cheerfully-bound copies of the poets—the kind that are given for birthday presents and prizes, beautiful outside, and inside very small print on thin paper that lets the printing on the other side show through. Charlotte found this out as they waited, by the light of their one candle, for it to be twelve o'clock.

Caroline was plucking fronds of fern, carefully, so that the lack of them should not disfigure the plants.

'It's all duffing,' said Charles. 'Don't

forget I said so. And how are you going to
pound the beastly stuff? You'll wake the
Wilmington and the Uncle and the whole lot
if you pound.'

'I thought,' said Caroline, hesitating with
the fern-fronds in her hand, and her little short
pig-tail sticking out like a saucepan handle, as
Charles put it later, 'I thought—it sounds
rather nasty, but it isn't really, you know, if
you remember it's all *you*—I thought we might
chew them. Each do our own, you know, and
put them on our eyes like a poultice. I know
you hated it when Aunt Emmeline chewed
the lily leaves and put them on your thumb
when you burnt it,' she told Charles, 'but then
her chewing is quite different from you doing
it.'

'*I* don't care,' said Charles; 'it's only a bit
more of your nonsense. Give us the beastly
seeds.'

'They won't come off the leaves,' said
Caroline. 'We shall have to chew the lot.'

'In for a penny, in for a sheep,' said Charlotte cheerfully. 'I mean we may as well be
hanged for a pound as a lamb. I mean——'

'*I* know what you mean,' Caroline inter-
rupted. 'Here you are. It's just on twelve.
Chew for all you're worth, and when the
Wilmington's clock begins to strike put it on

your eyes. And when it's struck six of them take it off. Yes. I've thought about it all. I'm sure that's right. Now, then, chew.'

'I hope it's not poison,' said Charles ; 'you'll remember I told you——'

'Of course it isn't,' said Caroline. 'I've often licked ferns, and I'm not dead. I say— I daresay nothing will happen—but think how silly we should feel if we hadn't tried it. And this is the only night. He said so.'

'Oh, all right,' said Charles. 'At any rate, if we do it you can't be always saying we ought to have.'

'Chew,' said Charlotte ; and the clock began to strike.

'One, two, three, four, five, six,' said Mrs. Wilmington's highly ornamented pink china clock ; and each child thrust a little bunch of fern fronds into its mouth.

'Seven,' said the clock.

'Now,' said Caroline.

And each child. . . . But you picture the scene.

'Eight, nine, ten, eleven, twelve, purr,' said the clock, and said no more.

'I don't like to take it off,' said Charlotte, her hands to her eyes. 'Suppose we *did* see something.'

'We shan't,' said Charles.

'You must,' said Caroline.

'Oh, well,' said Charlotte, and took away the little poultice of chewed fern from each eye.

'There's nothing,' she said.

'I knew there wouldn't be,' said Charles. 'Perhaps another time you'll know I'm right.'

'Never mind,' said Caroline. 'We did it. So we can't keep bothering about what might have happened if we had. Let's go to bed. It was decent of you to try, Charles, when you didn't want to so much—Oh!'

'What?' said the others.

'Poisoned,' said Charles gloomily. 'I knew it wasn't safe. I expect you chewed harder than we did, and—Oh!'

Charlotte had already said her 'Oh.' And now all three children were staring straight before them at the window. And there, where a moment ago was just black bare outside night, was a face—a white face with wide dark eyes.

'It's true,' gasped Caroline, 'it is true—the fern-seed does——'

'It's not true,' said Charles stoutly, his eyes on the face.

'Oh, but it is,' said Charlotte. 'Oh, what's going to happen now?'

And each child felt that the fern-seed had done what no one had, in the deep heart, believed that it would do, and that their eyes now gazed—seeing—upon the unseen.

'I wish we hadn't,' said Charles. 'I told you not to.'

The lips of the face outside moved, as though it were speaking.

'No,' cried Charlotte. 'I don't *want* it to be true.'

A hand was raised—a hand outside the window. Would it knock at the window? The fern-seed only made you see the unseen, not hear the unheard. If the hand knocked at the window—and plainly it was going to knock,—if the hand knocked, would they hear it?

The hand knocked.

A hand was raised.

CHAPTER V

THE MIDNIGHT ADVENTURE

Now, the fern-seed was only warranted to show the invisible, not to make the unhearable heard. If there should be no sound when that raised hand tapped at the window, then the children would know that the fern-seed was doing what it was warranted to do by the Latin book. If, on the other hand, the hand tapped and made, in tapping, the usual noise produced by a common tapper, then one of two things might be true. Either the fern-seed was stronger than the Latin book bargained for, and was able to make people hear the unhearable even if they did not cover their ears with the charm that had covered their eyes, or else the fern - seed spell was all nonsense and the face outside the window was a real person's face and the hand was a real person's hand, and the tap that was coming on the window was a really-tap that would sound hard and rattly on the glass of the window, as taps sound when fingers of bone and flesh make them.

All the children felt quite sure that they were not at all sure whether they wanted the face to be the face of a real person, or whether they wished it to be the Invisible made visible by fern-seed. But when the hand tapped at the window and a sound came to the children within—a sound quite distinct, and just the noise you or I might make if we tapped at a window and didn't want every one in the house to hear us—the children, though startled, no longer felt any doubt as to what they wished that face to be.

'It's only a real person,' whispered Charles, and sighed deeply.

'It's only a boy,' said Caroline. 'What does he want?'

'It's that Rupert chap we saw in the train,' said Charlotte.

Every one breathed much more freely, and they all smiled and nodded towards the window; and the face nodded back, but it did not smile.

'He must have run away,' said Charles, 'like I told him to.'

'It wasn't you; it was me,' said Charlotte promptly.

'I like this much better than its being invisible people,' said Charles, changing the subject a little. 'This is something *like* an adventure.'

'We shouldn't have had it without coming down for the fern-seed,' Caroline reminded him. And again they all nodded and smiled. The face outside moved its lips. It was saying something, but they could not hear what it said.

'It *is* that Rupert boy,' Caroline insisted; 'and he's run away to *us*. What larks!'

And again she nodded, and so did Charles. But Charlotte said, 'Don't let's go on nodding like Chinese pagodas. Of course, it wants to come in.' And at once the others saw that this was the case.

' He can't get in here,' Charlotte said; and, indeed, to have moved that table on which the fern - filled bell - glass stood surrounded by unhappy-looking little ferns in little dry pots, with bits of old tumbler arched protectively over them, would have been dangerous, and probably noisy. And, unless they removed the ferny difficulties, it was quite plain that the window could not be opened.

'The morning-room is next door—Mrs. Wilmington called it that,' said Caroline. 'It's a French window. She said so. It opens all right. I know how the fastenings go.'

'Why "French"?' asked Charlotte, eager for information even at that exciting moment, while Caroline was trying to explain to the face by signs that if it would just go along till it came to a French window it would find some one ready to let it in. 'Why "French"?'

'Because it's like a door,' said Charles, joining in the sign-message. 'Everything in France is the opposite of here. They say "we" for "yes," and "two" is "you," and "four" is an "oven." Silly, I call it.'

'Hush!' whispered Caroline. 'Tread softly, and don't tumble over the wolf-skins.'

Candle-bearing, the little procession passed along to the morning-room. The face had understood the signs. At any rate, there it was, framed in glass panes; and when the French window, which was, indeed, just like a door, was opened, there was the face, as well as the hands, arms, legs, body, and feet, of Rupert, the platform boy, or somebody exactly like him.

'Come in,' said Caroline, holding the door open. And Charlotte added, 'Fear nothing! We will baffle your pursuers. We are yours to the death.'

He came in, a drooping dusty figure, and the French window, which had permitted itself to be opened with the most gentle and noiseless submission, now, in closing, uttered what was little less than a tactless squawk.

'Fly!' whispered Caroline, swiftly turning the handle that fastened it. 'But your boots will betray us.'

Flight was the only thing, you see, and they had to risk the boots. Yet Rupert in his flight was noiseless as the others, who were all bath-slippered, and therefore shod with—if you were only reasonably careful and looked where you were going—the shoes of silence.

When the whole party was safe in Charles's room, with the door shut, they blew out the candles and stood holding each other and their breaths as they listened in the dark for what they fully expected to hear — the opening click of Mrs. Wilmington's lock, the opening creak of Mrs. Wilmington's door, the approaching rustle of Mrs. Wilmington's gown, the mincing amazement of Mrs. Wilmington's voice.

But all was still—still as the inside of a palm-house, which, as no doubt you know, is very much quieter than most of the few quiet places in this noisy world.

The four fugitives let their breaths go cautiously, and again held them. And still the silence wrapped them round, thick and unbroken as the darkness in which they stood.

'It's all right,' whispered Caroline at last. 'Light up.'

Fortunately, each silver candlestick had its box of safety-matches in a silver holder fastened to its handle by a silver chain. This does happen in really well-managed houses. The candles were lighted.

'We are saved,' said Charlotte dramatically.

'You came up like a mouse,' said Caroline to Rupert,—'a quiet mouse.'

It was then seen that Rupert's boots were not on his feet, but in his hand, very muddy, and tied together by frayed boot-laces.

'I took them off,' he explained, 'when I got into your park. My feet hurt so, and the grass was so soft and jolly. Oh, I am so tired—and hungry!' His voice broke a little, and if he had not been a boy I think he would have cried.

'Get on to the bed,' said Charlotte, with eager friendliness, 'and lie down. You be a wounded warrior and we'll be an Arab oasis that you've come to. That's the tent of the sheikh,' she added, as Charles gave the weary Rupert a 'leg up' and landed him among the billows of the vast feather-bed. 'Repose there, weary but honoured stranger. Though but humble Arabs, we are hospitable to

strangers. We will go and slay a desert deer
for you.'

'There are lots of biscuits in the sideboard
in the dining-room,' said Caroline. 'I'll stay
with the wounded—or else you can stay and
I'll go with whichever doesn't.'

Though it was the middle of the night no
one even thought of being sleepy. Perhaps
it was the excitement of this most real adventure, or perhaps the seeds of the fern have an
awakening effect. At any rate, the three C.'s
were as ready to begin a new game as though
it had been ten o'clock in the morning of the
first day of the holidays, instead of half-past
twelve of a night that wasn't any night in
particular except the Eve of St. John.

Charlotte and Charles set off, important and
tip-toeing, on a biscuit-hunt, and Caroline, like
a good little nurse, fetched a basin and sponge
and washed the face of the stranger, taking no
notice of his objections that he was not a baby,
and earnestly hoping that in her long dressing-
gown she looked at least a little like an Arab
maiden ministering to a Feringhee warrior.

'Now I'm going to wash your weary feet,
if you will stick them out over the side of the
bed,' she said. 'They always do in Saracen
countries; and if you think it's like a baby I'll
call it dressing your wounds.'

She brought a chair and a basin of water very carefully, and a big sponge, and then she peeled off Rupert's stockings and bathed his tired, swollen feet with great care and gentleness.   And if a little of the water did go on the bed—well, you can't think of everything all in a minute, and she did put a towel under his legs afterwards.

'That's jolly,' said the wounded knight, more graciously.

'You are terribly wounded,' said Caroline comfortingly.   'You must have been fighting dragons or walking over red-hot ploughshares, or perhaps it was a pilgrimage with peas in your shoes.   We play pilgrims sometimes, with cockles in our hats and pilgrims' staffs— only we always pretend the peas.   I think it's quite fair to pretend the shoes, don't you?'

When the others came back from their hunting, with a good 'bag' (it was a tin, really) of biscuits, the Saracen maiden greeted them with—

'Hist! The stranger sleeps. Let's pretend he's fainted, and we'll rouse him with a skin of wine.   Get some water in the tooth-mug.   And where are the biscuits?'

'We might as well have turbans,' said Charlotte, hastily twining a bath-towel round her head. 'All really Arab maidens are turbaned Turks.'

'Let's make it more tent-like before we wake him,' Charles suggested, drawing the curtains round two sides of the four-poster; 'and we might put the candles out of sight and pretend they're Arabian knights' lanterns.'

'Or put them in a line on the chest, and let them be the sun rising over the sands of the desert,' said Charlotte, putting the three candlesticks in a row.

When all was arranged, the three towel-turbaned children climbed into the tent and looked at the wounded knight, who lay asleep, looking very tired indeed, his feet still wrapped in the towel and his head half fallen off the pillow.

'Let him sleep a little longer,' said Caroline, 'ere we rouse him to eat of the flesh of the deer which my brothers have brought to the wigwam for the benefit of the poor pale-face.'

'We're not Indians, silly,' said Charlotte. 'We're Arabs, and I could do with a bit of the flesh of the deer myself, if you come to that.'

'So could I,' said Charles, his turban over one eye. 'It's jolly not being asleep. They say you get sleepy and cross if they let you sit up—but look at us.'

'Yes, look at us,' the others agreed, and ate the best mixed biscuits in a contented silence, broken only by the sound of crunching.

The familiar sensation of biscuit in the mouth seemed somehow to calm the excitement of the three C.'s.

The adventures of the night, which had seemed, as they happened, not so very wonderful, now began to appear more surprising, and at the same time more real.   And the silence which biscuit-eating demands (unless you are prepared to behave really badly and talk with your mouth full and have the crumbs all over the place) was favourable to reflection—a friend to thought.

'Do you know,' said Caroline at last— 'pass the mug, please—do you know, I don't at all know what we're going to do with him.'

'*I* was just thinking that,' said Charlotte.

'So was I,' said Charles.

'But I've been thinking——'

'So have I,' said the other two together.

'What?' asked Caroline, stopping short.

'What you have,' said Charlotte, and Charles repeated her words.

'Then I needn't tell you what I thought,' said Caroline briefly.

I think they were all getting, perhaps, a

little sleepy—or the effect of the fern-seed was wearing off.

'Oh, don't be crabby,' Charlotte said. 'We only meant we didn't see what on earth we could do with him. I suppose he must sleep with Charles. There's lots of room.' She leaned back on a pillowy bunch of featherbed and closed her eyes.

'No, you don't,' said Caroline firmly, pulling her sister up again into a sitting position by a limp arm. 'I could go to sleep myself if it comes to that. Take your turban off. It'll cool your sleepiness.'

'I said'—Charlotte spoke very slowly and distinctly, as people do when they are so sleepy they aren't quite sure whether they can speak at all—'I said, "Let him sleep with Charles."'

'Oh yes!' said Caroline. 'And be found in the morning when they call us, and taken alive and delivered back to the Murdstone man. No, we must hide him, and wake him before they call us. I can always wake up if I bang my head the right number of times on the pillow before I go to sleep.'

Charlotte was nodding happily.

'Get up!' said Caroline, exasperated. 'Get up! Get down! Get off the bed and stand on your feet. Now, then, Charles!'

But Charles was deeply slumbering, with

his mouth very much more open than it ought
to have been.

'That's it!' said Caroline, as Charlotte re-
sponded to her pull. 'That's it. It's just you
and me! Women always have to do the work
of the world! Aunt Emmeline said so once.
She said it's not "Men must work and women
must weep"; it's "Men must talk and women
must work." Come on and give me a hand.'

'All right. I'm awake now,' said Charlotte
cheerfully. 'I've been biting my tongue all
that awful time you've been talking. What's
the idea?'

'We'll make him an upper berth, like in
ships,' Caroline explained, 'and then we'll wake
him up and water him and biscuit him and
explain things, and get Charles into bed and
all traces concealed. It'll be just you and me
that did it. That's glory, you know.'

'Oh, *do* stop talking,' said Charlotte. 'I'll
do anything you like, only stop talking.'

There was a great mahogany wardrobe in
the room, with a mahogany hanging-cupboard
at each side, and between the mahogany cupboards a space with mahogany drawers below
and mahogany shelves above. And the shelves
were like shallow drawers or deep trays, and
you could pull them in and out. There was
nothing on the shelves but clean white paper,

and on each shelf a little bag made of white muslin and filled with dried lavender, which smelt very sweet through the fine mesh of the muslin.

The girls took out two of the trays and hid them under the bed. This left as much space above the lowest tray and the highest as they leave you on a steamer between the upper and lower berths. The girls made up a shake-down bed with blankets and pillows, and when all was ready they woke the boys gently and firmly by a damp sponge on the forehead and a hand over the mouth in case the sleeper should wake up yelling.

But both boys woke quietly. Charles had just enough wakefulness to submit to being got out of his overcoat and slippers and bundled into bed, but Rupert was thoroughly awake— ate biscuit, drank water, and understood exactly where and how he was to spend what was left of the night, as well as why he was to spend it there and thus.

He got into the wardrobe by means of a chair. The girls took away the chair and almost shut the doors of the wardrobe.

'We'll have a grand council to-morrow,' said Charlotte. 'Don't be anxious. Just re-member we're yours to the death, like I told you on the platform.'

'It was *me* said that,' said Charles, almost in his sleep.

'And don't move out of here, whatever you do,' said Caroline. 'I shall come quite early, and we'll hide you somewhere. I expect I shall think of something in my sleep. I often do. Good night.'

'Good night,' said Rupert, in the wardrobe. 'I say! You are bricks—and you won't let them catch me?'

'Of course not,' said the three C.'s confidently. (Charles said it quite in his sleep.)

Five minutes later the others were sleeping as soundly as Charles, and out Tonbridge way the Murdstone man and his groom and his gardener and the local Police were still looking for Rupert with anxious feelings, with lanterns that flickered yellow in the pale grey of dawn.

'Just remember we're yours to the death.'

CHAPTER VI

HUNTED

I don't know exactly how it happened. Perhaps Caroline was too sleepy to bump her head seven times on the pillow before she went to sleep. Or perhaps that excellent spell cannot always be relied upon to work. At any rate, none of the children woke till Jane came to draw up the blinds and let the half-past seven sunshine into their rooms.

Then Caroline woke quite thoroughly, looked at her little watch, and leaped out of bed.

'What's the hurry, Miss?' asked Jane, as Caroline stood, a little unsteadily, in the middle of the room, rubbing her eyes and yawning. 'It hasn't but just gone the half-hour.'

'I was dreaming,' said Caroline; and when Jane was gone she shook Charlotte and said, 'I say! *Did* anything happen last night?'

'No,' said Charlotte, behaving like a dormouse.

83

Caroline caught up her dressing-gown and crept along to Charles's room.   He was sitting up in bed, looking wildly at the wardrobe. Its doors were open, and there was nothing on the shelves (which were all in their proper places) except clean paper and little bags of lavender that smelt sweet through their white muslin veils.

'Whatever's happened?' asked Caroline, fearing the worst.

'Oh, nothing,' said Charles, rather crossly. 'Only I had a silly dream, and when I woke up I thought it was true, and of course it wasn't.'

'*I* thought it was a dream, too, when I first woke.   And Charlotte says nothing happened last night.   What did you dream?'

He told her a little.

'But I dreamed all that, too,' said Caroline anxiously.   'About the fern-seed and Rupert, and our playing Arab Saracens and hunting the biscuits.   We *couldn't* both dream the same thing.   Where did you put the biscuits in your dream—what was left of them?'

'You put them on the dressing-table.'

'Well, they aren't there now,' said she.

'Then it *was* a dream,' said he; 'and we both dreamed it.'

The two looked at each other blankly.

'I dreamed I dressed his wounds—sponged his feet, I mean,' she added, after a pause full of doubt. 'The mud was thick—if it wasn't a dream it'll be in the basin.'

But Jane knew her duty too well for there to be anything in the basin except a bright brass can of hot water with a clean towel laid neatly across it.

'Well, the fern-seed did something, anyhow, if it only made us both dream like that,' said Caroline. But Charles wanted to know how she knew they hadn't dreamed the fern-seed as well.

'Oh, you get dressed,' said his sister shortly, and went to her own dressing.

Charlotte, when really roused, owned that she remembered Rupert's coming. But, if he had come, he had gone and left no trace. And it is rare for boys to do that.

The children agreed that it must have been a dream, after the eating of the fern-seed, for all of them, for some reason that I can't understand, agreed that the fern-seed eating, at any rate, was real.

Breakfast seemed less interesting than usual, and when, after the meal, Mrs. Wilmington minced a request to them to go out for the morning, 'the same as you were requisted to do yesterday,' they went with slow footsteps and boots strangely weighty.

D

' Let's get out of sight of the house,' said Charlotte heavily.

They went away beyond the shrubbery, to the wood where there were oak-trees and hazels and dog-wood and silver birches and here and there a black yew, with open bracken-feathered glades between. Here they found a little glade between a honeysuckle and a sweet chestnut and a hazel thicket, flattened the bracken, and sat down amid the sweet scent of it.

' To hold a council about the wonderful dream we've all of us had,' said Caroline slowly.

But the council, if it could be called one, was brief and languid.

' I'd rather think first,' said Caroline. And the others said so would they.

' I could think better with my head on your lap, Caro,' Charles said.

And Charlotte murmured, ' Bunch the fern up closer under my back, Caro.'

And when the sun came over the top of the sweet chestnut it fell upon a warm and comfortable heap of children asleep.

You really can't stay up all night, or even dream that you stay up, and then hold important councils next day just as though nothing had happened.

When the children awoke, because the sun had crept up over the sweet chestnut and was shining straight into their eyes, everything looked different and much more interesting.

'I tell you what,' said Charlotte. 'Let's do fern-seed again.'

'It's only on the eve of——' Charles began, but Charlotte interrupted.

'The seed goes on when once you've planted it—chewed it, I mean. I'm certain it does. If we don't *see* anything, we may *dream* something more.'

'There wouldn't be time for a really thick dream before dinner,' Charles objected.

'Never mind! Let's try. If we are late for dinner we'd tell the truth and say that we fell asleep in the woods. There's such heaps of fern here it would be simply silly not to try.'

There was something in this. Fern-seed was chewed once more. Bracken, I have heard really well-educated people say, is not a fern at all, but it seemed a fern to them. And it certainly did its best to act up to what was expected of it. For when the three removed the little green damp pads from their eyes and blinked at the green leaves, there in the thick of them was Rupert, looking at them between the hazel thicket and the honeysuckle

—a real live Rupert, and no dream-nonsense about him.

'*Was* it a dream last night?' they all asked him, in an eager chorus. 'When you came to the window?'

'Of course it wasn't,' he said flatly. 'Only I was so afraid of being nabbed. So I got out early and put the shelves back and the pillows on the bed, and I took the biscuits; I thought you wouldn't mind——'

'Not a bit. Rather not'—chorus of polite hospitality.

'And I got out of your dressing-room window and down the ivy; it was quite easy. And I cut across the grass and in under those fancy sort of fir-trees, the ones that drag their branches—you know—in the avenue. And I saw you come out, but the place was all thick with gardeners and people. So I waited till their dinner-bell rang, and then I crept out here, and I was just going to say "Hi!" when you stuck that green stuff on your eyes. It looks nasty. What did you do it for?'

They told him.

'That's rummy,' he said, sitting among them quite at his ease, with one hand in his pocket. 'Because I knew fern-seed *made* you invisible—it says so in Shakespeare, you know, —and I ate a bit coming along, just on the

chance it might be some good—so that no
one should see me, you know—and nobody
did till you did. So,' he went on more slowly,
'perhaps I was *really* invisible until you put
the fern-seed on your eyes.'

'What a perfectly splendid idea!' cried
Charlotte. 'Because that makes it all true.
We were most awfully sick when we thought
it had only just made us dream. I say! Do,
now, do tell us how you ran away and why—
and what you're going to do, and everything.'

'I thought,' Rupert answered carelessly,
'of running away to sea. But it's a long way
to the coast. I would much rather stop here
with you. Couldn't you hide me in a log-hut
or something, like a runaway slave? Just till
they stopped looking for me. And I could
write to my father in India and ask him to
let me stay here instead of with old Mug's
brother. Couldn't you hide me till the answer
came?'

'We could try,' said Charles, a little doubtfully.

But Charlotte said, 'Of course we can
—we will! Only, why are you so different?
You seem miles older than you were when we
saw you on the platform.'

'*You'd* look miles older if you'd locked your

master in his study and then done a bunk—
and been running and hiding for half a day
and a night,' said Rupert, a little crossly.

'But what did he *do* to you?' they asked.

'Well, you saw what he was like in the
train.'

'But you seemed so frightened of him. I
wonder you dared to run away.'

'That wasn't funk—in the train. That
was just suppressed fury,' Rupert explained
tranquilly. 'I was wondering where I should
run to if I had to run. And then I did have
to run—like Billy-o! And when I saw the
name on a sign-post I remembered what you'd
said about "true to the death"—and I kept
behind the hedges, because I wasn't sure about
the fern-seed being any good, and I got up a
tree and I saw you go by, and when you came
back with the parson I just followed on quietly
till I got to outside your house. I hoped
you'd come out, but you didn't. And I hid
under one of those fancy firs, and then, I
suppose, I went to sleep, and when I woke up
there was a light in a window, and I went
towards it, stupid, like a bird. You know
how sparrows come out of the ivy if you show
a light?'

They didn't.

'Well, they do. And then I saw you

monkeying about. I *was* glad, I tell you. And I tapped on the window, and—you know the rest,' he ended, like a hero in a book.

'But what did the Murdstone man *do* to you?' Charlotte insisted on knowing.

'He was playing up for a row from the very first,' said Rupert; 'and when we got to his beastly house that night'—Rupert lowered his voice and spoke in a tone of deep disgust and bitterness—'he gave me bread and milk to eat. Bread and milk—with a teaspoon! And when I said I'd rather not, he said I must learn to eat what was set before me. And he talked about discipline and showed me a cane. He said he was glad there were no other little boys there—little boys!—because he could devote himself entirely to breaking me in.'

'Beast!' said Charlotte.

'He thought I was a muff of a white rabbit,' said Rupert; 'but he knows the difference now.'

I hope you will not think base scorn of Charles and Caroline when I own that they were both feeling a little uncomfortable in the presence of this young desperado. Fernseed is all very well, and so is the idea of running away from school, but that any master should really be so piglike as to make running away necessary—this came too near to the really terrible for them to feel quite easy about it.

'He must be like the Spanish Inquisition,' said Charlotte indignantly. 'Why isn't he put in prison now there are proper laws?'

But Charles and Caroline still felt that it was less likely that the Murdstone man should be so hateful than that Rupert should be drawing long-bows to excuse his running away. If he had been timid and miserable they would have believed him more. As it was, he was easy when he wasn't defiant.

You know that feeling—when you are not quite sure of some one you want to be kind to —when you can't be quite certain that if you believe what they say you won't be being unjust to somebody else. It is a hateful feeling. There is nothing more miserable than not being able to trust some one you want to trust. You know, perhaps, what that sensation is? Rupert, at any rate, must have known it, and must have known that the others were feeling it, for he suddenly pulled his hand out from his pocket.

'Look here, then,' he said. 'But—no, I don't blame you. I know it's not the sort of thing you'd expect to be true. Yes. He did it. The first night. About the bread and

'*I* believed you—without that,' said Charlotte.

milk.   Came and did it after I was in bed.
With a ruler.'

'It' was a blue bruise and a slight red
graze across the back of the hand that, till
now, had been hidden.

'*I* believed you — without that,' said
Charlotte, with hot cheeks.   '*I* know there are
people like that.   Like *Uncle Tom's Cabin.*'

'We do believe you,' said Caroline
earnestly.   'Who said we didn't?'

And Charles said, 'Of course we do—what
nonsense!   We'll bring you a paper and
pencil and an envelope, and you can write to
your father.   And we *will* conceal you.'

'Right O!' said Rupert.   'Hush!'

They hushed, and, Rupert pointing through
the blue gap between the oak and the honeysuckle, their eyes followed the pointing of his
finger.   A figure was coming up the drive—a
figure in blue.

'Go and see what it is,' whispered Rupert,
'but don't let on.'

'I'll go,' said Charlotte, jumping up.

'But what'll you say if they ask you what
you've come in for?' Charles asked.

'I shall say I've come in to fetch you a
pocket-handkerchief,' said Charlotte wither-
ingly, 'because you wanted one so badly.
You always do.'

She went.

'Look here,' said Caroline, once more thrilling to the part of the protecting Saracen maiden. 'Suppose they're after you? Let's cover you up with leaves and bracken, so that your tweediness won't show through the trees if they look—and bracken over your head. Creep through the bracken; don't crush it more than you can help.'

Rupert was entirely hidden when Charlotte returned, very much out of breath, from an unexpected part of the wood.

'I came round,' she whispered, 'to put them off the scent.'

'Who?' asked Rupert, under the leaves.

'The Police,' said Charlotte, with calm frankness and a full sense of the tremendous news she was bringing. 'They're inquiring after *you*. They've traced you to Hadlow.'

'What did they say at the house?'

'They said they hadn't seen you, but the Police might search the grounds.'

'What did you say?'

'I wasn't asked,' said Charlotte demurely. 'But I'll tell you what I did say. You lie mouse-still, Rupert; it's all right. I'm glad you're buried, though.'

'What *did* you say?'

'I said,' Charlotte answered, glowing with

the pride of a successful strategist—' I said we'd help them to search! Come on, the three C.'s. Round the back way! *We'll* help them to search for their runaway boy—so we will! And when they've gone we'll bring you something to eat—something really nice —not just biscuits. Don't you worry. The three C.'s *are* yours to the death.'

CHAPTER VII

BEING DETECTIVES

IF you are Jack Delamere, the Boy Detective, who can find out all secrets by himself, pretending to be a French count, a young lady from the provinces, or a Lincolnshire labourer with a cold in his head, and in those disguises pass unrecognised by his nearest relations and by those coiners and smugglers to whom in his ordinary clothes he is only too familiar,— if you can so alter your voice that your old school-fellows believe you to be, when dressed for the part, an Italian organ-grinder or a performing bear——

I am sorry, this sentence is too much for me. I give it up. What I was going to say was that persons accustomed to the detective trade, or, on the other hand, persons who are used to keeping out of the way of detectives, no doubt find it easy to play a part and to look innocent when they are guilty, and

ignorant when of course all is known to them.
But when you are not accustomed to playing
a part in a really serious adventure—not just
a pretending one—you will find your work cut
out for you. This was what Charles and
Caroline felt.

It was all very well for Charlotte to have
arranged that they should help the Police to
look for Rupert, and the other two said cordially
that it was very clever of her to have thought
of it, and they all started together for the side
door where the policeman was still talking to
Mrs. Wilmington. But their feet seemed
somehow not to want to go that way; they
went more and more slowly, and when they
were half-way to the house, Caroline said:

'I don't think I will. I don't know how.
I should do something silly and give the show
away. I shall say I'm too tired.'

'You *are* too bad,' said Charlotte, exasperated. 'I go and lay all the plans and then
you funk.'

'I don't,' said Caroline. And so anxious
was she not to have to play the part of pretending to look for Rupert when all the time
she knew where he was, that she added
humbly, 'Don't be snarky. I'm only saying
I'm not clever enough. I'm not so clever as
you, that's all.'

I am sorry to say that Charlotte only answered 'Rats!' and added, 'I suppose Charles is going to cry off next?' She did not think he was: she just said it. And Charles most unexpectedly answered:

'I think I'd rather not, if you don't mind.'

Charlotte stamped her foot. 'Oh, all right!' she said; 'but for goodness' sake come on. They'll think there's something up.' And they walked on.

'Look here,' said Caroline suddenly, 'I *will* pretend to help. It was only that I was so awfully afraid they'd find him. Only if I disappear, you'll understand it's just because I felt sillier than I could bear. You help too, Charles. I'm sure you can—only don't pretend too much. I shouldn't talk much except asking questions, if I were you.'

'Right O!' said Charlotte.

And Charles said, 'Oh, well, only if I give it away without meaning to, don't blame me.'

And by this time they were quite near the house, by whose side door of many-coloured glass the group of talking grown-ups awaited them. Mrs. Wilmington was there with her handkerchief over her head. And William and the gardener's boy and the gardener, and a tall stout young man with fat red hands who was the Police.

'I can't and won't,' Mrs. Wilmington was saying. 'The Master's orders is—are—that he's not to be disturbed in the mornings on any pretence—not if the house was on fire. I couldn't face him with this vulgar tale of runaway boys. *I* give you leave to search for him,' she said in proud refined accents. 'I'm quate competent to take *that* upon me; quate.'

The Police turned from her to the children, who said 'Good morning!'—all but Charlotte, who had said it before.

'Good morning to *you*,' said the Police, 'and so you young ladies and gents is going to join the search-party?'

'Yes, please,' said Caroline.

'What'll you do with him if you catch him?' Caroline asked abruptly.

'Send him to gaol, in course,' said the Police, winking at William. 'An' you're all going to help the law in the execution of its duty. And very useful I daresay you'll be,' he added affably, 'knowing the place and what not. Now see here,' he went on, condescending to them in a way which, it was remarked later, was like his cheek; 'let's have a game of play, make-believe, you know. Let's pretend this runaway lad is a friend of yours' (a cold shiver ran down three youthful backs; for a moment it seemed that all was discovered, but the Police went on, still playfully)—'a friend of yours, and you and him has settled to play a little game of hide-and-seek. And he's He. Now where,' he ended, more affably almost than they could bear,—'where would you look first?'

'I don't know,' said Charles miserably.

'Oh! just anywhere,' said Charlotte.

But Caroline said slowly, 'I should look in the wood over there,' and pointed straight to the spot where Rupert lay buried in fern and leaves.

'Right you are,' said the Police, delighted to have got a suggestion. 'Then here goes.'

Charlotte dared not look at her sister lest her face should show her detestation of this traitorous act. Charles put his hands in his pockets to express indifference, and decided not to whistle for fear of overdoing his part. He told himself that he never would have believed it of Caro—never.

And now Caroline was speaking again, looking confidingly up into the large patronising face of the Police.

'That's where I should look,' she was saying, 'if we were playing hide-and-seek. But as it is—— You see we've been there all the morning, and he couldn't have come into the wood without our hearing him, you know.   Have you tried the other wood, beyond the garden? And the thatched summer - house?   And the lodge that isn't used?   Over by the other gates, you know.'

'The old lodge,' the Police echoed. 'A very likely spot, I shouldn't wonder. You lead the way, young gentleman,' he said to Charles.

'Good old Caro—oh, *good* old Caro!' Charlotte was saying to herself as the party started.

'I'll dispose my search-party proper later on,' said the Police importantly, and turned to say, 'Ain't you coming, Miss?' to Caroline, who was stooping down, doing something to her foot.

'I can't,' she said; 'I've got a stone in my shoe. And it hurts,' she added, standing up firmly on it.

Caroline went indoors, and the search-party threaded the woods and converged at last on the empty lodge. Its lattice-paned windows were dusty, its door hung on a broken hinge, and little black balls of hard moss were dotted between the flagstones of its yard. Its thatch was loose in places, ruffled like the plumage of an old stuffed bird, and its garden had been so long untilled that it had ceased to be the weed-grown earth patch that a neglected garden first becomes, and had grown green all over, covered itself with grass and fern and bramble and baby oak-trees, and become just a fenced-in patch of the wood beyond.

'Halt!' said the Police; 'just the place. I'll warrant we've run the young gentleman to earth this time.'

But they hadn't. There was nothing in the lodge but an old hamper with a hole in it, a litter of straw and old damp paper, some cold ashes in the grate, and in the upper rooms two last year's birds'-nests, and a chair with three legs and half a back.

The Police stooped his helmeted head to the low door lintel, and came out into the sunshine a disappointed man.

'Thought we'd got him,' he said; and that was what he said at the thatched summer-house and in the larch wood, and at various other parts of the park and grounds where Rupert was not.

'Isn't it nearly dinner-time?' Charles asked, as the search-party pushed through a very brambly brake and came out once more at the back of the deserted lodge.

'Your kind governess, she put back dinner an hour for you to assist in the search,' said the Police reassuringly.

'Best try the other side, Mr. Poad,' said William; 'you've drawed this blank.'

'I will now whistle to the gentleman as owns the runaway,' said the Police suddenly and terribly, and whistled.

'Where is he?' Charlotte asked, with a sudden vision of the Murdstone gentleman seeing everything with half an eye, capturing Rupert and carrying him off in half a minute. Charles was wondering 'what they do to you for helping runaway boys.'

'Along the road,' the Police answered, 'with Mr. Binskin from the Peal of Bells. Keeping watch. I'd best report to him.'

'Will he come with us?' Charles could not help asking.

'I'm of opinion he's best where he is,' said the Police. 'I'm just a-going to tell him to keep on up and down outside. The ostler from the Peal is over the other side, case he gets out that way. Unless he's had to get back to his work already.'

'Let's go and have another look at those birds'-nests while we're waiting,' said Charlotte, with great presence of mind. And so it was through the little diamond panes of the lodge that they saw again the Murdstone gentleman, in evening dress and an overcoat, with his tie in a crumpled state under one ear, and his face, as Charlotte said, exactly like the face of a baffled executioner.

He stood talking to the Police for a few moments, with the old familiar scowl that they knew so well. They felt like that about it, though they'd only met the scowler, as you know, on one occasion. Then he went back through the gate, and the children, when they were quite sure that he was gone, rejoined the Police, rather tired, and feeling as though this silly game of looking for what they knew, or at any rate hoped, they weren't going to find, had been going on for ever, and seemed as though it would never stop.

'I thought it best,' the Police explained to William, 'to keep the gent on the outside of the place. He seems peppery-natured, and if he was to spy his boy among your glass-houses, which is where I propose to conduct my search in next, I wouldn't answer for it but what he'd leap upon him among the glass like a fox at a duck, and damage untold, as like as not.'

Need I tell you that Rupert was not discovered among the glass?

Less brisk than at its starting, the search-party returned to the side door where the coloured glass was, to be met on its doorstep by Caroline, rather out of breath and very hot. She carried her sun-bonnet by its strings (Aunt Emmeline believed in sun-bonnets and made dozens of them, as presents for all her friends).

'Well?' said Caroline.

'We haven't found him, Miss, if that's what you mean,' said the Police, taking his helmet off and wiping his face. 'I suppose you ain't seen anything?'

Caroline looked nervously at the others.

'I *heard* something,' she said, 'in the wood over there. I went back,' she went on in a sort of wooden way—and now she was not looking at the others at all—'because I left something there; and I heard a rustling sound, and I saw footmarks, in the boggy part of the wood, and I thought it looked like boy's boots.'

Charlotte said afterwards that she really thought she should have burst into little pieces. And Charles said the same.

To hear their own elder, and till now loved and esteemed sister, quietly betraying the refugee, and to be quite unable to say what they thought of her without having to explain the lack of candour in their own conduct! It was a terrible moment.

'You don't say so,' said the Police, and turned to William. 'It's a thirsty job,' he added carelessly, and William said he'd ask indoors.

A tray with glasses and a jug of something cool resulted. And the Police and William both seemed the better for it. The gardener had retired. It was too far the wrong side of dinner-time for him, he said.

The Police drew a long breath, and wiped his mouth with the back of his hand.

'Now then,' he said; 'you lead the way, Miss.'

Caroline led. The others followed. They could hardly bear to go, yet they could still less bear to be left behind. Across the hot sunny grass they went and into the wood. Even that, though shady, was hot, and there seemed to be more flies than could possibly be needed for any useful purpose. Caroline, still carefully avoiding the eyes of the others, led the way straight to the ferny lair where they had left Rupert, the others following in helpless fury.

'Hullo!' said the Police, 'this looks something like.'

For there the lair was—plainly to be seen— a lair and nothing else, but a lair that was deserted.

'I think we're on to him now,' said the Police; 'which way did you say them footstepses was, Missie?'

'Farther on,' said Caroline. 'I tied my handkerchief to a tree to mark the place.'

'You never!' said the Police admiringly; 'why, you deserve to be in the Force, Miss.

It's not every constable, even, would have thought of that.'

And I believe he spoke the truth.

Following Caroline and the Police, pushing miserably through the bushes that sprang back as the others passed through and tried to hit them in the face, Charlotte and Charles exchanged glances full of meaning.

The whole party made a good deal of noise: there was the rustling of leaves, both the green and the dead kind; the snapping of twigs underfoot; the grating of bough against bough as the searchers pushed through the hazels and sweet chestnuts and young oaks.

'You'd do fine for keepers,' said William, coming last.   'No poachers wouldn't never hear *you* a-coming.'

'That your handkerchief, Miss?' the Police at the same moment asked smartly, and pointed to a white thing that drooped from a dogwood branch; 'you identify the handkerchief?'

'Yes,' said Caroline in a stifled voice, 'and there'—she pointed down.

There were footprints, very plain and deeply-marked footprints, not very large, yet not small like a girl's.   They were the footprints, beyond any doubt, of a boy.

'Now we've got him,' said the Police for

about the fifteenth time that morning, and proceeded to follow the steps, as was remarked later, like any old sleuth-hound.

William said, 'Remarkable deep for the time of year,' but nobody took any notice of him. The boot-boy took a pleasure in planting his own steps beside the tracks they were following, till the Police admonished him.

'Them tracks is evidence,' he said; 'you needn't tread so nigh them.'

The tracks led them down a steep place, a sort of gorge, and ended at the tall oak fence.

'He must have escaped this way,' said the Police.

'I'll take my Sunday Sam he never,' said William.

'There's another footprint here,' said Caroline anxiously.

'So there be,' said the Police. 'You 'ave been a 'elp, Miss. I shall name you in my report.'

It was now seen that a further line of footprints led along the fence to a place where a pale was loose.

'This is where he got through, you may depend,' said the Police.

'I'll easy wrench another pale loose, if you want to follow on,' said William, and as he did so Charlotte saw him wink, distinctly wink at

They were the footprints, beyond any doubt, of a boy.

Caroline. How hateful everybody was! Oh, poor Rupert!

Every one got through, Charles and Charlotte rather doubtfully looking up and down the road first to see if the Murdstone master was in sight. 'Which way?' the Police now asked himself and the others anxiously.

That was quickly settled. A whitish object lying in the middle of the road ten yards away, beckoned them to the right. The Police stooped stiffly, picked it up and examined its corners.

'Rupert Wix,' he read solemnly. 'I shall now sound my whistle and acquaint the gentleman as owns the boy with our discovery of the ankercher belonging to the runaway.'

But Caroline laid a hand on his arm and arrested the whistle on its way to his lips.

'Isn't that something else white, farther along?' she said.

'Don't tell me 'e got two ankerchers,' said William; 'no boy was ever bred as 'ad two ankerchers at the one time.'

'I don't see nothing,' said the Police, but he walked in the direction of Caroline's gaze.

'It's wonderful what eyes you've a-got, Miss,' said William; 'none of the rest on us didn't spy it.'

Charlotte and Charles walked apart from Caroline in a marked manner.

There certainly was something white in the road—a piece of paper with a stone on it, and also, as the Police saw when he picked it up, writing, pencilled, with that kind of black blunt pencilledness which happens when you have a pencil whose point has seen better days, and you encourage its efforts with your tongue.

'To any kind Bypasser,' the Police read out, 'please put the inside in the post for me.'

The paper on which this was written was a leaf torn from a note-book and folded across. Inside was another leaf with a stamp in the corner, as though it had been a post-card. On one side was an address, 'Mr. and Mrs. Wix, The Nest, Simla, India,' and on the other these lines which the Police read out:

DEAR PARENTS—I am running away to sea through being so ill-treated by Macpherson. I will write from the first port. I shall get a ship at Hastings, I expect.—Your affecate son,

RUPERT.

'Well!' said the Police; 'if that don't beat all! Lucky we saw this.'

'Yes, ain't it,' said William, 'and this the Hastings road and all. You ought to catch up easy if you start right away now.'

'I shall now blow my whistle,' said the Police as usual, 'and acquaint the boy's guardian with our discovery.'

'If we can't be any more use,' said Caroline hastily, 'perhaps you wouldn't mind our going back to our dinners. They'll be getting dreadfully cold for the time of year,' she added a little wildly.

'Best go back through the gap,' said William. 'It ought to be mended, though. Here, you,' he said to the gardener's boy, 'go round by the lodge and tell Peters to get it seen to.'

'There is no need to detain you,' said the Police, 'and thanking you for your assistance, which shall be mentioned in my report. Good morning to you.' He blew his whistle and they hastened back through the gap.

Once through it the others refused to meet Caroline's eye. But she did not seem to notice it.

'I know listening's wrong,' she said; 'but when you're playing detectives the rules are different, and I should like——'

'Slip along by the pale, Miss,' said William. '"All's fair in love an' war," as the saying is.'

She slipped, and the others could not help following her. William went too.

The boots of the Murdstone tutor were now heard on the road. Then came the voice of the Police, explaining how clever he had been in finding the footsteps, the handkerchief, and the letter. 'And you'd best read the letter,' the Police added.

A brief letter-reading silence was broken by the Murdstone man, very angry indeed.

'Monstrous!' he said; 'and left in the public road for any stranger to see! Monstrous! There's not a word of truth in it.'

'You can tell that to the Magistrate,' said the Police. 'Beg pardon, sir, I mean I think I've cleared up this little difficulty for you.'

'I suppose I can get a trap in the village?' the Murdstone man asked.

'At the Green Dragon, sir.

'Right,' said Mr. Macpherson smartly. 'Good morning!' And he turned and walked quickly away, leaving the Police planted there, as they say in France.

'Well—I'm—dished!' said the Police aloud, after a moment's silence, to what he supposed to be solitude; 'not so much as tuppence to drink his blooming bad health in. The stingy blighter! He can look for his own boys after this. And I hope the young 'un gets off, so I do.'

'Same here,' whispered William behind the grey oak paling.

The Police walked heavily away.

'Best go in to dinner,' said William, and the four walked in silence across the park. When they got to the side door William spoke.

'You're a fair masterpiece, Miss Caroline,' he said; 'that I will say.'

'Thank you,' said Caroline.

Charles and Charlotte both felt — they owned it afterwards—almost choked by all the things they wanted to say to Caroline and couldn't, because of William. They drew long breaths and almost snorted with mixed emotions.

'I say,' said Caroline eagerly, as William turned away. But Charles interrupted.

'We don't mean to speak to you,' he said.

And just then Mrs. Wilmington appeared at the door, and no one could say anything further; anything that mattered, that is.

She escorted the girls to their room. In her superior lady-like way she was curious about the missing boy. Charlotte told the story briefly, while Caroline buried her hot face in a big basin of cold water and blew like a grampus. Then there was dinner, and Mrs. Wilmington stayed all through that to hear more details. When dinner was over Caroline disappeared.

'I expect she's gone away to cry,' Charlotte

whispered to her brother. 'I say, I wish we hadn't. But we did agree we oughtn't to speak to a traitor till it was sorry: you said so yourself in the wood.'

'It's all very beastly,' said Charles. 'I wish it hadn't happened, upsetting everything.'

'I say,' Charlotte said, 'let's forgive her now. I expect she thought she was doing right, being like a Spartan boy or something. Caro is silly like that sometimes. Let's go and find her and forgive her, and talk it all over comfortably, the three of us.'

'I don't mind,' said Charles; 'let's find her, if you like.'

But they couldn't find her.

CHAPTER VIII

THE HEROINE

It was William who, when they had searched house and garden and park for nearly an hour, greeted the two as they trailed forlornly into the stable-yard on the last wild chance of finding her there. By this time both were thoroughly sorry and remorseful, and very anxious indeed to know what had become of their sister.

'I suppose you haven't seen Caroline any-where about?' they said to William, who was sitting in the harness-room door, with a rose in his button-hole, smoking a black clay pipe.

'She was out in the garden a bit back,' he said; 'give me this 'ere button-hole. She's a sister to be proud on, she is.'

'Why?' asked Charles blankly.

'What she done this morning,' William answered.

'I suppose she thought it was right.'

'I don' know about right,' said William, scratching his ear. 'Anyhow she went down along towards where you was messing about in the wood this morning. Just after dinner she went with a book under her arm and her pinny full of roses. I'm coming along that way myself when I've finished my pipe.'

Charlotte and Charles went down slowly to the wood, and they were both very uncomfortable. However right Caroline might have been . . .

'I can't understand how she *can*—the very place where *he* was—all safe only this morning,' said Charlotte, and walked slower than ever. They went so slowly that William had almost caught them up before they had reached the wood.

Just before they turned in among the dappled shadows of the wood, Charles said, 'Did you hear that?'

'Yes,' said Charlotte; 'it's only Caro talking to herself.' And they went on. They did not hear any more talking, and when they reached the lair Caroline was sitting there silent with a splash of red rose colour beside her among the fern.

'Oh, Caro!' cried Charlotte, almost weeping, and flumping down beside her sister; 'I'm sorry we were horrid. We see now you must

have thought you were being Spartan-boyish
or something. And it's too perfectly horrid.
And do let's make it up ; do.'

' I did think you'd more sense,' said Caroline,
but she kissed Charlotte too, ' or that you'd
know that I had—more sense, I mean. And
directly I began to tell you, you said *That*.'
She sniffed. It was plain that she had been
crying.

Charles sat down. ' I'm sorry too,' he said
handsomely. ' Now let's talk about something else. Our only hope is to forget poor
Rupert.'

'I'll try to forget him,' Charlotte said ; ' but
he *was* such a nice boy. I suppose you had to
do it, Caro. But, oh, I do wish he was back
again.'

Here Charlotte began to cry.

' Oh, don't ! ' said Caroline, putting her arm
round her ; ' do you mean to say you don't
understand yet ? I'd no idea you could be so
silly.'

' I don't think she's silly at all,' said Charles
loyally. ' *I* wish he was here too.'

' He *is* here,' said Caroline in an exasperated
whisper ; ' just behind you. We thought you
might be some one else, so he hid. Come back,
Rupert ; it's only them.'

And from the tangled thicket Rupert put

forth a head very rough as to the hair, which
bristled with twigs and pine-needles.

'Then you didn't run away to sea?'

'Not much,' Rupert answered, leaning on
his elbows and showing only the head and
shoulders part of him.

'But the letter said——'

'That was *her*,' Rupert explained, pointing
at Caroline with his head. (That looks odd
when you read it, but if you try, you will find
that it is quite easy to do.) 'That was her.
It was all her. I'll never say anything about
girls being muffs again. She absolutely ran
the show. She's a brick.'

'Oh, shut up,' said Caroline with hot ears.

'But *what* did she do?'

'Took them off the scent. Tell them all
about it,' said Rupert.

'No, you,' said Caroline, rolling over and
burrowing her nose among the roses.

'Well, it was like this. After you'd gone
off, I was in a blue funk, and I don't mind owning
it. And when she came back I thought it was
the Police, and about all being lost except
honour—and precious little of that. Then she
explained it all to me, and I got my boots off.'

'Explained *what*?' Charles had to ask.

'Her plan, you duffer; her glorious Sherlock-
Holmes plan.'

'You *might* have told us,' Charlotte couldn't help saying.

'How could I ?   All among William and the Police ? '

'Well, go on.'

'She'd got her pocket-book, and I wrote that letter.   She thought of that too.   And I gave her my hankey, and she carried my boots off in her hand, and when she got to the swampy place she put them on and made the footmarks.'

'I stamped them in as deep as I could,' Caroline broke in, 'and I found the fence and got out and put the letter, and simply tore back round by the lodge.   Didn't you notice how hot I was ?   I saw the Murdstone man, but I'd got my sun-bonnet.   He was cutting the heads off nettles with his stick like some one in the French Revolution.'

'And she led them off the scent completely. They'd have been certain to find me here, with the fern all trampled about.   She thought of that too,' Rupert said.

'But where were you then ? '

'Up that tree.'   He pointed to a leafy beech. 'I saw you all go by, your Police with his nose on the ground like any old hound.   Not one of you looked up.   She's a regular A1, first-class brick, if you ask me.   And now if you can hide me a bit here till I've written

to my people and got an answer—— Yes,
she is a brick. And I shall always stand
up for it that bricks are bricks even if they're
only girls.'

'You do make such a fuss,' said Caroline,
delighted with his praise and trying not to be,
and feeling it the duty of a modest heroine to
turn the subject. 'And now I thought we'd be
the Royal Order of the Secret Rose. The rose
is the emblem of secrecy. Two buds and a
full-blowner you have to wear. It's the badge.'

She chose flowers and buds from the crimson
heap and presented them to the others. The
needed pins she produced from the front of her
pinafore.

'I've got one too,' said Rupert, grinning
from his covert. 'A badge, I mean, and——'

'Hush!' whispered Charlotte; 'there's some
one coming. It's William!'

'Oh, that's all right,' Caroline said amaz-
ingly. 'William knows. He's one of us.
He's wearing the Royal Rose too.'

'And he isn't going to tell?' Charles could
hardly believe it of a grown-up.

'No, he ain't a-going to tell'; it was William
who answered, pushing through the leaves and
sitting down squarely on a stump. 'I don't
give away a good sport like what Miss Caroline
is—not me.'

'But when did you find out?' Charlotte asked.

'I had my suspicions from the first—Miss Caroline going off so artful. And then when she come back, of course I knew.'

'Why "of course"?' Charles wanted to know.

'Well, nobody except the Pleece would cotton to it as a young lady like Miss Caroline would set out to give away a runaway dog as 'ad trusted her, let alone a young gentleman.'

Charlotte and Charles never wish to feel less pleased with themselves than they did then.

'An' the bootmarks,' William went on; 'much too deep and plain they was for anybody as was out to get off, with somebody arter them. Let alone as I see a bit of young master's jacket up in the tree as we come over the park. And the ankercher dropped so handy. Not but what I own I thought it was all up when we come to that letter. I did think that was a bit too thick. As if people on the bolt 'ud stop to write letters and lay them convenient like in the middles of roads. I thought you'd killed the cat with kindness that time. But no—'e swallowed it all, old Poad did, like mother's milk it went down. And so did the schoolmaster. And off 'e goes. And off *he* goes. And off *you* goes to your dinners,

and I come along to the young chap in the tree
and fetches him a bite of something, and
whistles him down that all's serene. And Miss
Caroline she comes along and makes me a
member of her ancient order of Rosy Buffaloes,
or whatever it is, and here we are as jolly as
you please, and safe as you please. Only my
advice is, tell the Master.'

'We can't,' said Caroline earnestly. 'It
wouldn't be fair. He might think it was his
duty, or something——'

'Ah!' said Charles, relieved; 'we're not the
only ones. We thought that of *you*. It's just
the same.'

'There's only one difference,' said Caroline
—and this was the only time she hit back
that day, so we may forgive her for it—'one
difference, and that is that I'm right and you
were wrong.'

'Oh!' said Charles blankly.

'Best tell the Master.' William's tone was
persuasive.

'You said you were ours to the death.'

'You asked me if I was, and I wasn't going
to contradict a lady,' William corrected. 'And
as far as keeping my tongue betwixt my teeth,
and lending a hand in the victualling depart:
and a rug and a truss in the straw-loft that
I've got the key of, and where the Master

'Fetches him a bite of something.'

hisself wouldn't presume to show a nose—as far as that goes, I'm your man. More especially since I seen your governors, teachers, pastors, and masters in that nasty white rage with his face all twisted. I wouldn't 'and over a blind kitten to 'is tender mercies. But my advice is——'

'Don't!' Caroline implored; 'because really we can't, you know.'

'Well, I must be getting along,' said William, rising stiffly; 'I ain't talked so much since the election. And I wasn't a-going to say what you thought I was a-going to say. What I was a-going to say was, get out of this. It's all trampled, and some one's sure to notice—if it's only that Jim. You go deeper into the wood, and come night-time I'll fetch him away and bed him down all right. So long!'

He tramped away, crunching sticks and stalks as he went.

'How glorious,' Charlotte said slowly, 'to have a real live heroine for your sister.'

'Yes, but,' Charles asked anxiously, 'are you sure William will keep the secret?'

'I'd answer for him with my life,' said Rupert. 'You don't know how jolly he was when he brought me the bread and cheese, and water in a medicine bottle. It tasted a little of camphor. Awfully decent chap he is!'

'He can't help keeping the secret,' Caroline spoke with impressive earnestness; 'he wears the Royal Rose and the twin buds, the badge of secrecy. If you wear *that* you simply can't betray a secret. It says so in the *Language Of*, page 37.'

She picked up the book from under the roses, fluttered its leaves, found page 37 and read:

'"The red or damask rose, full-blown and worn with two of its own buds, is the emblem and pledge of inviolet"—inviolable, I mean—"secrecy, and he who wears the Royal Queen of flowers accompanied by two unopened promises of her future magnificence, by this eloquent symbol binds himself to preserve uncontaminated the secret trust reposed in him by the more delicate and fragile portion—fragile and delicate as the lovely flower which is the subject of our remarks—of the human race."'

'I see,' said Charlotte, relieved; 'then he can't tell, even if he wants to.'

'If the book knows,' Charles added.

'Well, it's all right, you know,' said Rupert, 'because I'm a judge of human nature, and I know that William is the soul of honour, and wouldn't want to tell even if he could.'

'So that's all right.' Charlotte breathed deeply. 'I say, Rupert, aren't you afraid?'

'What of?'

'The Police.'

Rupert laughed. 'I think William was right,' he said, wriggling out a little farther from the fern so that the red rose in his button-hole burst suddenly upon public view; 'if the Police would swallow that letter they'd swallow anything. And if the eyes of the whole *vox populi* were upon me,' he ended with a grand if vague remembrance of old Mug's careful teaching, 'Caroline would find a *via media*, or way out.'

'Rats!' said Caroline briefly.

'I say!' said Charles, gazing awe-struck, 'what a jolly lot of Latin you know!'

CHAPTER IX

THE MORNING AFTER

'Wake up!' whispered Charlotte, sitting up very wide awake and pinching her sister gently but firmly.

'Why?' Caroline asked, very warm and sleepy. 'We aren't called yet, and it's quite dark.'

'Called!' Charlotte echoed in contempt. 'And the curtains aren't drawn, so of course it's dark. Wake up, silly; don't you remember?'

'All right!' Caroline murmured, and went to sleep again.

'You can't have forgotten yesterday, and how we were detectives, and you were Sherlock Holmes wrong way out, and about Rupert, Rupert, Rupert?'

And at that Caroline did wake up, and sat up in bed and rubbed her eyes.

'Isn't it glorious?' Charlotte asked, jumping

up and down on the bed; 'our splendid secret
and the rose and everything?   I do think we're
lucky, don't you?'

'I suppose so,' Caroline answered, yawning;
'but what are we going to do with him?'

'Conceal him, of course,' Charlotte answered
briskly, 'and answer for him with our lives.
Until the answer comes to the Indian letter.'

'The letter didn't go, you know,' Caroline
reminded her, and put one foot out of bed.

'What's the matter with you?' Charlotte
asked.   'You don't seem a bit keen.'

'I don't feel keen,' Caroline answered.   'I
wish it hadn't happened.   I feel as if I didn't
want to do anything but to be quiet and have
nothing happen, like it used to.   My inside
mind feels quite stiff and sore.'

'That's using it so much yesterday; being
so clever, you know.   Of course your mind
feels stiff.   It isn't used to it,' said Charlotte
brightly, bounced off the bed and ran to draw
the curtains.   'Oh!' she said, and stood quite
still with the curtain in her hand.

'What?' Caroline asked anxiously, for the
tone was tragic.

'It's raining,' said Charlotte; 'that's all.
Hard.'

'How awful,' said Caroline.

Somehow no one had expected it to rain.

The sun had shone now for days and days, and it had seemed as though it must always go on shining.

'Rupert won't be able to hide in the wood, will he?' said Charlotte after a dismal silence.

'Oh, Charlotte,' said Caroline in deep reproach, holding up her little silver watch, 'it's only a quarter to five. I'm going to sleep again. You know how thin and rotten you feel in the afternoon if you get up too early. Come on. Perhaps it won't be raining when it's proper getting-up time.'

But it was, as hard as ever. And it was a dismal little breakfast-party. The dining-room, usually so sunny and delightful at this hour, was sombre and brown and dull. The books all looked like lesson-books, and even the portrait of the Lady with the ruff had but little interest for the children. It seemed as though some one had turned off all sunshine and all magic at the very meter.

Anxiety about Rupert mingled with the usual wet-day feelings, and every one was at first too miserable even to tell the others how miserable it was.

Almost in silence Caroline poured out the milk, Charles served the bacon, and Charlotte handed the toast. And quite in silence they ate and drank. But breakfast soon began its

healing work, and before it came to the marmalade, Charlotte was able to say :

'This is the time to do something desperate.
I'll have some tea, please, Caro.   Aunt
Emmeline says it's a dreadful drug and people
take it instead of beer.   I don't like it,' she
hastened to add.   'It's only to show how
desperate we are.'

'Yes, but your drinking tea won't help
Rupert.   He'll be soaked in the woods,' said
Caroline heavily.

'Still, he'll be safe,' Charles pointed out.
'No one will go looking for him in the sopping
wet.   I'll have tea too.   Let's call it a carouse
in the smugglers' cave.'

But the others thought this was going a
little too far.

'I don't feel as if we ought to play till
we know about Rupert and whether he's had
any breakfast.   And I know the Wilming-cat
won't let us go out in the rain,' Charlotte
said.

'One of us must go out and see William,
that's all,' said Caroline.   'I'll go if you like,
and chance the Wil-cat.   No ; we can't all go.
People notice you so much more if there's a
lot of you.'

Thus William at work in the harness-room
was visited by a small figure in a damp

mackintosh and a red tam-o'-shanter frosted
with raindrops.

'Where is he?' it whispered, 'and has he
had his breakfast?'

'Now you be off, Miss,' said William, very
loud and plain. 'I ain't up to talking so early.
My jaws is hung crooked with talking so much
yesterday. Be off with you.' As he spoke he
pulled a piece of chalk from his pocket and
wrote on the table:

'Come at 12,' and smeared it out with his
cuff, just as the gardener came to the door and
said:

'Don't look like clearing up.'

Caroline understood.

'We shall be wanting some flowers,' she
said, 'to send in a letter. And it's too wet to
go and get them. I thought perhaps William
would.'

'Flowers ain't William's business, nor yet
his pleasure,' said the gardener, 'or he
wouldn't 'ave a dead un in his button-hole like
what he's got.' He pointed to William's coat,
hanging on a saddle-perch and still bearing in
its button-hole the withered rose of secrecy.

'Perhaps *you* would, then?' Caroline suggested. 'I want four red roses, no—five, and
ten buds. And is there any stephanotis? I
think it means absent friends.'

'No, there ain't,' said the gardener.

'Well, then, traveller's joy.   That means safety.'

'Plenty of that — nasty weed,' said the gardener, but not unkindly. 'Right you are, Miss.   I'll bring 'em to the dining-room window to save my boots on cook's flagstones.'

'So that's all right,' said Caroline, returning to the others. 'We're to go at twelve.   Only now we must write to Aunt Emmeline and send her the traveller's joy, because I said we wanted to send it in a letter.   Yes, you must, too, Charles.   We shall be doing an unselfish act, because I'm sure no one wants to write to Aunt Emmeline, and she says un-selfishness makes the sun shine on the cloudiest days.'

'All right, we'll try it on,' said Charles, but not hopefully; and soon there was a deep stillness, broken only by the slow scratching of pens.

Presently the gardener brought the roses and clematis to the window.

'That's what you want?' he asked, handing in the wet red and green bouquet.

'Quite,' said Caroline; 'and do you know it's just as well you hadn't any stephanotis, because I see it doesn't mean what I thought it meant.   It means 'Will you accompany me to the East?' and Aunt Emmeline would have been so upset wondering what we meant.'

'She wouldn't 'a been the only one,' said the gardener, and clumped away on those boots which were not considered suitable for cook's flagstones.

When the letters were done, it was only eleven o'clock, and it was decided that, as Rupert must have had his breakfast, it wouldn't be unfeeling to play desert islands, just to pass the time till it should be twelve.

The dining-room table made an excellent island, and the arm-chair was a ship which held the three of them, and could, with reasonable care, be wrecked quite safely on the deep waters of the hearth-rug. The card-table from the window, turned wrong way up, made a charming raft; and the girls' pinafores, fastened to the poker and tongs, did for sails. You steered with the fire-shovel and brought bags of biscuit (which looked like cushions) from the good vessel, the *Golden Vanity*, which, disguised as the sofa, lay derelict across the Carpet Bay. It was a grand game, and when some one began to say 'Twelve o'clock,' the shipwrecked sailors were quite astonished. The person who began to say 'Twelve,' was, of course, the tall clock with the silver face inlaid with golden roses.

'We ought to go at once,' said Caroline, putting the masts back in the fender; 'but if we leave everything like this, the Wil-cat——'

'We'll clear up,' said Charlotte with a noble effort, 'to make up for being beastly yesterday. You go, Caro. We'll come out as soon as we've done, and stand in the door till you tell us it's all right.'

'That's jolly decent of her,' Charles told Caroline. 'And I say the same.'

'Jolly decent of *you*,' said Caroline, and went.

It was still raining. Caroline stood at the back door with a rose and two buds in her hand, and watched the rain splashing in the puddles and on to the sack-covered shoulders of the gardener and the gardener's boy and the stable boy as they went off to their dinners. As soon as she could be quite sure that they had really gone and wouldn't be likely to come back for anything they'd forgotten, she ran across to the harness-room.

'Here's your new secret rose,' she said, 'and now can I see Rupert? The others'll be out directly.'

'Go and tell them to stay where they be,' said William crossly; 'there won't be much secret rosing left if you're all hanging about here. And Mrs. What's-her-name's equivalent to a bit of secret nosing herself, if you come to that. Hurry up now, afore they comes along.'

The others were not pleased, but they had to own that most likely William knew best.

Thus it was Caroline alone who followed William through the stable and up the ladder into the straw-loft, which at first seemed to have nothing in it but straw, very dark in the corners and very yellow under the skylight.

'Where is he?' Caroline asked, and the straw rustled and opened, revealing Rupert, rather tousled and strawy about the head, and the bright eyes and black ears of a small fox-terrier.

'I hid when I heard you on the ladder,' he said. 'You can't be too careful.' He spoke in a low hoarse voice.

'Now I'll keep about down in the stable,' said William, 'and if I whistle, you lay low.'

He retreated down the ladder, and they heard him say 'Over' to one of the horses.

'I wish *this* was over,' said Rupert, rather fretfully.

'It is beastly having it rain,' said Caroline sympathetically; 'but it'll be fine to-morrow, I expect, and I've brought you a secrecy rose.' He took it and said 'Thank you!' but not enthusiastically. 'And,' she went on—'wait till I get it out—it's rather a tight fit for my

'If I whistle, you lay low.'

pocket—I've brought you *Robinson Crusoe*, and a pencil and paper to really write to your father and mother. And I'll post it as soon as the rain stops.'

'Well, you are a brick,' he said. 'I shall be all right with something to read. But you've simply no idea how slow time goes when you're in concealment. I can't think how those Royalist chaps stood it as they did ; and the Man in the Iron Mask and Sir Walter Raleigh and Mary Queen Of.'

'I *am* sorry,' said Caroline again. 'How long will it take to get an answer from India?'

'Oh, weeks,' said Rupert wearily. 'I was just thinking I couldn't stick it, and perhaps I'd better really run away to sea, only not Hastings, of course. But it doesn't seem so bad now I've got the book, and Pincher's rather jolly, and you too, of course,' he added with sudden politeness.

'Tell me all about last night.' Caroline settled comfortably into a nest of straw. 'What happened after we left you?'

'Oh, William came and brought me in and gave me a rug and the dog and some more bread and cheese. And bread and bacon this morning.'

'I say, you *are* hoarse.'

'Oh, it's nothing. I say, don't think me a pig, but I should like something to *eat*. I feel as if I'd been eating bread and cheese and cold bacon for long years, and it's all fat—the bacon is, I mean.'

Caroline said how stupid it was of her and she'd bring him something when the men went home to their teas. And then suddenly there seemed to be nothing more to say.

There was a silence, broken by Rupert's putting his head under the blanket to cough in a suppressed manner.

'I hope you haven't taken a chill,' said Caroline with motherly anxiety. 'Aunt Emmeline says you never take them if you keep your windows open at night; but of course you can't here, because there aren't any.'

'No,' said Rupert. 'I say, do you play chess, or draughts, or halma or anything?'

'I could bring them,' she said; 'but I only know the moves at chess and when you bring down the Queen and the Bishop, and the other person is called the Fool's Mate—only they always see it before you get it finished.'

'I'll teach you,' said Rupert yawning. 'I say, everything is pretty beastly, isn't it? It's jolly in India. I wish I was there.'

'So do I,' said Caroline. 'At least I don't mean that. But I wish you were not so mizzy.'

'There ought to be a Society for the Prevention of Schools,' Rupert went on; 'then everything would be all right.'

'I'll tell you what,' said Caroline; 'I think this is a dumpy day. I felt quite flat this morning, as if nothing mattered. But it got better. I'll look in my book when I get back and see if there's any flower that means cheer up. And if there is I'll bring it to you, and perhaps it will work a cheering charm on you.'

Caroline herself, sitting among the straw, wrinkling her forehead in the effort to think of some way of cheering the prisoner, was almost a cheering charm herself. Rupert perhaps felt something of this, for he said:

'I'm all right. Only I feel so jolly rotten.'

'You write the letter,' said Caroline. 'I don't feel half as flat as I did. I'll think of all sorts of things to amuse the captive. And I'll bring you——'

William whistled below. The two children stiffened to the stillness of stone and held their breaths. Voices. Mrs. Wilmington's voice.

'Have you seen Miss Caroline, William?' she was saying. 'I am afraid she has run out in the reen.'

'She's up in the loft, Mum,' said William. 'I let her go up just to 'ave a peep. 'Ere, Miss, you come along down. You seen all there is to see.'

Caroline rustled through the straw and down the ladder. Mrs. Wilmington, cloaked and with a brown plaid shawl over her head, stood in the stable door.

'I'm quite dry, really I am,' said Caroline, as William climbed the ladder to padlock the trap-door.

'You best come in at once,' said Mrs. Wilmington. And at that moment a faint sound was heard from the loft. Rupert had coughed again.

'What's that?' Mrs. Wilmington asked, pausing on one galosh to listen.

'My dawg's up there,' said William; ''e catches rats now and again.'

'It was a strange noise for a dog,' said the housekeeper with a thoughtful air.

'Weren't it now?' said William admiringly. 'Can't think 'ow they does it! You wouldn't believe the noises dogs make when they're after rats. It's the way it takes 'em, you see.'

'I see, said Mrs. Wilmington, and turned away, picking her galoshed steps delicately, and followed by Caroline, who now ventured to breathe again, and splashed in all the puddles.

'Your uncle,' said the housekeeper, taking off her shawl and shaking it at the back door, 'was inquiring for you. He does not weesh you to go out in the reen.'

'No,' said Caroline.

'And I always understood,' said the house-keeper, 'that young ladies was, were, better away from low company.'

'If you mean William,' began Caroline hotly, but Mrs Wilmington interrupted her with—

'I mean dogs in straw-lofts. Now you know.'

Caroline decided to get Mrs. Wilmington a soothing bouquet as soon as the rain cleared off.

'Your uncle's in the dining-room,' said the housekeeper. 'Wipe your shoes on the mat, please.'

From the dining-room came the sound of talking. Caroline heard :

'You see, uncle, you just sit on the wreck and we'll come and rescue you with the raft.'

She paused in the doorway. Could it be true that the Uncle was playing? No, it could not.

'Thank you,' said the Uncle ; 'I feel safer on the wreck. I'm glad you've been having a game,' he said, blinking kindly at her.

'I hope you don't mind the room being a little untidy, uncle,' said Caroline. For, indeed, the others had decided that the clearing-up bargain was off, and had gone on with the game.

'Not at all, if you don't break things,' he said a little nervously.

'We're most *awfully* careful,' Charles explained. 'You see we keep the raft on the carpet for fear of scratching it.'

'*I* think it polishes it, being dragged about on this Turkish sea,' Charlotte told them.

'And so you're not dull, even on this rainy day? I feared you might find it wearisome.'

'Oh *no*,' said every one; 'it's the loveliest house in the world.' And Charlotte asked him kindly how his magic was getting on.

'Poorly,' he said; 'poorly. And yours?'

There was a silence, full of the thoughts of the magic of fern-seed and of the great Rupert-secret.

'We've invented a Secret Society,' Caroline said difficultly and in haste: 'the Secret Society of the Rose. You wear one full blown rose and two buds, you see.'

'I see. And what is the secret?' asked the innocent and kindly uncle.

Every one became scarlet except the Uncle, who looked more like oyster shells than ever, and said:

'I beg your pardon.'

'We'd tell you in a minute if we could. But you see it *is* a Secret Society.'

'I see. I am very sorry I was so indiscreet. But tell me this,' he added hastily. 'You haven't broken anything, have you?'

'Not a thing.'

'I thought you wouldn't,' the Uncle assured them. 'Mrs. Wilmington was of opinion that you would break almost everything in the house. But that was before she saw you, of course. If you *do* break anything you'll tell me, won't you?'

'Of course,' they answered in various tones of surprise.

'Quite so. I might have known. I wish I could do something to amuse you. If you had any friends in the neighbourhood you might have the carriage and drive out to see them. But of course you have no acquaintances here.'

'The clergyman is a friend of ours,' Charles remarked.

And Caroline said if only they might go and see him.

'By all means,' said the Uncle; 'bring him back to tea with you. I am sincerely glad to find that you are making yourselves at home.'

With that he went away.

F

'Do you think that was snarkasm? About making ourselves at home?' Charles asked.

'Not it,' Charlotte assured him. 'I'm sure the Uncle's open as the day.'

'All the same we'd better clear up,' said Charlotte, and on the word Harriet came in to lay the cloth. Mrs. Wilmington followed. And it was she who cleared up, with pinched lips and a marked abstaining from reproaches.

The children dined alone, and the cook remarked on the sudden growth of their appetites. How was she to know that generous double helpings of beef, Yorkshire pudding, potatoes, summer cabbage, rhubarb pie and custard were hidden behind the books on the dining-room shelf, for the later refreshment of a runaway boy at present lurking in the straw-loft?

'We must put the things in tumblers,' Caroline said, 'because plates would be missed; but the tumblers live in the sideboard, and there are dozens.'

So a row of tumblers, containing such greasy things as never before had profaned their limpid depths, stood in a row like beakers on the bench of a secret laboratory.

'It's all very well,' said Charlotte, replacing the last book and ringing the bell, 'but how shall we get them to him?'

'William will manage it at tea-time,' Caroline was sure.

'But we've got to bring the clergyman home to tea.'

'Oh, bother!' was the remark that sprang to the lips of Caroline.   'I never thought of that.'

CHAPTER X

BREWING THE SPELL

IT was awkward, certainly. And the awkward-
ness kept worrying and worrying at the back
of Caroline's mind all through the pleasure of
going out in the carriage to make a call by
themselves, and the delight of the call, which
was diversified by peppermints, a fine collection
of butterflies, and being allowed to try and
play the harmonium.

It was while Charles and Charlotte were
busy with this in the large bare room which
had been the last rector's drawing-room, and
was now used for all sorts of parish parties,
that Mr. Penfold took Caroline into the con-
servatory to show her a pet newt.

'A friend of mine with an orange waistcoat,'
Mr. Penfold said.

He was a very nice newt, but even his
orange-coloured stomach could not drive away
the worries from the back of Caroline's mind.

How were the tumblers of food to be got to
Rupert?   Altogether she felt worried; the
whole adventure was beginning to feel too big
and too serious.   And when Mr. Penfold,
suddenly asking her if she could keep a secret,
showed her a green parrot sitting on a nest
behind a big geranium, she longed to say that
she would keep his, and to tell him her own.

What she did say when she had admired
the parrot was:

'You're a clergyman, and so I suppose you
know all about right and wrong?'

'I do my best to know,' he said. 'Well?'

'Well, aren't there some secrets you ought
to keep, even if you know that some people
would say you oughtn't to if they were to
know you were keeping them—only of course
they don't?'

I think it was rather clever of Mr. Penfold
to understand this; but he did.

'There are some things we all have to
judge for ourselves,' he said. 'Could you
give me an instance of the sort of thing you
mean?   Not the real thing you were thinking
about, of course; but something like it.'

'Of course not the real thing,' she said,
and paused.

The temptation to be very clever came to
her. She would tell him the real thing, and

he would never think it could be the real one.

'Well, suppose,' she said slowly, and stopped.

'Suppose?'

'You heard about that boy who ran away, and they were looking for him yesterday?'

'He wasn't found, was he?' the clergyman asked, carefully picking dead leaves from a salmon-coloured fuchsia.

'No,' said Caroline. 'Well, suppose the boy had come to you, what would you have done? You wouldn't have given him up, would you?'

'I don't know any of the facts of the case,' he answered slowly.

'But suppose it was a runaway slave.'

'Certainly not.'

'Well, then,' said Caroline.

'But, you see, it wouldn't stop with not giving him up. He would have to be fed and clothed, and have somewhere to sleep, and it would be impossible, quite impossible, to keep him concealed. They would be sure to find him.'

'Ye-es,' said Caroline; 'but what could you do?'

'Well, leaving the boy out of the question —he was just given as an instance, wasn't he

Showed her a green parrot sitting on a nest.

—suppose *you* were in any other sort of difficulty, the thing for you to do would be to tell your uncle. You take it from me, you can trust him absolutely. He'll decide what's right. Unless you'd like to tell me. I'd help all I could.'

'If ever I have a secret I *can* tell you, I will,' Caroline promised. 'We're a Secret Society just at present. That's why we're all wearing red roses.'

'I wish I could have joined it,' said the Unusual Clergyman; 'perhaps you'll let me join later?'

'If I ever can, I will,' said Caroline cordially. And then the others came to look at the newt, and they all went home in the carriage to tea. The Uncle and the Unusual Clergyman talked about things which the children did not understand, or perhaps they might have understood if they had listened, but their thoughts were in tumblers full of beef and pudding behind the books on the shelves, and though they caught a few words, 'golden bough,' 'myths,' 'folk-lore,' they did not pay much attention till they heard the words 'secret rites' and 'symbolic,' and then the Uncle suddenly said:

'Well, come along to my room, won't you? I'll show you that passage I was speaking of.' And he and the clergyman went off.

Of course the three C.'s hastened to the stable-yard. The men had gone to their tea and the servants were having theirs, so it was quite safe. The tumblers of food, now thinly iced with congealed fat and looking very uninviting, were carried in the side-pockets of Charles and under the pinafores of the girls.

William received the visitors with marked disapproval.

'You're late,' he said. 'I've got to go down to the village to see about a new axle for the light cart. What's all that rubbish? Ain't what I gives him good enough for his lordship?' He looked sourly at the tumblers the children had stood upon the corn-bin.

'Of course it is,' said Caroline, feeling that a fatal error had been committed. 'We only thought he'd like a change. Don't be cross, William. You know you're our beanyfactor.'

'Well, beany or no beany, you don't see 'im to-night. Off with you. I'll see 'e's all right. Yes, you can leave the grub. You come 'bout eight in the morning if you can, and then we'll see.'

It was a disappointed party that returned to the dining-room.

'I did think it would be different,' said
Charlotte. 'It's all so dull. And it'll go on
being like this for weeks.'

'It's the dreadful anxiousness *I* don't like,'
said Caroline. 'The clergyman said secrets
were awkward pets to keep, and they are.'

'Why is everything always different from
what it was when you thought it was always
going to be the same?' Charlotte asked, with
the air of an inquiring philosopher.

'You see,' said Caroline, 'we are rather
young for rescues.'

'Yes, but,' Charles urged, 'we couldn't do
anything *except* rescue. We can't do anything
else *now*, however young we are.'

They talked about it for an hour, and said
the same things over and over, and then Mr.
Penfold came in to say good-bye.

'I'm translating that book. I'm getting
on with it,' he said; 'it's most interesting.
I've got some of the manuscript in my pocket.'

'Oh do let us look!' they all said at
once.

'Well, just one page then, only one, or I
shall be late for the choir practice.'

He laid down a type-written page and they
all sprawled over the table to read it.

'To obtain your suit,' it said. 'Herbs
favourable to the granting of petitions . . .'

There was a blank for the names of the herbs, which Mr. Penfold hadn't yet had time, he told them, to translate.

'Suitors to kings and those in high places shall note well these herbs,' the translation went on, 'and offer the flowers and leaves in bunches or garlands when they go to tender their suit. More efficacious it is, however, if the herbs be bruised and their juices expressed, and a decoction given to drink in a little warm sack or strong waters or any liquor convenient. But for this ye need interest with the household of the king or him who has the granting of the desire. These herbs have the virtue to incline the heart favourably towards suitors if gathered in the first quarter of Luna by the hand of the petitioner in his proper person.'

That was the end of the page. The children had to own that they couldn't understand it.

'Oh,' said the Unusual One, 'it only means if you're going to ask a favour of any one. One of the herbs was balsam, I believe. Now I must fly. Keep the page till to-morrow if you like.'

They did like. And when he was gone Charlotte spoke.

'Look here. We shall have to tell the

Uncle. Let's decoct him some balsam and then tell him.'

But the others wouldn't hear of it. They had to hear of it, however, next day, when at twelve o'clock William allowed them to visit Rupert in his loft. Rupert's eyes were very bright and his hands were very hot, and he coughed almost all the time—a very little cough, but most persevering.

'William,' Caroline came down the ladder to say, 'we must tell uncle. I'm sure Rupert's ill. He ought to have a doctor.'

'You're right, Miss,' William replied. 'What did I tell you from the first?'

Caroline expected stern opposition from Rupert, and even feared that he might say that rather than have his secret given to an uncle he would indeed run away to sea. But he only turned his head restlessly on the straw and said, 'Oh, I don't care! Do what you like.'

The day was, most fortunately, fine. So after dinner they all went into the garden to get the balsam. But they couldn't find any balsam.

'I'll get the *Language Of*,' said Caroline, 'and we'll take the herbs that seem most likely to make a person do what you want.'

In finding suitable 'herbs,' first in the book

and then in the garden, the time went quickly : there was a good deal of talk, of course.

'I *really* don't think we need worry,' said Caroline again and again. 'I think with the herbs it's sure to be all right, and the Uncle will let us keep him.' She spoke as if Rupert were a stray kitten or an ownerless puppy. 'You see the fern-seed came right, and the sorry bouquet we gave to the Wilmington came right, and you'll see this will. We'll give him some in his tea as well as the bouquet, and that'll make quite certain.'

'It's all nonsense,' said Charlotte. 'Besides, he'll spit it out. I know I should. You can lead an uncle to the teapot but you can't make him drink.'

'We'll have calceolaria,' Caroline finally decided, 'because it means "I offer you pecuniary aid," or "I offer you my fortune"; and, of course, Rupert'll cost something to keep. And double china aster, if we can find it, because it means "I share your sentiments." Straw means agreement, so we'll have that too. It needn't show in the bouquet. And eschscholtzia, because that signifies "do not refuse me."'

They got the calceolarias and the eschscholtzias, but the gardener said the asters weren't out yet.

'It's only two flowers,' said Charlotte;
'suppose we wear something in our button-
holes to mean "we trust in you"?'

Nothing meaning just that, however, could
be found in the book. The nearest was
heliotrope, 'I turn to thee,' and rhododendron,
'danger.' A bouquet of rhododendron and
heliotrope was, however, found to be incom-
patible with the human button-hole, so these
flowers were added to the Uncle's bouquet.

'And now,' said Charlotte, 'let's go in and
express the juices. We can't chew them this
time, because it would be disgusting.'

'Scissors and tea, I think,' Charles said, and
this bright suggestion was acted on.

The Unusual Clergyman was perhaps partly
to blame for what followed. Calceolaria,
rhododendron, and eschscholtzia (a word I
spell with the greatest pain and difficulty)
were cut up very fine indeed with Caroline's
nail-scissors, and secreted in Charles's handkerchief—a clean one fetched down for the
purpose. When the tea-tray was brought in,
and the maid had gone to ring the bell which
summons uncles, the lid of the teapot was
hurriedly raised and a good handful of chopped
leaves and petals thrust in.

The magic bouquet was placed on the
Uncle's plate.

He came in, pale and shadowy as ever, and yet looking, the children thought, somewhat different, and took up the bouquet. It was rather an odd one. The eschscholtzias were drooping miserably among the strong rhododendrons; so was the heliotrope. And the calceolarias seemed shrivelled and unhappy; and the straw, of which in his enthusiasm Charles had brought a large double handful, showed much more than Caroline had meant it to.

'What's all this, eh?' the Uncle asked.

'It's a sym-what's-its-name bouquet.'

'Simple?' asked the Uncle; 'it's anything but that. Sympathetic?'

'No,' said Charlotte, 'sym-—what Mr. Penfold was saying to you yesterday about magic.'

'Symbolic. I see. And what does it symbolise?' he asked kindly, but without smiling.

'We'll tell you when you've had your tea,' they all agreed in saying.

The Uncle sniffed the bouquet, and that was perhaps why he did not sniff the tea. They wondered how he could possibly not smell it, for as Caroline poured it out it seemed to fill the room with its strange mixed scent. However, he just stirred it and talked about the

He screwed up his nose.

weather, not at all amusingly, and presently
he lifted the cup to his lips.

Six anxious eyes followed his every move-
ment; and his movements from the moment
the tea entered his mouth were brisk and
unusual. He screwed up his nose in a way
that at any less important moment would have
been funny, went quickly to the window, leaned
out, and did exactly what Charlotte had said
he would do.

'Excuse me,' he said, coming back to the
table and taking up the cup; 'I beg your
pardon for that natural if impolite action. I
think this tea must be poisoned. Don't drink
any of it, and please ring the bell. I must
inquire into this.'

Nobody moved.

'We aren't going to drink any,' said
Charles.

'Oh, don't inquire!' said Charlotte
anxiously.

'Was it *very* horrid?' asked Caroline. 'I
am so sorry.'

'Will you kindly ring?' the Uncle asked
coldly. It was a terrible moment, but
Caroline met it bravely.

'No,' she said; 'don't ask the servants,
please, uncle; it's not their fault. *We* put the
stuff in the teapot.'

'You put poison in the teapot? For me?'
The Uncle suddenly sat down.

'No, no, dear uncle,' cried Caroline; '*not*
poison. Only calceolaria and eschscholtzia
and straw and rhododendron; it isn't poison.
It's just a little magic spell to make you say
"Yes" to what we want.'

'Have I given you reason to suppose that I
could not grant your requirements without
spells?' he asked severely.

'Oh no! But we wanted to make sure.'

Charlotte held out the translation and the
Uncle read it.

'But this doesn't say calceolaria and all the
rest of it,' he objected.

'No, it doesn't say. That's just it. So we
had to get the nearest things we could. Straw
for agreement, because we want you to agree
to what we want; and calceolaria, because it
means "I offer you pecuniary aid"; and rhododendron to show it's dangerous not to; and es-
what's-its-name for "do not refuse me."'

'Do not refuse you *what*?' said the Uncle in
an exasperated voice.

The three of them looked at each other and
two of them said, 'You tell, Caro.'

Caroline clasped her hands very tight, and
drew a long breath, and said very fast indeed:

'There was a boy ran away from school

called Rupert his master was cruel to him and
he came here and we hid him and put the
Police off the scent and he's such a nice boy
and his father's in India like ours and he's in
the straw-loft now with such a dreadful cold
and I know the doctor ought to be sent for and
if you give him back to that Murdstone man I
know he'll die and I can't bear it and I'm very
very sorry it was silly putting the stuff in your
tea but we weren't taking any chances and if
you're angry about the tea do punish us but
stick to Rupert and oh uncle I don't know
what to say but what would you have done if
you'd been us?'

'There, there,' said the Uncle gently, and
not seeming as surprised as they expected;
'don't cry. Don't *you* begin,' he added with
more sternness to Charles, who was becoming
subject to sniffs. 'There, go and wash your
faces. We'll have some fresh tea made in
another pot, and talk it over.'

'It's hopeful, I tell you,' said Caroline, washing her face; 'he's not said "No." Oh, I
believe the spell's working. Stop snivelling,
Charlotte. There's nothing to cry about, *yet*.'

'You began,' said Charlotte truthfully.

'I didn't,' said Caroline; 'and if I did, you
put it all on to me, and I didn't know what I
was saying or doing. Come on down. We

mustn't let him think it over by himself too
long.'

Over tea, for which nobody felt very hungry,
the Uncle asked many questions, and heard
the full story of the escape and the Royal
Order of the Secret Rose.

'And don't blame William, will you?'
Charlotte begged; 'because he's done nothing
but say tell you ever since it began.'

'I shall not blame William,' said the Uncle.

'I wanted to tell you,' said Caroline; 'at
least next day I did, but it wasn't my secret.
And Rupert agreed for us to tell now.'

Tea was over and there was a silence.
Uncle Charles was looking from one to another
of the children.

'And you really believed,' he said slowly,
'that putting that abominable stuff in my tea
would make me agree to keep your runaway
boy?'

'There was the fern-seed, you know,' said
Charlotte; 'and it said in the book that the
decoction of balsam would make you grant our
desire, and calceolaria's as good as balsam any
day.'

'And you really thought it would?'

'Won't it?' asked Caroline, and her eyes
filled with tears. 'Oh, uncle, if you only knew
how I hated giving you that horrid stuff

instead of your nice tea.   It hurt me far more
than it did you.'

The Uncle laughed faintly, but he did
laugh.

'Then you *will* grant our desire,' cried
Charlotte.   'You couldn't laugh if you weren't
going to.   So you see the herbs did do the
magic.'

'Something seems to have done it,' said the
Uncle.   'You had better give me a red rose
and two buds and enrol me as a member of
your Royal Order of the Secret Rose.'   He
found himself suddenly involved in a violent
threefold embrace.

'I will give you a word of advice,' he said,
settling his neck-tie when it was over.   'Never
try to administer philtres or potions *inwardly*.
Outward application is quite as efficacious.
Indeed I am not sure but what your bouquet
was in itself enough to work the spell.   Something has certainly worked it.   For I may
now tell you that Mrs. Wilmington had her
suspicions, and by a stratagem surprised the
secret this afternoon.   She told me and wished
to send for the Police.   But I heard William's
story, and decided not to send for the Police
till after tea.   But now Mrs. Wilmington has
seen the boy, you may as well make her a
Royal Rose too.   She will not betray you.'

The children looked at each other amazed.

Mrs. Wilmington? It was unbelievable.

'The doctor is coming at once,' said the Uncle. 'I hope it isn't measles.'

'Then, if we hadn't spelled you, should you have given him up to the Police?' Caroline asked.

'Your telling me, or the spell, or something has stopped that. Now run away and play in the park. If the illness is not infectious you shall see your little friend later.'

'Oh, uncle,' said Charlotte in heartfelt tones, 'it's a long lane that never rejoices. We have been so sick about it. And now it's all right. And you *are* a dear.'

'The dearest dear,' corrected Caroline.

'I call him a brick,' said Charles, with the air of a man of the world.

'There's only one thing more,' said the Uncle; 'go and get me that red rose, and then I shall know that you'll let me into the next really important secret you have.'

They ran to get it, and the Uncle took it and the petition bouquet away with him to his study.

. . . . . .

When the doctor had paid his visit they were allowed to see Rupert for a few minutes before bedtime—not in the straw-loft as they had expected, but in the blue room, which is hung with tapestry, and has blue silk curtains to windows and four-poster.

'They brought me in at tea-time,' Rupert told them. 'That Mrs. Wilmington of yours is first-class. I don't know what you meant by saying she was a rotter. And your uncle— isn't he a brick?'

Charles was glad he had thought of that word himself, Rupert's using it showed it was the correct thing to say.

'I'm jolly glad you told him,' Rupert went on. 'Of course we couldn't have gone on the other way. And he's sent a telegram a mile long to my people in India to ask whether I mayn't stay on here till school begins again.'

'How splendid,' said Charlotte, awestruck; 'how awfully splendid! I didn't think uncles *could* be like that.'

'Uncles are all right,' said Rupert, 'if you treat them properly.'

Then he began to cough, and Mrs. Wilmington came in with lemonade and honey, and told the others that they were tiring him, and it was bedtime anyhow.

'If you treat them properly,' said Charlotte dreamily, as she brushed her hair, 'uncles are all right. Do you think *he* would have been all right if we hadn't treated him just as we did?'

'No,' said Caroline. 'Just unhook me, will you, Char? I don't. I think it was the spell.'

'So do I,' said Charlotte. 'Stand still or I can't unhook you. What the eye doesn't see, the hook doesn't come out of. I expect the tea was like what Miss Peckitt's sister's mistress had when their house was burglared—nervous shock. I expect that is the same as electric shocks making people walk that couldn't before. I expect the nervous shock made that part of uncle that grants favours wake up and walk, don't you?'

'You make haste into bed,' said Caroline. 'What's the good of talking all round it? We did what it said in the book, and it happened like it said in the book it would happen. I believe you could manage everything with spells if you only knew the proper ones. When I grow up I shall be a professoress of magic spells and have my business office in a beautiful palace, and kings and queens will come in their golden chariots to ask me what spells they ought to do to make their subjects happy and not poor, and for everybody to have a chicken in the pot, and——'

'Talk about talking!' said Charlotte. 'Come along to bed; do.'

CHAPTER XI

THE ROSICURIANS

THE door of the drawing-room at the Manor House was kept locked, and Mrs. Wilmington dusted the room herself and carried its key in her pocket. After the Uncle had said that about Mrs. Wilmington having expected the children to break everything in the house, the three C.'s began to wonder whether the drawing-room had always been kept in this locked-up state, or whether it was only done on their account.

'Out of compliment to us,' as Charles put it.

'I almost think it must be that,' Caroline said; 'because of course drawing-rooms are for people to sit in, and the Wilmington must expect some one to sit in it or she wouldn't dust it so carefully.'

'I looked in the other day when she was dusting,' said Charlotte. 'I couldn't see much

175

just a bit of the carpet, pink and grey and
pretty, and the corner of a black cupboard-
thing with trees and birds and gold Chinamen
on it, and a table with a soup tureen with red
rabbits' heads for handles, and a round looking-
glass that you could see some more of the
room in, all tiny and all drawn wrong somehow — you know the sort; convict mirrors,
Harriet says they are. I asked her.'

'When?' said Charles.

'Oh, I don't know. Just after. And
Harriet goes in to sweep it. She says its
full of lovelies.'

'Why don't you ask her if it was shut up
out of compliment to us?' Charles asked.

'Because I wasn't going to put ideas into
Harriet's head, of course.'

And Caroline agreed that such a question
would have been simply giving themselves
away.

Each of the three C.'s had turned the handle
of the drawing-room door many times to see
whether by chance Mrs. Wilmington had just
this once not remembered to lock it. But
she always had. And their interest in the
room had steadily grown. And now here
was another wet day, just the day for examining golden Chinamen and looking at yourself in convex mirrors; and the room was

locked up so that no one could enjoy these advantages.

Rupert was still in bed, the doctor had decided against measles; but the feverish cold which had given rise to the measle idea was still too bad for Rupert to be anywhere but where he was. And the others were only allowed to see him for a few minutes at a time. Mrs. Wilmington had, so Harriet explained, 'taken to the new young gentleman in a way you'd hardly believe,' and was spending the afternoon reading *Masterman Ready* to him after a baffled attempt to read him *Eric, or Little by Little*, which she fetched from her own room on purpose, and which Rupert stopped his ears with his fingers rather than listen to.

'It is *the* time,' said Charlotte; 'there is a time in the affairs of men that they call the Nick. And this is it. Let's try to get in. The Wilmington is safely out of the way. Let's!'

'Yes, let's,' said Charles.

'No, don't let's,' said Caroline. 'The Uncle mightn't want us to. Perhaps compliments to us aren't the real reason. Perhaps there's some wonderful secret kept in there, known only to the head of the house and his faithful Wilmington. The Uncle's been so jolly decent. Let's ask the Wilmington for the key.'

The others laughed, and Charles said, ' You know well enough *that's* no earthly.'

Caroline did not think there could be a secret, because the Uncle was now a member of the Royal Order of the Secret Rose, whose unchangeable motto was 'halves in all secrets.'

' So if there'd been anything like *that* he'd have told us without preservation,' Charles added. 'Yes, I agree with Caro.'

'And,' said Charlotte, 'I don't see—— Oh, I say, I've got an idea! Let's have another hunt for that second book the Lady in the picture's got under her elbow. We really ought to find it. It's a sacred duty we owe the Uncle for being so decent about Rupert.'

' The drawing-room door's knob is just the same as this one's,' Charles pointed out ; 'and the morning - room's and the library's door knobs are the same too. Let's see if this key won't fit the drawing-room.' He rattled the key of the dining-room door as he spoke.

' I wish you wouldn't,' said Caroline. ' It's jolly rough on me. Everybody always blames the eldest. I wish you'd been the eldest, Charles.'

'I would have if I could, you bet,' said
Charles. 'Come on.'

'No, look here,' said Caroline desperately,
'please don't. And I'll go and ask uncle if
we mayn't. There!'

'But we're forbidden to disturb him.'

'I'd rather disturb him than go poking into
places he doesn't want us to go poking into.
Don't you see? If he doesn't mind us going
in he'll say "Yes," and if he does mind he'll
say "No," and then we shall be glad we didn't
without asking him.'

'But what could be in there that he doesn't
want us to see?' Charles wanted to know.

'Oh, anything! Clouds of live butterflies
that are let out after lunch, and go back to
their cages when the tea-bell rings. I think
Caro's right about asking the Uncle,' Charlotte
said.

'Butterflies are simply piffle,' Charles
pointed out. 'They'd be laying their eggs all
over everything and turning into cocoons all
the time. I know, because of silkworms.'

'Well, a snake then,' said Charlotte briskly:
'an enormous king-serpent, with a crown on its
head, and yards and yards long, that comes out
of a cupboard from two to four every day, and
twines pieces of itself round the legs of the
furniture, or your legs if you go in. It wouldn't

mind what legs they were it twined round, I
expect.'

'I like snakes,' said Charles briefly.   'Let
Caro go to the Uncle if she wants to.'

They all went.   It was deemed respectful
to wash a little.

'They like you to be clean when you ask
for things,' said Caroline.

'It's always "wash!" whatever you do,'
Charlotte complained.   'While there's life
there's soap.'   But she washed too.

There was an agitated pause on the sheep-
skin mat outside the Uncle's study door.

'Shall we knock?' Charles asked.

'You don't knock at sitting-room doors,'
said Caroline, turned the handle, and opened
the door three inches and three-eighths.

'Who's that?' said the voice of the Uncle.
'How often am I to give orders that I am not
to be disturbed on any pretence?'

'There isn't any pretence,' Charles was
beginning, when Caroline broke in with:

'It's a depredation of the Secret Rose.'

'So I perceive.   But I am too busy to play
now,' said the Uncle; and you could tell by
the very way he spoke that he had his thumb
in a book and was afraid of losing his place.

'It isn't play.   We want to ask your per-
mission for something.'

'Well, if I receive this deputation, will it undertake not to do it again for a week, on any pretence?   Then come in.'

They came in, to a room that seemed quite full of books.   There were books on the tables, books on the floor, books on the mantelpiece and on the window - ledge, books open and books shut, books old and new, books handsome and ugly.   The Uncle seemed even to have used books to cover the walls with, as ordinary people use wall-paper.   He was sitting at a wide green leather-covered writing-table, and sure enough he had his thumb in a tall brown folio.

They all said 'Good morning' politely, and Caroline coughed and said :

'If you please, uncle, we want to explore the whole house to look for the other book— the book, I mean, that is lost out of the picture. Dame Eleanour's book, I mean.   You said we might.   But the drawing-room door's locked.'

'Dear me,' said the Uncle impatiently, 'can't you unlock it.'

'No,' Charles told him.   'The Wil — I mean Mrs. Wilmington keeps the key in her under-pocket.'

'Oh, she does, does she?   You won't break anything?   But of course you won't,' said the Uncle rather in a hurry.   'Well, as members

G

of the Society of the Secret Rose, I'll let you through my secret door.'

He put a folded paper in his book to mark the place, got up, and crossed the room to a low narrow door by the fireplace that looked as though it led to a cupboard. He went through the door and the children followed him. They found themselves in a little carpeted corridor. At the left was a door, closed and barred; to the right a flight of stairs, and in front another door. This the Uncle opened.

'Here is the drawing-room,' he said; and there it was. They could see a corner of its carpet, and it was the same pink and grey rose-pattern as the other corner that Charlotte had seen.

'Now come up here,' said the Uncle, and led the way. At the top of the stairs was another door. The Uncle opened it, and behold, the well-known corridor, with the stuffed birds and fishes, from which their bed-room doors opened.

'I will give you the key of this door to keep,' said the Uncle, 'and then you can visit the drawing-room when you please. If you do not disturb anything, and refrain from making your visits in muddy boots, Mrs. Wilmington need never know. It will be a secret between

us—my little contribution to the Society of
the Rose. Like a conspiracy, isn't it?' he
asked anxiously.

'Just exactly like,' every one agreed, and
asked whether it was really a secret staircase.

'It is now, at any rate,' said the Uncle. 'It
used to be merely the humble backstairs, but
I had it shut up because I dislike noise.'

'We'll always come down in our bath
slippers,' Caroline promised him. 'Oh, uncle,
you are a darling!'

The Uncle submitted to a complicated threefold embrace, and went back to his brown
folio.

'Now, then,' said the three, and entered the
drawing-room.

You went up three steps to it. That was
why you could not reach up from the outside
to look through the windows, of which there
were three. They were curtained with grey
and pink brocade that rhymed with the carpet.
There were tall gold-framed mirrors set over
marble console tables with golden legs, and
round mirrors whose frames had round knobs
on them, and oval mirrors with candlesticks
branching out from underneath them. There
was a golden harp with hardly any of its strings
broken, in one corner, and a piano with inlaid
woods of varied colours, on which Caroline

would have dearly loved to play 'The Blue-
bells of Scotland' and Haydn's 'Surprise'; but,
as this would have meant Mrs. Wilmington's
surprise too, it was not to be thought of.
There were carved Indian cabinets with
elephants and lions on them, and Chinese
cabinets with mandarins and little-footed gold
ladies, and pagodas in ivory under glass cases,
and wax flowers also glass-cased. There were
statues, tall and white and cold, and boxes of
carved ivory and carved ebony, and one of
porcupine quills, and one of mother-of-pearl and
silver — a work-box that was. There were
cushions and chair-seats of faded needlework;
old and beautiful and straight-backed chairs
and round-backed chairs; two crystal chan-
deliers that looked like fountains wrong way
up; china of all sorts, including a Chinaman
who wagged his head when you came near
him.

In fact, the room was the kind of room you
sometimes find in houses where the same
family has lived for many many many years,
and each generation has taken care of the
beautiful things left by its ancestors, and has
added one or two more beautiful things, to be
taken care of by the generation that is to come
after. You could have amused yourself there
for an hour just by looking; and the three

C.'s remembered joyously that they had not been forbidden to touch.

It is wonderful how careful children can be if they do not allow their minds to wander from their determination to be careful. The three C.'s looked at everything and touched a good many things, and did not break or hurt anything at all. They examined the cabinets, opening their doors and pulling out every drawer in the hope of discovering some secret place where The Book might be. But they only found coins and medals and chessmen and draughts and spellicans, bright foreign sea-shells, a sea-horse and a snake skin, some mother-of-pearl counters and ivory draughts, and an ivory cribbage board inlaid with brass that shone like gold.

'It's no good,' said Charles at last, pulling out one of the lacquered drawers; 'let's play spellicans. It's a nice quiet game that grown-ups like you to play, and we owe the Uncle *something*.'

'Let's have just *one* more look,' Charlotte pleaded. 'Oh, I say, we haven't looked at the books yet.'

There were books, not many, on some of the tables—large books with pictures, and one, a photograph book, so heavy that Caroline could not lift it up.

'I say. Look here,' she called out; 'this book's only got about three pages of uncles and aunts, the rest is solid, like a box made to imitate a book. Suppose *the* book were inside the box part?'

'Won't it open?' The others were crowding close to look.

'There's a sort of catch there,' said Charles, putting his finger on a little brass button.

'Oh, crikey!' he started back. So did the others. For a low whirring sound had come from the book, and Charlotte had hardly time to say, 'It's a Nihilist bomb, come away!' before the book broke into the silvery chiming cadence of 'Home, Sweet Home.'

'It's a musical box,' Charlotte explained needlessly. And then the same thought struck each mind.

'Mrs. Wilmington!' For the musical box was a fine one, and its clear silvery notes rang out through the room. Mrs. Wilmington must hear wherever she was. She would hear and come.

'Fly!' said Caroline, and they fled. They got out, locked the door, rushed softly yet swiftly up the stairs and waited behind the upper door till they heard Mrs. Wilmington's alpaca sweep down the front stairs. Then out, and down after her, quickly and quietly,

'It's a Nihilist bomb, come away!'

so that when, having found the musical box
playing with sweet tinkling self-possession to
an empty drawing - room whose doors were
locked, and having satisfied herself that no
intruder lurked behind brocaded curtain or
Indian screen, she came to the dining-room,
she found the three C.'s quietly seated there
each with a book, a picture of good little
children on a rainy day. She could not see
that Charles's book was a *Bradshaw* and
Caroline's *Zotti's Italian Grammar*, wrong
way up.

'Oh, you *are* here,' she said ; 'did you hear
that musical box ? '

'Yes,' said the children meekly.

Mrs. Wilmington stood a moment in the
door. She did not understand machinery, and
to her it seemed quite possible that a musical
box might begin to play all on its own account
without any help from outside. On the other
hand, it had never chosen to do it before these
children came.

'You ought not to wear bedroom slippers
in the sitting-rooms,' she said, and went away
without more words.

'I nearly burst,' said Charles then ; 'especially when she noticed our feet.'

'But she'll find out,' Charlotte said. 'She
found out about Rupert. Let's go back *now* ;

because she won't think we're *there* now she
knows we're *here*. There was another book,
all heavy too. We'll start that and wake her
up again.'

'I say, isn't it a lark?' Charles whispered,
as they crept up the stairs.

CHAPTER XII

THE OTHER BOOK

They found the second book. It was not so heavy as the other, but in it, too, there were only three or four pages of ladies in crinolines and gentlemen in whiskers and chokers, leaning against marble pillars with velvet curtains loosely draped in the background.

'Be careful,' Charlotte urged; 'be quite ready to fly before you start it.'

But when they pressed the little catch and sprang towards the door ready to 'fly,' no silvery sound met the ear. In an awe-struck silence they went slowly back to the table.

And now, looking more closely, they saw that the catch was not made to press down but to slide along. Charlotte pushed it. A lid flew up, and there was a space that had perhaps once held a musical box, but now held a reel of silk, an old velvet needle-book with

a view of the Isle of Wight painted on it
outside, and inside, needles red with many a
year's rust ; a box of beads with a glass top, a
bone silk-winder, a netting needle, and a sheet
of paper with some finely pencilled writing on
it.

'Bother!' said Charles; 'let's start the
other.'

But Charlotte was looking at the beads and
Caroline was looking at the writing.

'What jolly little different beads, not a bit
like now,' said Charlotte ; and Caroline said :

'It's a list of books, that's all. I say,' she
added in quite another voice, 'that Thessa-
lonian book is underlined, *hard*, I wonder
why?' She unfolded the paper and turned it
over. 'There's another underlined, Pope's
Ill Something,' she said.

'*Iliad*,' said Charles, looking over her
shoulder. 'I always know Latin words the
minute I see them, even if I don't know what
they mean. Let's start the other musical box.'

'No,' said Caroline quickly, 'let's find Pope's
What's-its-name. There's only those two underlined. It's a clue, that's what it is. Come on
and don't make a row. I feel we're on the
brink of—the very brink. Punctuality and
despatch.'

'All the books in the dining-room's names

are in a book at the end of the bottom shelf,' said Charles. 'I know, because I thought it was *the* book; the cover's something like the one in the picture.'

It was easy to find Pope's *Iliad* in the Catalogue. '1 vol. Top shelf. Case 6. Number 39,' it said. Then there was a rush for Case 6 and a dragging of chairs to the spot. Caroline being the tallest, reached the volume and got it down.

' The cover feels loose in my hand,' she said. 'Oh, I do believe it is!'

It was. From the loose boards whose back pretended that they were covering Mr. Alexander Pope's translation of the Greek epic, another and quite different book came forth. A thin brown book, the second book of the picture! Charlotte climbed on a chair expressly to compare the two. There was no doubt of it. The two were the same. Inside was yellowy paper with a queer sort of waviness about it, and large print of that curious old-fashioned kind where the s's are all like f's, except at the ends of words.

'We can read this,' said Charles hope-fully. 'I mean even *you* can. It's not Latin this time. Let's take it to uncle and tell him we've found it. *Won't* he be delighted with us?'

'We promised not to bother for a week,'
Charlotte reminded him.   ' Let's keep it for a
week, and then we'll give him the two together.
He won't be able to believe his eyes.   It *is* an
eyesore, isn't it ? '

' I think what you mean's a sight for sore
eyes,' Caroline suggested.   ' Let's have a look.
Is it spells ? '

' It looks like all about being ill,' said
Charlotte doubtfully ; ' but it's very hard with
these s's pretending to be f's, and the spelling
is rum, isn't it ? '

' All spelling's rum, I think,' said Charles ;
' especially ie's and ei's.

' I.E., except after C,' said Charlotte absently.
' It says, " Government and Virtues.   It is
under the Moon ! " '

' What is ? '

' *I* don't know.   It goes on : " It is a good
wound-e herb-e and the juice taken in wine
helpeth the jaundice, and is fovereign for the
plague, if fo be the fufferer be not too far gone
in it." '

' What does ?   What is ? '

' " The flowers," ' Charlotte read on, ' " be
large and yellow in forme and in others paler
and fmaller.   The ftalk is two feet high and
divideth himfelf into many fpreading branches." '

' What does ? '

'Rugged wort. It's all about plants, I think, and what they're good for.'

'How glorious!' Caroline cried and clapped her hands. 'Now we've got all three. The spells, and the medicine, and the *Language Of*. And what one won't do, the other will. Hist! not a word!' She had only just time to throw the book into a chair and sit down on it as the door opened, and Harriet entered with the tea-tray.

The Uncle did not come in to tea. Only Mrs. Wilmington looked in for a moment to say that Rupert's cold was worse, and that they had better not see him again that day.

'And please don't be up and down stairs all the time in your heavy boots,' she added.

'Our feet don't seem to please her to-day, somehow, whatever we put them in,' said Charlotte. 'I wish we could give her something to make her like us. We might just as well be black-beetles.'

'What we've got to do,' said Caroline, pouring out milk, 'is to get Rupert better. I felt all the time in the drawing-room how hateful it is for him to be out of things like this. If we could work something out of the three books, I'm sure he would get all right in no time. A threefold spell; that's what we want.'

'Well, we can't have it then,' said Charlotte. 'I should think *two* books would be ample. It's only a cold he's got. It might want the three if it was plague or wounds or jauntry— jaundice, or whatever it is.'

They spread out the book on the table as soon as tea was cleared away, and put their heads together over the yellow pages. But it was some time before they could find anything that seemed as though it could possibly do Rupert any good.

'What a beastly lot of herbs there are in the world,' Charlotte remarked. And Charles reminded her that they called any old flower an herb in books.

'What I can't understand,' he added, 'is how people can possibly have so many disgusting things the matter with them—palsy and leprosy and quinsy, and all the other things as well.'

'I don't suppose people have them now,' said Caroline consolingly. 'Aunt Emmeline says Hygiene has got on so nicely, people don't have nearly such awful things the matter with them as they used. Look at the Black Death in fourteen hundred something. You never hear of black deaths now.'

'I wonder whether funerals are black because of that,' said Charles. 'I think there's something in Latin about Black Death knocking the back of the horseman with an even foot.'

'I always did think Latin was nonsense,' said Charlotte.

Their eyes were quite tired of the yellow paper and the long s's before the great idea occurred to them. It was Caroline who had it.

'Let's look up Roses,' she said. 'I'm sure the rose is Rupert's lucky flower. Perhaps if we made a conserve, or a decoction, or a tincture or something——'

'We promised not to give any one anything for their insides. I've just remembered,' said Charles. 'How rotten!'

'Never mind—let's look! We'll make it a spell as well. Out of the *Language Of*. I expect it'll work all right. Find Rose.'

They found Rose—pages and pages of it. The author of the *Herbal* had plenty to say. As he himself put it : 'If I ſhould ſet down here all uſes of the roſe my booke would be already too long.'

But after diligent search they found out that the rose is under the dominion of Venus.

'That's all right,' said Charles. 'She had a little boy of her own. So she'd know.'

Also, that the decoction of roses 'is proper to cool the heat of fevers.'

'Only we don't know what fever Rupert's got,' Charles said. 'It might be the scarlet kind or the swine kind, if humans have that.'

They also found that the rose was 'a confiderable reftorative. The bitternefs of the rofes when they be frefh is of good ufe to cure choler and watery humours.'

'I suppose watery humours means when you're in the humour to cry: he isn't that,' said Charlotte.

Farther down the page they found: 'The moift conferve of rofes mixed with mithridate and taken together is good for thofe that are troubled with diftillations of rheum from the brain to the eyes and the nofe.'

'That's it!' cried Caroline. 'I knew the rose would do the trick! I know a cold in the head is rheum. That's French. I daresay it's Latin too,' she added hastily. 'But I never knew before that colds come from your brain. I expect that's what makes you feel so duffing when you've got a cold.'

If a doubt was still left in any breast, it was set at rest when they learned that 'Red rofes procure reft and fleep,' and that 'a ftrong tincture of the rofe maketh a pleafant julep, calmeth delirium, and helpeth the action of the bark.'

'Rest's what he wants; the Wil-cat said so,'

Caroline shut the book with a bang, 'and if roses
help the action of the bark, that's the very
thing. She said the cough wanted easing.'

'Does bark mean cough?' Charles asked
doubtfully.

'You may depend it did in those old times,'
Caroline assured him. 'Aunt Emmeline told
me lots of the words they call slang now, were
book-words once. "Swank" wasn't slang in
Shakespeare's time, she said. And it's stopped
raining. Let's get the roses, and we can
think about how we'll give them afterwards.
Perhaps if he just smelt them.'

'There was an old Roman Johnny,' said
Charles instructively ; 'he asked all his friends
to a party, and let down tons of rose leaves on
them till they died. Couldn't we do that to
Rupert? Not till he died, of course, but till
he got better.'

'We might cover him with rose leaves,' said
Caroline, delighted with the romantic idea,
'like babes in the wood. Let's get pillow-
cases full—I know where the linen-room is—
and hide them till every one's in bed. And
then put them over him. We ought to put
something out of the *Language Of* as well.
Iceland moss means health, I believe. Only
there isn't any.'

A hasty search in the *Language of Flowers*

informed them that nemophila meant 'success everywhere'; and as nothing more suitable could be found, it was decided to mix a few nemophila flowers with the rose leaves.

'There was a secret Society once called The Rosicurians. Aunt Emmeline told me,' said Caroline. '*We* shall be that if the roses cure Rupert. I like being long-ago things, don't you?'

The garden was very wet indeed. Even in mackintoshes it was difficult to avoid getting wet through. Every tree dripped on the children's heads, and the water from the soaked rose leaves ran up their sleeves and down their necks. There were so many fully-blown roses that it was easy enough to fill the three frilled linen pillow-cases, though of course it isn't the sort of thing that is done all in a minute.

It was nearly bedtime when the three dripping children, each carrying a dripping sack of rose leaves, stood outside the arbour which led to the secret passage. They had gone out that way.

'I know we were told not to,' Charlotte had said, 'but it was only the Wil-cat who told us, and it was only because the Uncle doesn't like other people to use the passage. And of course we'll tell him afterwards, and he'll say it was all

right. When we've cured Rupert every one
will say how clever.'

Yet now at the last they hesitated.

'I do wish I could remember,' said Caroline
frowning, 'whether we *did* promise not to go
through the passage or whether it was only
that we were *told* not to. It really does make
all the difference, doesn't it?'

(It often happens that grown-up people think
children are disobedient because really and truly
the children *can't* remember whether they
promised or not, and naturally they give themselves the benefit of the doubt. Sometimes
the grown-ups do not, in their turn, give the
children this benefit.)

Neither Charles nor Charlotte could remember having promised.

'Then here goes!' said Caroline, pushing
open the door. The candle they had put there
in readiness gave them enough light to fasten
the bolts by, and also to find the recess in the
vault of the passage which they had decided to
use to hide the rose leaves in.

They listened at the other door, got safely
into the passage and up to their rooms. Caroline pulled off her wet things, put on her bath
slippers, and crept down with her bath towel to
rub away the water they had dripped on the
floor by the door of the room where the secret

staircase was. They feared so wet a patch
might prove a clue to Mrs. Wilmington. But
Mrs. Wilmington was with Rupert, putting
cold bandages on a very hot head, and before
she left him for the night, the stones were dry.

Perhaps you would not like to go down a
secret staircase in the middle of the night and
into an underground passage, even to fetch
rose leaves to cure a sick friend? But the
three C.'s were not afraid of the darkness.
Their mother had always accustomed them to
go about in the dark. It was a sort of game to
them, to feel their way about the house without
a light, and to fetch sweets which their mother
would put ready for them. She used to tell
them exactly where to find the little packets,
and so the dark was always mixed up in their
minds with sweets and expectation and pleasant
things. And they only had to go down the
house stairs in the dark. Directly they got to
the secret stair of course they lighted the candle.

And now you see them in their quilted red
dressing-gowns carrying up the wet sacks of
rose leaves. They felt their way to Rupert's
room. In it a night-light was burning dimly.
They lighted the dressing-table candles.

'Hullo!' said Rupert; 'who's that?'

'It's only us,' whispered Caroline. 'Is the
fever very hot?'

'It is now,' said Rupert; 'it was cold just now.
I wish I could go to sleep. I can't though.
I feel all hot and then all cold. It is beastly.'

'We've brought you something nice and
cool,' said Charlotte. 'You get out of bed and
you'll see.'

Rupert, his eyes very shining, and his cheeks
a bright scarlet, tumbled out of bed in a very
long night-shirt and rolled into the arm-chair by
the bed head. Caroline threw a blanket over
him.

'I *must*,' she said, when he protested; 'they
always do when you're ill and they're making
your bed.'

The children turned back the bedclothes and
emptied three sacks of dripping rose leaves on
to the bed.

'Now,' said Charles, shivering a little himself, 'get in. I should think that's enough to
cool the hottest fever.'

Rupert rolled into bed. He was really very
feverish—if he had not been, he would never
have rolled into that couch of wet red rose
leaves.

'Oh, how ripping,' he said; 'it's lovely; so
cold, so cold. You are bricks to bring them.
And how sweet they are. No! don't cover me
up. That's what Mrs. Wilmington does. Let
me get cool.'

'They always cover you up,' said Caroline
severely. 'Lie still, or the spell won't work.'

'Oh, is it a spell?' said Rupert. 'I thought
it was rose leaves. Sacks of them, sacks and
sacks and sacks and sacks and sacks. Each
sack had a cat, each cat had a kit, you know.
I say, if I talk nonsense, it's because I want to.
You're not to think I don't know it's nonsense.'

'You're not to talk at all, even if you could
talk sense,' said Charlotte, tucking the bedclothes very tightly round his neck. 'Lie still
and say, " I am much better. I am quite well."
I have an aunt called Emmeline, and she never
has a doctor, and she always says that.'

'I am much better. I am quite well,' said
Rupert obediently. 'I am much better. I am
quite well. I am much better. I am a bell. I
shall ring presently for Mrs. Wilmington. I
have a clapper inside my head. I am much
better. I am a bell.' And so on, for a very
long time.

'This is the delirium it talked about,' said
Caroline in a satisfied tone, and held the
blankets down more firmly.

Presently Rupert began to shiver, and
Charlotte fetched the eiderdowns from the
beds of the three, while the others held the
blankets tightly round Rupert, who now no
longer seemed to know at all what he was

Rupert rolled into bed.

saying, nor who he was saying it to.   He talked about India, and seemed to fancy that Charles was his ayah and Caroline his syce.   Charlotte he mistook for the Murdstone man, which was very painful for her.   But they held the blankets tightly round him, even when he said it was too hot out there in the sun and begged to have the punkahs set going.

Then quite suddenly he went to sleep; they waited a little, and when they were quite sure that he was asleep, they took up the fur hearth-rug and put that on his bed for fear he should take cold, and then, very cold indeed themselves, but quite certain that their spell had cured Rupert, they crept back to their own beds—rather chilly places without their eiderdowns.

'I *know* the spell will work,' were Caroline's last words.   'You'll see, Rupert will be all right in the morning.'

.   .   .   .   .   .

At five o'clock Mrs. Wilmington crept into Rupert's room to see if he needed anything. The floor was strewn with wet, cold, crushed rose leaves, and on it lay two wet sheets. Rupert, rolled in a tangle of blankets, eider-downs, and hearth-rug, was sleeping as a healthy baby sleeps.   She laid her hand very gently on his forehead.   It was cool and soft.

.   .   .   .   .   .

By breakfast-time Rupert was much better. The fever had gone.

'So you see the spell *did* work,' said Caroline. 'Rupert is much better. I sometimes think we are much cleverer than grown-up people think we are. Rupert is *much* better.'

But all the three C.'s had dreadful colds in their heads.

CHAPTER XIII

THE ROSY CURE

WHEN Mrs. Wilmington found Rupert asleep among the remains of the dewy, crushed rose leaves, she had the sense not to disturb him, but to put two more blankets over him and to let him go on sleeping, while she wrapped herself in a shawl and spent what was left of the night on the blue sofa at the end of the four-post bed.

Uncle Charles, coming down, neat and early, to his study, was met by a very pale housekeeper with prim lips tightly set, who said :

'If you please, sir, them children leave this house or else I do. I mean those children.'

'What have they been doing now?' asked the Uncle wearily. He had thought of a new idea about Coptic magic while he was shaving, and he wanted to be alone with his idea and his breakfast.

'Doing their very best to murder that poor young gentleman in his very bed,' said the housekeeper, looking like a thin portrait of Mrs. Siddons.

'Did they put flowers and things into the boy's food or drink?' the Uncle asked, frowning.

'Worse, sir, far worse. They put him into flowers and things. And I've taken the liberty of sending for the doctor. And, please, mayn't I pack their boxes? No one's lives is safe—are, I mean.' Mrs. Wilmington sniffed and got out her handkerchief.

'Please control yourself,' said the Uncle. 'I will inquire into what you have told me, and I will see the doctor when he has seen the boy. In the meantime, kindly refrain from further fuss. And, please, tell the cook to serve another omelette and some fresh tea. These are no longer warm enough for human food.'

Mrs. Wilmington put her handkerchief in her pocket and went back to Rupert, who was now wriggling among the blankets and asking what he could have to eat.

Rupert was much better. There was not a doubt of it. Harriet had told the children as much, in confidence, when she brought their breakfast.

'But Mrs. W. she is in a paddy and no

error,' Harriet assured them. 'A regular fanteague she's in. I wouldn't be you for something. However you come to think of such things beats me. An' she was on at the Master before he was up a'most about it, going on something chronic.'

'How do you know?' Charlotte asked.

'Oh, I know more then you think, Miss,' said Harriet, tossing her head. 'I've ways of my own of finding out what *I* want to know. I know a sure spell to find out the gentleman's name you're going to marry,' she added rather in a hurry. 'I'll show you some time, if this blows over and you don't have to leave on account of it.'

'Bother marrying,' said Charlotte briefly. 'I don't mean to marry any one. I shall be an Arctic explorer, and sail in the cold waters of the North.'

'It's hot water you'll be in first,' said Harriet. 'Don't answer her back's my advice. Then p'raps it'll blow over. Least said soonest mended's what I say. They can't go on at you for ever if you don't answer 'em back.'

'If you don't answer they say you're sulky,' said Charles, who sometimes noticed things.

'No, they don't, Master Charles; not if you keep on saying "Yes'm" and "No'm" every time they stops for breath. That's the way to egg-sauce 'em, trust me it is.'

The three C.'s did not quite see their way to exhaust Mrs. Wilmington by saying "Yes'm" and "No'm" in answer to her reproaches, and they felt that she would not understand if they tried to explain why they had done what they did do. So they had rather a poor time with Mrs. Wilmington, who said a good deal about the rose leaves, and told them they might have been the death of Rupert, 'when really,' as Caroline said afterwards, 'they had been the life and soul of his getting better.'

Mrs. Wilmington also told them that they were not to think of going out and getting into any more of their dangerous mischief, because their uncle was going to give them a right-down good talking to as soon as the doctor had been.

'But we may go out to-morrow, mayn't we?' Charles asked hopefully. And Mrs. Wilmington replied:

'Perhaps you won't be here to-morrow'—a very disquieting remark.

The children remained in the dining-room waiting for that right-down good talking to; and you know what a hateful thing that is to wait for. They sat there miserably, wondering whether Mrs. Wilmington could possibly

happen by any extraordinary accident to be
right for once, and whether they *had* done
Rupert any harm. They tried to console
themselves by saying every half minute or so,
'But Rupert is better, all the same,' and
'Whatever she says, Rupert is better,' and
things like that.

One thing all felt, that they must see the
doctor and know if they really had done any
harm. Thoughts of concealing themselves in
the wardrobe in Rupert's room, and listening
to the doctor's wise words at the bedside, were
dismissed, partly owing to an honourable feeling about listening, and partly because Mrs.
Wilmington didn't give them any opportunities
for that sort of concealment. Listening at the
Uncle's door when the doctor had come down
and been shown into the study was also impossible, for the same reasons. The only
thing they could do was to keep the dining-
room door open.

'And pounce,' said Caroline. 'If we
pounce, suddenly and well, we shall be able to
say, "How is Rupert; is he really worse or
better?" before any one can stop us. And the
doctor is a gentleman. He must answer a
lady's question.'

'You're not ladies, you're only little girls,'
said Charles. But the others made allowances.

H

It was a time of trial. Caroline answered with that soft answer which is sometimes so hard to bear:

'Yes, dear Charles, we are. Aunt Emmeline says you cannot begin to be a lady too soon, and that is why you must wipe your mouth before drinking as well as after, and never interrupt, and put on your gloves *before* you go out, and things like that. And when I gave my penny to the crossing-sweeper, you know, that muddy Friday, he said I was a real little lady. You *must* remember that day, Charles—the day you upset the ink over my *Hereward the Wake*.'

'Here, I say, chuck it,' said Charles, rather red. 'I never——'

'Oh, Pax, for goodness' sake,' said Charlotte; 'if we begin ragging just when we ought to stand by each other, we're like deserters. United we stand, divided we fall a victim to the Wilmington. Hark! that's the Uncle's door.'

They flung themselves into the hall; and the astonished doctor, just saying a few last words of politeness to Uncle Charles, was met by a charge of children all firmly asking, 'How is Rupert? Is he worse? Is he better? Did we really do him any harm?'

'He's much better,' said the doctor, rubbing

his hands cheerfully ; 'your rose leaves were a variant of what is known as the packing treatment.   You did him a world of good. But,' he added hastily, as Uncle Charles, behind him, uttered the ghost of a grunt, and Mrs. Wilmington, from the top of the stairs, coughed loudly and expressively, 'it might have been very dangerous, very.   Verdict : not guilty, but don't do it again.'

And with that he laughed in a jolly, red-faced way, and went out of the front door and on to his horse and rode away.

'And *now*,' said the Uncle, leading the way back into the dining-room.

I will draw a veil over that scene.   A right-down good talking to is never a pleasant thing to record.   And I am not sure whether the three C.'s deserved this one or not.   Was it chance or magic that made them do exactly the right thing for Rupert?   Of course they explained fully to the Uncle that as it was a threefold spell it was bound to act exactly as it had acted.   He shook his head, did not smile, and went on talking about responsibility and carefulness and so on.   He really did smile when Charlotte, very near to tears, explained that they had only been acting like the Rosi-curians in olden days.   But he hid his smile in his handkerchief, and the children did not see it.

'And now—' said the Uncle once again, and paused. The three children knew those words well, and each wondered what their punishment was to be.

'I hope it won't be lines,' Charles told himself. 'I'd rather anything than lines.'

'I hope it won't be keeping us in,' thought Caroline. 'I'd rather anything than be kept in. And such a fine day too.'

And still the Uncle paused, till Charlotte could bear it no longer. She did not stop to think what she would rather the punishment was or wasn't. She said, 'Oh, uncle, we really didn't mean to be naughty! And it really hasn't hurt him. But we don't want to shirk. Only don't keep us suspended. Let us know the worst. Are we to be hanged for a sheep as a lamb? You know you're hanged twice if you're hanged quickly. We'll do whatever you say, and we don't mind being punished if you think we ought. Only don't do what the Wil—I mean, Mrs. Wilmington, said.'

'What did she say?'

'She said perhaps we shouldn't be here to-morrow. Oh!' said Charlotte, and began to cry. So did Caroline. Charles put his hands in his pockets and sniffed.

'Don't!' said the Uncle earnestly; 'please

don't. I have said what I felt it my duty to say. But it is all over. I certainly have no intention of punishing you for what was a mistake. What I blame you for is—well, briefly, interference, and taking too much on yourselves.'

'Shoving our oar in,' sobbed Charlotte. 'But we did so want Rupert to be better.'

'He is better,' said the Uncle. '*Please* don't cry. It is over now. But I must ask for a promise.'

'We did keep the other promise,' Charles reminded him.

'I know you did. This is more comprehensive as well as more definite. I want you to promise me that you will not only refrain from administering your remedies internally, but that you will not make any external application of them to any of your friends—or enemies,' he added hastily.

'Not put them on to people's outsides?— yes,' murmured Caroline.

'Without consulting me. If you wish to try any more experiments, the simple presentation of a symbolic bouquet should be enough. It was enough in my case. You remember.'

'Of course we promise,' said every one.

'Oh, uncle, you are kind not to be crosser!'

'We don't really mean to do wrong.'

'But you can't do right without it turning out wrong sometimes. You can't just do nothing,' said Caroline; 'though really it's the only safe way. Things do so turn out wrong that you didn't think would.'

'They do,' said the Uncle. 'Now dry your eyes and run out and play. And if you see your way to letting Mrs. Wilmington know that you're sorry, it *would* perhaps be well.'

'Of course we will if you want us to,' they said; and Charlotte added:

'It *will* be well. She always says it is.'

'Always says what is what?'

'She always says everything's all very well when we say we're sorry.'

Then they went round to the terraced garden and sat on the grass and talked it all over.

'And if ever there was an angel uncle, ours is it,' said Charlotte.

'Yes,' said Charles, 'and Rupert is better. I'm glad we did it, aren't you?'

'I suppose so. Yes. No. Yes. I don't know,' said Caroline. 'You see the spell worked. That's a great thing to be sure of, anyhow.'

It was the one thing, however, that they couldn't persuade Rupert to be sure of. He was certainly better, but, as he pointed out, he might have got better without the rose leaves.

'Of course it was jolly decent of you to get them, and all that,' he said ; 'but the medicine the doctor gave me cured me, I expect. I don't want to be ungrateful, but what are doctors for, anyhow?'

'*I* don't know,' said Charles, 'but I know you jolly well tried fern-seed when you pretended to be invisible.'

'I feel much older than I did then,' said Rupert, biting ends of grass as he lay on the dry crisp turf. It was the first day of his being loosed from those bonds which hamper the movements of persons who have been ill. You know the sort of times when you feel perfectly well, and yet, merely because you have a cold or measles or something, you are kept in when you want to go out, and sent out (in what is called 'the best of the day') when you want to stay in, and little driblets of medicine are brought you when you feel least need of them, and glasses of hot milk and cups of beef-tea occur just when you are thinking fondly of roast beef and suet pudding, and you are assured that what *you* need is not heavy food like pudding and beef, but something light and at the same time nourishing. Also you have to go to bed earlier than the others and not to sit in draughts.

However, all this was now over for Rupert, and he was one of the others, on a natural meal-footing. His parents, by the way, had telegraphed thanking Uncle Charles very much, and accepting his invitation for Rupert to spend the rest of the holidays at the Manor House. They had also telegraphed to the Murdstone master telling him that Rupert would not return to him. So that now there seemed to be no bar to complete enjoyment, except that one little fact that Rupert wouldn't believe in spells.

'But the fern-seed acted,' said Caroline, 'and the secret rose acted, and the Rosicurian rose leaves acted.'

'I don't see how you can say the fern-seed acted. I wasn't invisible, because you all saw me through the window.'

'Oh, but,' said Charlotte eagerly, 'don't you see? You *wanted* us to see you. You can't expect a spell to act if you don't want it to act. I wouldn't myself, if I was a spell.'

'It wasn't that at all,' said Caroline; 'don't you remember *we* chewed the fern-seed to make us see invisible things, and we saw *you*. And you *were* invisible, because you'd chewed fern-seed too. It came out just perfectly.

Only you won't see it.   But let's try it again
if you like—the fern-seed, I mean.'

But Rupert wouldn't.   He preferred to
read *The Dog Crusoe*, lying on his front upon
the grass.   The others also got books.

CHAPTER XIV

THE MINERAL WOMAN

NEXT day Rupert felt more alive, as he
explained.

'Now, look here,' he said at breakfast,
'suppose we go and discover the North
Pole.'

'That *would* be nice,' said Caroline; 'the
attics? We've never explored them yet.'

'No, attics are for wet days,' said Rupert.

'Not the real North Pole, you don't
mean?' said Charles, quite ready to believe
that Rupert might mean anything, however
wonderful and adventurous.

'No,' said Rupert; 'what I thought of was
a *via medias res.*'

'Latin,' explained Charles to the girls.

'It means a middle way. You ask your
uncle to let us take our lunch out, bread and
cheese and cake will do; and to not expect
us till tea-time, and perhaps not then. We'll

just go where we think we will, and shut our
eyes when we pass signposts and post-offices.
We might get lost, you know, but I'd take care
of you.'

'We mustn't disturb the Uncle,' Caroline
reminded them. 'We promised. Not for a
week.'

'Write him a letter,' said Rupert. And
this is the letter they wrote. At least Caroline wrote it and they all signed their names.

'Dearest Uncle' ('Dearest is rot,' said
Charles, looking at Rupert to be sure that he
thought so too; 'put Dear').

'But Dear is rottener,' answered Caroline,
going on; 'it's what you say to the butcher
when you write about the ribs that ought to
have been Sir Something. *I* know.'

Please may we go out for the day and take our
lunch, bread and cheese and cake would do, Rupert
says he will take care of us, and not expect us home
till tea, and perhaps not then, with love

CAROLINE
CHARLOTTE
CHARLES.

'Rupert can't sign because he's "he" in the
letter. Only the "we's" can sign,' said Caroline. And Harriet took the letter to the
Uncle, and the Uncle wrote back:

By all means. I am sure you will remember not to administer spells internally or externally to any one you may meet. Be home by half-past six. If anything should detain you, send a telegram. I enclose 2s. 6d. for incidental expenses.——Your dearest
UNCLE.

'How sweet of him,' the girls agreed, and Charles wanted to know what sort of expenses he meant.

'"Incidental"? Oh, if you want an apple or some chocks in a hurry and don't happen to have any on you,' Rupert explained. 'Or ginger beer. Or raw eggs to suck as you go along; they're very sustaining when all other food's despaired of.'

The Uncle must have given orders, for Harriet soon brought in four neat brown-paper parcels.

'Your lunches,' she said. 'Hope you'll enjoy yourselves. You've got a nice day for your outing. Bring me a keepsake, won't you? from wherever it is you're going to.'

'Of course we will,' said Charlotte. 'What would you like?'

But Harriet laughed, and said she was only talking.

They put on their thinnest clothes, for it was a very hot day, and they got William to cut them ash-sticks, 'in case we want to be pilgrims

with staffs,' said Charles.   The girls were very
anxious for Rupert to wear his school blazer,
and so flattering were their opinions of it, and
of him, and of it on him, and of him in it, that
he consented.   Charles wore *his* school blazer,
and the girls' frocks were of blue muslin, and
they had their soft white muslin hats, so they
looked very bright and yet very cool as they
started off down the drive with their ash-sticks
over their shoulders and their brown-paper
parcels in knotted handkerchiefs dangling from
the ends of the sticks.

'Who shall we be?' Charlotte asked, as
they passed into the shadow of the woods
where the road runs through to the lodge gate.

'I'll be Nansen,' said Charles.   'I wish we
had some Equismo dogs and a sledge.'

'It's Eskimo,' said Rupert.

'I know it is,' said Charles.

'I don't believe you did,' said Rupert, and
Charles turned red and the girls looked at each
other uncomfortably.

'I didn't say I did,' Charles answered.   'Not
when I said it first.   I meant I know now you've
told me.   It looked like Equismo in the books.'

This was disarming.   Rupert could do no
less than thump Charles on the back and say,
'Sorry, old man'; and Caroline hastened to
say, 'What will *you* be, Rupert?'

'Why, Rupert, of course. Prince Rupert. He invented Prince Rupert drops that are glass and crumble to powder if you look at them too hard. And he fought at Naseby—Rupert of the Rhine, you know. "For Charles, King of England, and Rupert of the Rhine!"' he shouted.

'Oh, I say,' Charles urged, 'do let me be Charles if you're Rupert. It's only fair.'

'You can't keep changing,' said Rupert. 'Besides, Charles had his head chopped off afterwards.'

'Well, Rupert died too, if you come to that. You might, Rupert.'

And the girls said, 'Do let him'; so Rupert said, 'All right, he didn't mind.'

Charlotte said she thought she would be Charles the Second, because he was a merry monarch; but it was decided that it might be confusing to have two Charles's; so she had to be content with being Joan of Arc, while Caroline was Boadicea.

'She was British, you see,' Caroline explained; 'and Aunt Emmeline says you ought to support home industries.'

'Now we all call each other by our play names all day,' Charlotte said, 'and if you make a mistake you lose a mark.'

'Who keeps the marks?'

'You keep your own, of course—counting
on your fingers. And if you did it ten times,
you'd tie a knot in your handkerchief. Aunts do
it ten times if they play often. *We* don't.'

Here Boadicea, Joan of Arc, Prince Rupert,
and King Charles turned out of the lodge gate,
and the exploring expedition began at seventeen
minutes past ten, precisely. The three C.'s kept
up the game, calling each other by the new
names with frequency and accurateness ; but
Rupert grew more and more silent, and when
Charlotte addressed him as Prince Rupert the
stainless knight, he told her not to be silly.

At a quarter-past twelve, the four children,
very dusty, very hot and rather tired, reached
a level crossing. The gates were shut because
a train was coming, and already, as you looked
along the line, you could see the front of the
engine getting bigger and blacker, and the
steam from it getting whiter and puffier, and
you could feel the vibration of its coming in
the shuddering of the gate as you leaned
on it.

The train stopped, in a snorting, panting
hurry, at the little station just beside the gates,
let out a few passengers, shook itself impatiently, screamed, and went on. The big
gates across the road swung slowly back till
they stretched across the railway, and the people

who had got out of the train came down the sloping end of the platform and through the small swing-gates, and the four children, who were crossing the line, met the little crowd from the train half-way. There were two women with baskets, a man with a bandy-legged dog, and a girl with a large band-box partly hidden by brown paper, and—the four children were face to face with him before they knew that there was any one coming from that train whom they had rather not be face to face with—the Murdstone man himself. He was not a yard from them. Rupert threw up his head and backed a little as if he expected to be hit. The three C.'s breathed a deep concerted 'Oh!' and trembled on the edge of what might be going to happen. No one knew what Mr. Murdstone's power might be. Could he seize on Rupert and take him away? Could he call the police? Anything seemed possible in that terrible instant when they were confronted, suddenly and beyond hope of retreat, with the hated master.

And nothing happened at all. The Murdstone man passed by. He gave a cold, sour, unrecognising glance at the three C.'s, but he never looked at Rupert. He looked over his head as though Rupert had not been there, and passed on.

He looked over his head as though Rupert had not been there.

Rupert grew very red and said nothing. The girls looked at each other.

'Let's walk along by the river,' said Caroline, 'and then we'll tell you why he didn't look at you.'

'You'll tell me now,' said Rupert firmly, 'or I won't go another step.'

'He didn't look at you,' said Charlotte, 'because he didn't see you.   And he didn't see you because you were invisible just when you wanted to be.'

'I didn't want to be,' said Rupert ; 'at least —— Oh, well, come on.'

When they had reached a green meadow that sloped pleasantly to the willow-fringed edge of the river Medway, Charlotte said :

'You *were* invisible, to him.   That's the magic.   Perhaps you'll believe in spells now.'

'But there wasn't any spell,' said Rupert impatiently.

And the girls said with one voice, 'You take off your blazer and see.'

'I hate hanky panky,' said Rupert, but he took off the coat.

'Look, in there,' said Caroline, turning back that loose fold which the button-holes are made in—'*fern-seed*.   Char and I seccotined it on while you and Charles were washing your hands.   We meant to ask you to wish to be

invisible when we went into a shop or something, just to prove about spells, but you did it
without our asking. And now you *will* believe,
won't you?'

'I *can't*,' said Rupert; 'don't talk about it
any more. Let's have the grub out.'

They opened the parcels and 'had the grub
out,' and it was sandwiches, and jam-tarts packed
face to face, and raspberries in a card-board box
that had once held chocolates—that was in
Rupert's parcel—and biscuits, and large wedges
of that pleasant solid cake which you still get
sometimes in old-fashioned houses where baking
powder and self-raising flour are unknown.

'This is the first picnic we've ever had by
ourselves; don't you like it, Prince Rupert?'

Rupert's mouth was full of sandwich. He
was understood to say that it was 'all right.'

'King Charles is gracefully pleased to like
it,' said Charles. 'Boadicea had better pour out
the Rhine wine, for it's a thirsty day.'

'Oh,' said Boadicea in stricken tones,
'there isn't any!'

And there wasn't. Not a drop of milk or
water or ginger-beer or anything drinkable.
No nephew or niece of Aunt Emmeline's was
likely to do anything so rash as drinking water
from a strange river to which it had not been
properly introduced, so there was nothing to be

done but to eat the raspberries and pretend
that raspberries quenched thirst, which, as you
probably know only too well, they don't.

This was why, when they had eaten everything there was to eat, and buried the bits of
paper deeply in a hollow tree, so as not to spoil
the pretty picture of green willows and blue-
green water and grass-green grass, they set
out to find a cottage where ginger-beer was
sold. There was such a cottage, and they had
passed it on the way. It had a neat gay little
garden and a yellow rose clambering over its
porch, and on one of its red brick sides was a
pear-tree that went up the wall with level
branches like a double ladder, and on the other
a deep-blue iron plate which said in plain white
words 'Bateyes Minerals.' A stranger from
Queen Victoria's early days might have supposed this to mean that the cottage had a small
museum of geological specimens such as you
find now and then in Derbyshire; but Rupert
and the three C.'s knew that 'Minerals' was
just short for ginger-beer and other things
that fizz.

So, after making sure that they had not
lost their two shillings and their sixpence, they
unlatched the white gate and went in.

The front door, which was green and had
no knocker, was open, and one could see

straight into the cottage's front parlour. It was very neat and oil-clothy, with sea-shells on pink wool mats, and curly glass vases, and a loud green-faced clock on the mantelpiece. There was a horse-hair sofa and more white crochet antimacassars than you would have thought possible even in the most respectable sea-side lodgings. A black and white cat was asleep in the sun, edged in among the pots of geraniums that filled the window. In fact, it was a very clean example of the cottage homes of England, how beautiful they stand!

The thirsty children waited politely as long as they could bear to wait, and then Caroline tip-toed across the speckless brown-and-blue linoleum and tapped at the inner door. Nothing happened. So she pushed the door, which was ajar, a little more open and looked through it. Then she turned, shook her head, made a baffling sign to the others to stay where they were, and went through the door and shut it after her.

The others waited; the sign Caroline had made was a secret one only used in really serious emergencies.

'I expect there's a bird in there and she wants to catch it,' said Charles; but the others could not believe this, and they were right.

Quite soon Caroline returned bearing a

wrinkled black tray with three bottles of lemonade, three glasses, and the little round wooden thing that you press the glass marble down with into the neck of the bottle.

'Here,' she said in a hurry, 'you go round to the other side of the cottage, and there's a hornbeam arbour and a bench and table, and you're very welcome to sit there. I'll tell you all about it afterwards,' she added, whispering. 'Only *do* take it and go.'

'But what *is* it?' Rupert asked.

'She's crying dreadfully. I don't know what it is yet. Oh, *do go.*'

And she thrust the tray on him and went back through the door with an air of import- ance which even the others found just a little trying. However, they were thirsty and loyal, so they did as they were asked to do; found the hornbeam arbour, and settled down on the blue-painted benches to drink their lemonade and tell each other how thirsty they had been, drawing deep breaths between the draughts to say so with.

Caroline, in the meantime, was in the back kitchen of the strange cottage gently patting the shoulder of a perfect stranger, who sat with her elbows on the mangle and her head in her hands crying, crying, crying.

'Don't! oh, please don't!' said Caroline,

again and again; and again and again the woman who was crying said, 'Go away. I can't attend to you. Go away!'

She was a middle-aged woman, and her dark hair, streaked with grey, was screwed up behind in a tight knob. Her sleeves were tucked up, and all round her were piles of those square boxes with wooden divisions in which lemonade and ginger-beer travel about. The boxes were dotted with greeny bottles, some full, some empty, and the boxes were everywhere—on the sink, under the sink, on the copper, on the bricks, and outside the open back door.

'Don't cry,' said Caroline in a voice that would have soothed an angry bear. '*Do* tell me what's the matter. I might be able to help you.'

'Oh, go along, do!' said the woman, trying to dry her eyes with a corner of a blue-checked apron. 'You seem a kind little gell, but it ain't no good. Run along, dearie.'

'But,' said Caroline, 'if you don't stop crying, how am I going to pay you for the lemonade I took when you said I might? Three bottles it was.'

'Sixpence,' said the woman, sniffing.

'You poor dear,' said Caroline, and put her arms round the woman's neck. 'Now,' she

'I can't attend to you.   Go away!'

said comfortably, 'you just fancy I'm your own little girl and tell me what's the matter.'

The woman turned her face and kissed Caroline.

'Bless you for a silly little duck,' she said. 'My own little gell's in service over Tonbridge way. It's silly of me taking on like that. But it come so sudden.'

'What did?' Caroline asked. 'Do tell me. Perhaps I can help. I've got an uncle, and I know he'd give me some money for you, if that's it. And, besides, I can make nice things happen sometimes—I really can.'

'It isn't money,' said the woman drearily, 'and I don't know why I should tell you.'

'It eases the heart, you know,' said Caroline; 'my aunt says it does. Do tell me. I'm *so* sorry you're unhappy.'

'You wouldn't understand,' said the woman, drying her eyes. 'It's silly, I know. But I only heard this morning, and just now it all come over me when I was sorting out the bottles. I was born in the little house, you see, and lived here all my life. And now to leave! A week's notice too! Where'm I to go to? How'm I to manage? What'm I to get my living by? You see, being right on the highroad I get all the thirsty customers as they comes by. Where'm I to go to?

There's a cottage back by Wright's farm; ne'er a bit of garden to it, and nobody passes it one year's end to another. I'd never sell a single bottle if I lived there to be a hundred.'

'But why must you leave here?' Caroline asked.

'Gentlefolks,' said the woman bitterly; 'got a grand 'ouse of their own up in London. But they gone and took a fancy to my little bit, 'cause it looks so pretty with the flowers I planted, and the arbour my father made, and the roses as come from mother's brother in Cambridgeshire.

'"Such a sweet pretty cottage to stay in for week-ends," they says; an' *I* may go to the Union and stay there, week in, week out, and much they care. There's something like it in the Bible, only there ain't no prophets now like there was of old to go and rebuke the folks that takes away poor folks' vineyards and lambs and things to make week-end cottages of. And of course they can pay for their fancy. An' it comes a bit 'ard, my dear. An' that's all. So now you know.'

'But that's dreadful,' said Caroline; 'the landlord must be a very wicked man.'

'It ain't 'is doing,' said the woman, sorting bottles swiftly; ''e's but a lad when all's said and done. Comes of age in a week or two.

Ain't never been 'is own master yet, so to say.
It's 'is cousin as manages the property. 'E's
got it into 'is 'ead to screw another shilling or
two out of us somehow ; 'ere, there, and everywhere, as they say. To pay for the harches
and the flags when Milord comes of age, I
suppose. Now you see you can't do anything,
so run along, lovey. You're a good little gell
to trouble about it, and you're the only one
that has. It'll come home to you all right,
never fear. Kind words is never lost, nor
acts neither. Good day to you, Missy.'

'Good-bye,' said Caroline ; 'but I'm not so
sure that I can't do anything. I'll ask my uncle.
Perhaps he knows my Lord, whoever it is.'

'Andore,' said the woman; 'but nobody don't
know him about here. He's been abroad for
his education, being weak in the chest from a
child. But it ain't no good, dearie. I'll 'ave to
go, same as other folks as 'ad to go afore me.'

'I shall think of something, you see if I
don't,' said Caroline. 'I've got an aunt as
well as an uncle, and she says you can make
things happen. You just keep on saying,
"Everything's going to be all right. I'm not
going to worry." And then everything *will* be
all right. You'll see. And I'll come again
to-morrow or next day. Good-bye, dear.'

She kissed the woman, paid the sixpence,

and went out to the hornbeam arbour with the
air of one who has a mission.

'Come on,' she said; 'I'll tell you as we go
along. No, I'm not thirsty now. Oh, well, if
you've saved some for me. That was jolly
decent of you.' She drank. 'Now,' she said,
'there's not a moment to be lost; it's a matter
of life and death to the Mineral woman. Come
on.'

And as they went back along the dusty road
she told them what had happened.

'I must ask the Uncle *at once* if he knows
Lord Andore,' she said; 'and he can telegraph
to him like he did to India, and then everything
will be all right.'

'But,' said Charlotte, 'we promised we
wouldn't disturb him *for anything*. Suppose
he doesn't appear at tea?'

'Then we must do something else,' said
Caroline. 'It's the realest thing I've ever had
the chance of doing—except you, Rupert,' she
added politely; 'and if we can't get at the
Uncle we'll try a spell. Every single spell
we've tried has come right. First the fern-
seed; then the——'

'Yes, I know,' said Rupert hastily, 'and it's
all right to play at. But this is a real thing.
I've got a godfather that's a baronet. I'll write
to him to go to the House of Lords and tell

this Lord Andore.   Appeal to Cæsar himself,
don't you know.   How's that?'

'Yes, do,' said Charlotte ; 'but we'll work the
spell as well.   We may as well have two
strings to our harp like that blind girl in the
picture.   What spell can we do?'

'We'll look it up in the books,' Caroline said
importantly ; 'and, Rupert, if we pull it off and
she doesn't get turned out of her house, you
will believe the spell, won't you?'

'I'll try,' said Rupert cautiously ; 'and, anyway, I'll write to my godfather.   Only he's in
Norway.   I'd better telegraph, perhaps?'

'It'll cost pounds, won't it?' said Charles
admiringly.

'Never mind,' said Rupert carelessly.   'Mrs.
Wilmington will lend me the chink till I get
my allowance.   Let's do the thing properly
while we're about it.   You may as well be
hanged for a sheep as——'

'As a cow.   Yes, indeed,' said Charlotte with
approval.

CHAPTER XV

JUSTICE

THE great discovery was Charlotte's. When they got home and found that the Uncle had gone to Tonbridge for the day, every one felt that something must be done, and Rupert began to write out the telegram to his god-father. It was quite a nice telegram, very long, and explaining everything perfectly, but Mrs. Wilmington unexpectedly refused to lend more than ninepence, so it could not be sent. Caroline sat rocking herself to and fro, with her fingers in her ears to shut out Charles's comments and advice, and tried in vain to think of some way of using a spell to help the Mineral woman.

'It's no use, you know,' Charles said, 'looking up the spells in the books until we know how we're going to use it.' And Caroline had to agree that this was so. So she rocked herself and racked her brains and felt herself growing slowly more and more stupid, as you do when you are trying very hard to think of something that has made up its mind that it is not going to be thought about.

'You see,' Charlotte went on, 'we mustn't give the wicked cousin anything to eat to make him good, and most likely we couldn't get at him to make him eat it, even if we were allowed. What a pity we can't get at the Lord with a foreign education, weak from a child. I daresay we could make him take things. When you're weak from a child they give you just anything.'

'That's true,' said Rupert. 'I knew a chap with a flat chest that had cod-liver oil given him —with oranges. But he said even the oranges weren't worth it.'

'But we aren't allowed to give people things to eat,' Charlotte reminded him.

'Besides,' Rupert reminded *her*, 'we don't know the weak Lord's address.'

'I do,' said Caroline, taking her fingers out of her ears, though really she could hear almost as well with them in.

'Then,' said Charlotte, 'let's go and see him. Let's appeal to Cæsar.'

'But he's got two addresses,' said Caroline, 'and we don't know which he's at. I mean, the Mineral woman didn't.'

I

'Try both,' suggested Rupert.

'But one's in London,' said Caroline. 'The Mineral woman said : "He's all right : he's got the castle and he's got his mansion in Belgrave Square ; I can't expect him to bother about me and my little house."'

Charlotte sprang up. 'Let's go to the castle, and if he's not there, we'll get another take-your-lunch-with-you-cheese-and-cake-will-do day and go to London and see him there.'

The brilliant daring of this idea made the others gasp.

'Do you mean go *now*?' said Caroline.

'Why not? There's lots of the day left. It's not half-past three yet.'

'You don't know where the castle is,' Rupert objected.

'Yes, I do,' said Caroline; 'so there! William said the day of the Rupert hunt—he said, "I hoped the boy'd got into the castle grounds. Milord's men 'ud have sent Poad about his business pretty sharp if he'd gone trespassing there." So it can't be far off.'

'I'll tell you what,' said Charlotte. 'You know uncle said the day after we'd been Rosicurians would we like the carriage to go and see Mr. Penfold, only we didn't, because we knew he'd gone to Canterbury. Now if we could only persuade William that going to see

Lord Andore is the same thing as going to see
Mr. Penfold, and that to-day is the same as the
other day, well then—— People think so much
more of you if you go in a carriage—servants,
I mean, and people who don't know about
sterling worth, and its being better to be good
than pretty, and all not being gold that
glitters.'

'And what will you do when you get there?'
Rupert asked doubtfully.

'Why, give him a bunch of magic flowers,
and tell him about the Mineral woman.'

'You'll look very silly,' Rupert told her,
'driving up to a lord's house with your two-
penny-halfpenny flowers, when he's got acres
of glass most likely.'

'I don't care if he's got miles of glass, and
vineries and pineries of every modern incon-
venience. He hasn't got flowers that grow as
true and straight as the ones in the wonderful
garden. Thomas told me nobody had in all
the country-side. And they're magic flowers,
ours are. Oh, Rupert, I wish you wouldn't be
so grown-up.'

'I'm not,' said Rupert; 'it's you that's
silly.'

'You're always being different from what
we'd made up our minds you were,' said
Charlotte hotly; 'there, now it's out. We

were sorry for you at first. And then we liked you; you were so adventurous and splendid. And then you catch a cold and go all flat. Why do you do it?'

'*Non semper vivens arcus*,' said Rupert, and Charles hung on his words. 'You can't be always the same. It would be dull. Besides, I got such a beastly cold. And I'd had the adventure. You don't want to go on having one dinner after another all day. You want a change. I'm being sensible, that's all. I daresay I shall be silly again some day,' he added consolingly. 'A chap has to be silly or not *moresuis*, that means " off his own bat," Charles.'

'Yes,' said Charles, 'I'll remember.'

'Well, look here. I'll go and try it on with William if you like,' said Charlotte; 'but he likes Caroline best because of what she did on the Rupert hunt day.'

'You do rub it in, don't you?' said Rupert. 'I wish sometimes you *hadn't* helped me that day.'

There was a silence. Then Charlotte said, 'You go, Caro. And Charles, whatever happens, you must wash your hands. Go on, like a sensible, and do it now, so as not to waste time.'

'*Cui bono?*' said Rupert. 'It'll be all the

same in a hundred years, or even in five minutes, if it's Charles's hands.'

But Charles went, when Charlotte assured him that if he didn't they would go without him. The moment the door closed behind him she turned to Rupert.

'Now, look here,' she said ; 'I know what's the matter with you. You've got the black dog on your back. I don't know what dog it is or why. But you have. You haven't been a bit nice to-day ; you didn't play up when you were Rupert of the Rhine—not a bit, you didn't—and you think we're silly kids. And you think you're letting yourself down by playing with us. You didn't think that the first day when we saved you. Something's got into you. Oh, I do believe you're bewitched. Rupert, *do* you think you're bewitched? Because if you are we know how to unbewitch you.'

'You're a very silly little girl,' was all Rupert found to say.

'Not a bit of it,' said Charlotte brightly. 'You only say that because you haven't got any sisters of your own, so of course you don't know. We've been as nice to you as ever we could be, and you're getting nastier and nastier. If you like to be nice, *be* nice. If you don't, I shall know it's not your fault but because you're

bewitched, and I shall pity but not despise you.
So now you know.'

Rupert was twisting and untwisting the
fringed tassel of a sofa-cushion and looking at
the floor.

'So you hate me now, I suppose?' he said.

'No, I don't. But I hate the black dog.
I thought you were splendid at first. And
even now I think you're splendid inside,
really. Only something's happened. It *is*
like bewitchment, I do think. Couldn't you
do anything to stop it? I'd help you, really I
would. I say, I'm sorry if I've scratched too
hard.'

'You don't understand,' said Rupert with
what was plainly an effort. 'Sometimes I'm
like this. I feel as if I was some one else. I
can't explain. Now you can laugh if you like.
I only thought I'd tell you. Don't tell the
others. It's perfectly beastly. I suppose I
could help it if I knew the way. Only I don't.'

'Suppose you had a bath,' suggested Charlotte. 'Aunt Emmeline says when children
feel naughty you should always wash their
faces; and if it's true of children, it must be true
of bigger people,' she added hastily, answering
Rupert's frown, 'because your face is made of
the same sort of stuff, however old you are.'

'That was part of it,' said Rupert, 'when

I saw the river to-day. Can you swim? I can. And I promised my father I'd never go into the water to swim unless there was some man there, and—— My father's in India, you know,' he said unnecessarily. 'It was he taught me to swim.' He walked to the window and looked out. 'I thought I was going back to India with him. And then the doctors said some rotten rigmarole, and my father went without me, and I was all right again three months after, and I might as well have gone with him, only then it was too late; and then things began to happen that I never thought could. And nothing will ever be right again.'

'Look here,' said Charlotte, 'I'm *frightfully* sorry I scratched you, and about your father and your not going. Look here, don't come with us this afternoon. You go down to Mr. Penfold's. He's the clergyman. He said the other day he'd teach Charles to swim, so I know he can. If you go directly, he'll take you down to the river and you can drown dull care in the Medway.'

'Do you think he'd mind?'

'Mind? He'd love it,' said Charlotte. 'Just go and say the three C.'s said I could swim, and I can too!'

'I can't like that,' said Rupert; 'but if you sent me with something, a book or anything,

then I could bring in swimming in a natural
sort of way and see what he said.'

'Say we said was there any more of the
translated Latin book we could have. Will
that do? You know Latin, so that will be all
right. I say, I hope they haven't gone without
us. They're a most awful time. Look here,
cut off to Mr. Penfold's before they come back,
if you like. I shall just say you're gone. You
just *go*.'

'You're not a bad sort,' said Rupert, thump-
ing her on the back as he went out, but keeping
his face carefully turned away; 'I think I will.'

Charlotte and Charles met in the doorway,
and the meeting was rather violent, for both
were in a hurry—Charlotte to find out what
William had said and Charles to tell her. I am
sorry to say that he had not been washing his
hands, as indeed their colour plainly confessed,
but helping William in the toilet of the horse;
for Caroline had succeeded in persuading
William that to-day was, for all practical pur-
poses, the same as the other day, all the more
readily perhaps because Mrs. Wilmington had
come out and said that she didn't think it was,
at all. And Caro had said she thought perhaps
they'd better *all* wash, and not just Charles.
And William said that he would drive them to
Lord Andore's lodge gates, because he had to

go down to the station to meet the Master anyhow, and it was on the way, or next door to,
but they'd have to walk back. 'And we've
forgotten to decide what flowers to get, and
Caro says bring up the books so that she can
look at them while you're washing your hands.
Because William says he must start in a
quarter of an hour.'

Thus Charles ended breathlessly, adding,
'Where's Rupert?'

'He's not coming with us. Get down Pope
IV. and I'll get the *Language Of*'; and carrying the books she went up the wide shallow
stairs, three at once.

There was but little time to make a careful
selection of the flowers most likely to influence
a youthful peer. Charlotte was all for repeat-
ing, flower for flower, the bouquet designed for
suitors, which had been so successfully used
in the case of Rupert and the Uncle. But
Caroline argued that what suited uncles might
very well be the worst possible thing for lords
who were no relations, and that it would be
much better to start afresh with an entirely
new floral selection.

'Look in the *Language Of*, then, while I
wash,' she said. 'Look for duty and justice and
being kind to the poor.' Charlotte fluttered
the pages obediently.

'Jealousy, Jest, Joy, Justice. Gladiolus and sweet-scented tussilage. What's tussilage?'

'I don't know,' said Caroline, soaping fervently; 'try the medicine book.' The medicine book admitted that tussilage was another name for *Tussilago Farfara*, or coltsfoot.

'But coltsfoot comes in February,' said Caroline, 'and we don't know it when it's grown up.'

'There's rudbeckia: justice,' said Charlotte hopefully. But the medicine book, when consulted, pretended not to know anything at all about rudbeckia, and as the children knew nothing about it either, it was ruled out.

'There's justice shall be done, Cornflower,' said Charlotte; and the medicine book, after saying 'See Bluebottle,' informed them that cornflowers 'being naturally cold and dry are under the dominion of Saturn'; also that 'taken with water of plantain or the greater comfrey is a remedy againſt the poiſon of the ſcorpion.'

'That's all right,' said Charlotte gaily; 'it must be sharper than a scorpion's teeth to have a wicked landlord. Now——'

'I'll look now,' said Caroline; 'you wash, quick!'

Caroline chose red columbine because it

meant 'anxious and trembling'; 'and I'm sure
we shall be *that* soon enough,' she said. The
medicine book confirmed her choice by assuring
her that columbine was an herb of Venus,
commonly used, with good success, for 'fore
mouths and throats.'

'Ours will be, before we've done,' she said.
'We shall have to explain to him a lot.'

The liverwort polyanthus, though signify-
ing confidence, was rejected as being too
difficult to find most likely; but the daily rose
('Thy smile I aspire to') seemed the very
thing, and it was agreed that lemon verbena
('Unexpected meeting') would be both scented
and appropriate.

'And I've got a little straw too,' said
Caroline—'I got it while William was harness-
ing—it did so well with uncle; and wistaria
means 'Welcome, fair stranger,' so we'll have
that. There was no time to look these up in
the medicine book, except liverwort, and of
this they had only to read that 'It is true that
Mizaldus and others, yea, almoſt all aſtrological
phyſicians hold this to be an herb of Jupiter,
but the truth is it is an herb of Mercury, and a
ſingular good herb for all ſadneſs of ſpirit,'
when Charles came to say 'Hurry up! or
William will be off without us.'

'To gather the flowers will be but the work

of a moment,' said Caroline; 'you two go in the carriage, and I'll tell William to drive out by the deserted lodge and pick me up at the garden gate.'

Unfortunately the flowers were not easy to find. The gardener had to be consulted, and thus the gathering of Lord Andore's presentation bouquet was the work of about a quarter of an hour, so that William was waiting and very cross indeed when Caroline came running out of the garden with the flowers—a mere bundle, and no bouquet, as Charles told her—in her held-up skirt.

'No time now to drop people at lodge gates,' he said. 'I'll set you down at the turning, and even that I didn't ought to do by rights, being late as it is, and I shall have to fan the horse along something cruel to get to the station in time as it is.'

So the splendour of driving up to the castle in the carriage was denied them; they could not even drive to the lodge. And all they got, after all Caroline's careful diplomatic treatment of William, was, as she said, 'just a bit of a lift.'

'It saves time, though,' said she, 'and time's everything when you've got to be home by half-past six. I do hope Lord Andore's in, don't you?'

'I don't know,' said Charles. 'I think it would be more noble if we had to sacrifice ourselves and go to London to see him. We should have to break open our money-boxes. I've always wanted to do that. I do wish Rupert had been here. He could have made up something to say in Latin, and then Lord Andore would have had to pay attention.'

'He'll have to in English,' said Caroline quietly, 'if he's there. Oh, I do hope he is! The Mineral woman is most likely crying all this time. She only stopped for a minute, I'm certain, to sort the bottles because of the man coming for them with the cart at three. Won't it be glorious going and telling her that it's all right and she needn't go?'

'But suppose it all *isn't*, and she *need*,' said Charles gloomily.

'The spells have never failed us yet,' said Caroline.

'I believe it's something to do with the garden and our being the ancestors of Dame Eleanour,' said Charlotte; 'of course it'll be all right, Charles.'

'Rupert didn't think so.'

'Rupert doesn't know as much as we do, when it isn't Latin,' said Charlotte. 'We're going to teach Rupert a lot, by and by. You see if we don't. All right, William; we're getting out as fast as we can, aren't we?' for the carriage had stopped, and a voice from the box was urging them to look slippy.

The carriage rolled away, leaving them at the corner, with the big bouquet which Caroline had hastily arranged as they drove along.

'If we see him, you'll let me tell him, won't you?' she said; 'because the Mineral woman told about it to me.' And the others agreed, though Charles pointed out that the Mineral woman only told her because she happened to be there.

CHAPTER XVI

THE APPEAL TO CÆSAR

So far all had gone well with the project of calling on Lord Andore to tell him about his unfortunate tenant and the week-ending admirers of her cottage. But at Lord Andore's lodge gate a check occurred.

As the long gate clicked itself into place after they had passed through it, an elderly person in a black cap with violet ribbons put her head out of the lodge window and said:

'No, you don't!'

'Yes, we do,' said Charlotte unguardedly.

'No village children allowed in,' said the black and violet cap.

'We aren't,' said Charles. And then the cap disappeared only to reappear a moment later at the lodge door, on the head of a very angry old lady with a very sharp long nose, who might have been Mrs. Wilmington's grandmother.

'Out you go, the way you came,' she said; 'that's the order. What do you want, anyhow?'

'We've got a bouquet for Lord Andore,' said Caroline, showing it.

'Keep it till the fifteenth,' said the woman; a silly thing to say, for no bouquet will keep a fortnight. 'No village people admitted till the gala and fête when his lordship comes of age. You can come then. Out you go. I've no patience,' she added; and it was quite plain that she had not.

They had to go back. I wish I could conceal from you that Charles put out his tongue at her as he passed. It is a dreadful thing to have to relate, and my only comfort is that Caroline and Charlotte did not do it. Charlotte made a face, but Caroline behaved beautifully.

Only, when they were out in the road again, it was Caroline who said, almost 'between her set teeth' as heroes do in moments of crisis, 'You know that broken paling we passed?' The others instantly understood. They went back, found the broken paling and slipped through. It was Caroline's dress that was really badly torn. Charlotte's was only gathers, which you can tuck into your waistband and it only makes a lump and the skirt rather

Found the broken paling and slipped through.

uneven lengths, and it was not the fence but a nail that tore Charles's stocking so badly.

The shrubbery in which they found themselves was very thorny and undergrowthy, and nearer to the lodge than they would have chosen. They could see its white walls quite plainly every now and then, and they feared that it, or the managing director of it, might be able to see them. But it makes all the difference whether you are looking for a thing or not, doesn't it? And certainly the last thing the cap woman expected was that any one should dare to defy her.

So, undiscovered and unsuspected, the children crept through the undergrowth. The thorns and briars scratched at the blue muslins, no longer, anyhow, in their first freshness, and Charlotte's white hat was snatched from her head by a stout chestnut stump. The bouquet, never the handsomest of its kind, was not improved by its travels. But misfortunes such as these occur to all tropical explorers, and they pressed on. They were all very warm and rather dirty when they emerged from the undergrowth into the smooth spacious park, and, beyond a belt of quiet trees, saw the pale grey towers of the castle rise against the sky. They looked back. The lodge was not to be seen.

'So *that's* all right,' said Caroline. 'Now we must walk fast and yet not look as if we were hurrying. I think it does that best if you take very long steps. I wish we knew where the front door was. It would be awful if we went to the back one by mistake, and got turned back by Lord Andore's my-myrmidons.'

'I expect his back door is grander than our front,' said Charlotte; 'so we shan't really know till the myr-what's-its-names have gone for us.'

'If we'd had time to disguise ourselves like grown-ups—Char, for goodness' sake tear that strip off your hat, it looks like a petticoat's tape that's coming down,' said Caroline—'they'd have thought we'd come to call, with cards, and then they'd have had to show us in, unless he wasn't at home.'

'He must be at home,' said Charlotte, tearing a long streamer from the wretched hat, which now looked less like a hat than a fading flower that has been sat on; 'it would be too much if he wasn't.'

They passed through the trees and on to a very yellow gravelled drive, hot and gritty to the foot, and distressing to the eye. Following this, they came suddenly, round a corner, on the castle. It was much bigger than they expected, and there seemed to be no doubt which was the front entrance. Two tall grey towers held a big arched gateway between them, and the drive led straight in to this. There seemed to be no door-bell and no knocker, nor, as far as they could see, any door.

'I feel like Jack the Giant Killer,' said Charles ; 'only there isn't a trumpet to blow.'

His voice, though he spoke almost in a whisper, sounded loud and hollow under the echoing arch of the gateway.

Beyond its cool depths was sunshine, with grass and pink geraniums overflowing from stone vases. A fountain in the middle leapt and sank and plashed in a stone basin.

There was a door at the other side of the courtyard—an arched door with steps leading up to it. On the steps stood a footman.

'He's exactly like the one in *Alice*,' said Caroline ; 'courage and despatch.'

The footman looked curiously at the three children, hot, dusty, and untidy, who advanced through the trim parterre. His glance dwelt more especially on the battered bouquet, on Charlotte's unspeakable hat, and the riven stocking of Charles.

'If you please,' said Caroline, her heart beating heavily, 'we want to see Lord Andore.'

' 'Slordship's not at heum,' said the footman, looking down upon them.

'When will he be back?' Charlotte asked, while Caroline suddenly wished that they had at least brought their gloves.

'Can't say'm sheur,' said the footman, doing something to his teeth with a pin ; and his tone was wondrous like Mrs. Wilmington's.

'We want very much to see him, said Charles. 'You see we've brought him a bouquet.'

'I see you 'ave—have,' said the footman, more like Mrs. Wilmington than ever. 'Would you like to leave it? It'll be a surprise for his Lordship when 'e comes in,' and the footman tittered.

'He *is* here, then,' said Caroline. 'I mean, he's not in London?'

'His Lordship is *not* in London,' said the footman. 'Any other questions? Always happy to say me catechism, 'm sheur.'

The children turned to go. They felt the need of a private consultation.

'Any particular neem?' said the footman, and tittered again. ' 'Slordship'll be dying to know who it was called,' and once more he tittered.

Charlotte turned suddenly and swiftly.

'You need not trouble about our names,'

she said, 'and I don't believe Lord Andore knows how you behave when he's not there. He doesn't know *yet*, that is.'

'No offence, Miss,' said the footman very quickly.

'We accept your apology,' said Charlotte; 'and we shall wait till Lord Andore comes in.'

'But, I say! Look here, you know'—the footman came down one step in his earnestness—'you can't wait here, you know.'

'Oh yes, we can,' said Caroline, sitting down on the second step. The others also sat down. It was Charles who said, 'So there!' and Caroline had to nudge him and say, 'Hush!'

'We never called before at a house where they didn't ask you in and give you a chair to sit on. But if this is that kind of house,' said Charlotte grandly, 'it does not matter. It is a fine day, luckily.'

'Look here,' said the footman behind them, now thoroughly uneasy, 'this won't do, you know. There's company expected. I can't have a lot of ragged children sitting on the steps like the First of May.'

'I'm sorry,' said Charlotte, without turning her head; 'but if you haven't any rooms fit to ask us into, I'm afraid you'll *have* to have us sitting here.'

The three sat staring at the bright garden and the dancing fountain.

'Look here,' said the footman, weakly blustering; 'this is cheek. That's what this is. But you go now. Do you hear? Or must I make you?'

'We hear,' said Caroline, speaking as calmly as one can speak when one is almost choking with mingled rage, disappointment, fear, and uncertainty.

'And I defy you to lay a finger on your master's visitors,' said Charlotte. 'How do you know who we are? We haven't given you our names.'

The footman must have felt a sudden doubt. He hesitated a moment, and then, muttering something about seeing Mr. Checkles, he retired, leaving the children in possession of the field. And there they sat, in a row, on Lord Andore's steps, with the bouquet laid carefully on the step above them.

It was very silent there in the grey-walled courtyard.

'I say,' whispered Charles, 'let's go. We've got the better of *him*, anyhow. Let's do a bunk before he comes back with some one we can't get the better of, thousands of stately butlers perhaps.'

'Never,' said Charlotte, whose hands were

cold and trembling with excitement. But Caroline said :

'I wish Mr. Checkles might turn out to be a gentleman, the everyday kind that we know. Lords' servants seem more common than other people's, and I expect the Lord's something like them. They say, Like master like man.'

As if in answer to Caroline's wish, a door in the wall opened, showing a glimpse of more garden beyond, and a jolly-faced youth came towards them. He was a very big young man, and his clothes, which were of dust-coloured Harris tweed, were very loose. He looked like a sixth-form boy, and Charles at once felt that here was a man and a brother. So he got up and went towards the new-comer with the simple greeting, ' Hullo !'

' Hullo !' said the sixth-form boy, with a friendly and cheerful grin.

' I say,' said Charles confidentially, as he and the big boy met on the grass, 'there isn't really any reason why we shouldn't wait here if we want to ?'

' None in the world,' said the big boy ; 'if you're sure that what you're waiting for is likely to come, and that this is the best place to wait for it in.'

' We're waiting for Lord Andore,' said

Caroline, who had picked up the bouquet and advanced with it. 'I'm so glad you've come, because we don't understand English men-servants. In India they behave differently when you call.'

'What have the servants here done?' the youth asked, frowning, with his hands in his pockets.

'Oh, nothing,' said Charles in a hurry; 'at least, I mean, we accepted his apologies, so we can't sneak.'

'I wouldn't call it sneaking to tell *you*,' said Caroline confidingly, 'because, of course, you'd promise on your honour not to tell Lord Andore. We don't want to get other people's servants into trouble when we've accepted their apologies. But the footman *was* rather——'

At this moment the footman himself appeared at the top of the steps with an elderly whiskered man in black, whom the children rightly judged to be the butler. The two had come hastily out of the door, but when they saw the children and their companion, the footman stopped as if, as Charles said later, he had been turned to stone, and only the butler advanced when the youth in the Harris tweed said rather shortly, 'Come here, Checkles!' Checkles came, quickly enough, and when he was quite close he astonished the three C.'s much more than he will astonish *you*, by saying, 'Yes, m'lord!'

'Tea on the terrace at once,' said the Harris-tweeded one, 'and tell them not to be all day about it.'

Checkles went, and the footman too. Charlotte always believed that the last glance he cast at her was not one of defiance but of petition.

'So you're him,' Charles was saying. 'How jolly!'

But to Caroline it seemed that there was no time to waste in personalities, however flattering. Lord Andore's tea was imminent. He was most likely in a hurry for his tea; it was past most people's tea-time already. So she suddenly held out the flowers, and said, 'Here's a bouquet. We made it for you. Will you please take it.'

'That's awfully good of you, you know,' said Lord Andore; 'thanks no end!' He took the bouquet and smelt it, plunged his nose into the midst of the columbine, roses, cornflowers, lemon verbena, wistaria, gladiolus and straw.

'It's not a very nice one, I'm afraid,' said Caroline; 'but you can't choose the nicest flowers when you have to look them out in

two books at once. It means Welcome, fair
stranger ; An unexpected meeting ; We are
anxious and trembling ; Confidence—no, we left
that out, because we hadn't any ; and Agreement, because we hope you will.'

·How awfully interesting. It *was* kind of
you,' said Lord Andore, and before he could
say any more Charlotte hastened to say :

'You see, it's not just an ordinary nosegay,
please, and don't thank us, please, because it
wasn't to please you but to serve our own
ends, though, of course, if we'd known how nice
you are, and if we'd thought you'd care about
one, we would have, in a minute.'

'I see,' said Lord Andore, quite as if he
really had seen.

'I'm sure you don't,' said Caroline ; 'don't
be polite, please. Say if you don't understand.
What we want is justice. It's one of your
tenants that had the cottage in your father's
time before you, and they're turning her out
because there are some week-endy people
think the cottage is so pretty, with the flowers
she planted, and the arbour her father made,
and the roses that came from her mother's
brother in Cambridgeshire. And she said you
didn't know. And we decided you ought to
know. So we made you the nosegay and we
came. And we ought to go, and here's her

name and address on a bit of paper, and I'm
sorry it's only pencil.   And you *will* see justice
done, won't you?'

'It's very kind of you,' said Lord Andore
slowly, 'to take so much interest in my
tenants.'

'There,' said Charlotte; 'of course we were
afraid you'd say that.   But we didn't mean to
shove our oar in.   We just went in for ginger-
beer, and Caro found her crying, and there's a
hornbeam arbour, ever so old, and a few shillings a week can't make any difference to you,
with a lovely castle like this to live in.   And
the motto on the tombs of your ancestors is
Flat Justicia.   And it's only bare justice we
want; and we saw the tomb on Sunday in
church, with the sons and daughters in ruffs.'

'Stop!' said Lord Andore.   'I am only a
poor weak chap.   I need my tea.   Come and
have some too, and I'll try to make out what
it's all about.'

Thanks awfully,' said the three C.'s, speaking all together.   And Caroline added, 'We
mustn't be long over tea, please, because we've
got to get home by half-past six, and it must
be nearly that now.'

'You shall get back at half-past six all
right,' said Lord Andore, and led the way, a
huge figure in the dust-coloured clothes, through

the little door by which he had come, on to a
pleasant stone terrace with roses growing all
over and in and out and round about its fat old
balustrades.

'Here's tea,' he said. And there it was,
set on a fair-sized table with a white cloth—a
tea worth waiting for. Honey and jam and all
sorts of cakes, and peaches and strawberries.
The footman was hovering about, but Charles
was the only one who seemed to see him. It
was bliss to Charles to see this proud enemy
humbly bearing an urn and lighting a spirit-
lamp to make the tea of those whom he had
tried to drive from even the lowly hospitality
of Lord Andore's doorstep.

'Come on,' said the big sixth-form-looking
boy, who was Lord Andore; 'you must be
starved. Cake first (and bread and butter
afterwards if you insist upon it) is the rule here.
Milk and sugar?'

They all drank tea much too strong for
them, out of respect to their host, who had
forgotten that when he was a little boy milk
was what one had at tea-time.

And slowly, by careful questioning, and by
making a sudden rule that no one was to say
more than thirty-seven words without stopping,
Lord Andore got at the whole story in a form
which he could understand.

' I *see*,' he would say, and ' *I* see,' and then ask another question.

And at last when tea was really over, to the last gladly accepted peach and the last sadly unaccepted strawberry, he stood up and said :

' If you don't mind my saying so, I think you are regular little bricks to have taken all this trouble. And I am really and truly very much obliged. Because I do mean to be just and right to my tenants, only it's very difficult to know about things if nobody tells you. And you've helped me a lot, and I thank you very much.'

' Then you will ? ' said Charlotte breathlessly.

' Not let her be turned out of her cottage, she means,' Caroline explained.

' She means the Mineral woman,' said Charles.

' Of course I won't,' said Lord Andore ; ' I mean, of course, I will. I mean it's all right. And I'll drive you home, and if you're a minute or two late, I'll make it all right with uncle.'

The motor was waiting outside the great arch that is held between the two great towers of Andore Castle. It was a dream of a car, and there was room for the three C.'s in front beside the driver, who was Lord Andore himself.

The footman was there, and the proudest

moment of the day for Charles was that in which Lord Andore gave the petition bouquet into that footman's care, and told him to see that it was put in water, 'Carefully, mind; and tell them to put it on the dinner-table to-night.'

The footman said 'Yes, m'lord,' as though he had never seen the bouquet before. Charlotte's proudest moment was when the woman at the lodge gate had to curtsey when the motor passed out.

Rupert was waiting for them at their own lodge gate, and when he saw the motor, his eyes grew quite round like pennies.

'Oh, do stop, it's Rupert,' said the three C.'s; and Rupert was bundled into the body of the car, where he travelled in lonely splendour. Yet, even after that, and when the motor had gone away, and the three C.'s had told him all their adventures and the splendid success of their magic nosegay, Rupert only said:

'It's Chance, I tell you. It's just accidental. Co—what's its name—incidence. It would all have happened just the same if you hadn't taken that hideous old mixed assorted hay-stack with you.'

'Still disagreeable?' said Charlotte brightly.

'Oh, been all the same, *would* it?' said Charles; 'that's all you know.'

Rupert was bundled into the body of the car.

Augustus Caesar directing the building of the city.

'It's *not* all I know,' said Rupert; 'as it happens, I know heaps of things that you don't. And I could find out more if I wanted to. So there!'

'Oh, Rupert, don't be cross,' said Caroline, 'just when we're all so happy. I *do* wish you'd been there, especially at tea-time.'

'I'm not cross,' said Rupert. 'As it happens, I was feeling extra jolly until you came home.'

'Oh, *don't*,' said Caroline; 'do let's call it Pax. We haven't told you half the little interesting things that happened yet. And if you can't believe in the magic, it's your misfortune. We know you can't help it. We know you don't unbelieve on purpose. We know we're right, and you think you know you are.'

'It's the other way round,' said Rupert, still deep in gloom.

'I *know* it is, when *you* think it, and when we think it, it's the other way,' said Caroline. 'Oh, Pax! Pax! Pax!'

'All right,' said Rupert. 'I had a good swim. Your Mr. Penfold's not half a bad sort. He taught me a new side-stroke.' But it was plain that Rupert's inside self still felt cloudy and far from comfortable.

Next day the three C.'s and Rupert, in the

middle of Irish stew, were surprised by the sudden rustling entrance of Mrs. Wilmington.

'A person wishes to see you,' she said to Caroline; 'quite a poor person. I asked her to wait till dinner was completed; but she says that she hopes you will see her now, as she ought to commence going home almost at once.'

'Of course!' said Caroline; 'it must be the Mineral woman.'

'She seemed to me,' said Mrs. Wilmington, 'to have an animal face.'

But Caroline was already in the hall, and the figure that rose politely from the oak chair was plainly—though disguised in her Sunday clothes—that of the Mineral woman.

'Oh, Miss!' she said; 'oh, Miss!' She took hold of both Caroline's hands and shook them, but that was not enough. Caroline found herself kissed on both cheeks, and then suddenly hugged; and 'Oh, Miss!' the Mineral woman said; 'oh, Miss!' And then she felt for her handkerchief in a black bag she carried, and blew her nose loudly.

Mrs. Wilmington had gone through the hall very slowly indeed; but even she could not go slowly enough not to be gone by the time the Mineral woman had, for the time being, finished with her nose. And as Mrs.

Wilmington went through the baize door, she heard again, 'Oh, Miss!'

Mrs. Wilmington came back five minutes later, and this time she heard:

'And it's all right, Miss; and two bright new five-pound notes "to buy more rose trees with," and a letter in his own write of hand thanking us for making the place so pretty; and I'm to be tenant for life, Miss. And it's all your doing, bless your kind heart. So I came to tell you. I never thought I should feel like I do about any strange little gell. It was all your doing, Miss, my dear.'

Which was a very mysterious and exciting thing to be overheard by any housekeeper who was not in the secret. And a very heart-warming and pleasant thing to be listened to by a little girl who was.

'You see,' said Caroline, when she had told the others of the Mineral woman's happiness, 'the magic always works.'

CHAPTER XVII

THE LE-O-PARD

'WE simply must write to Aunt Emmeline,' said Caroline earnestly. 'I've got three new pens and some scented violet ink. I got it at the shop yesterday; it's lovely. And I've been counting up the picture post-cards she and Uncle Percival have sent us. There are forty-two, and twenty-eight of those have come since we wrote last.'

'I'd almost rather not have the post-cards; they make you feel so horrid when you don't write,' said Charles. 'Suppose *we* send picture post-cards. You don't have to write nearly so much.'

'I think that would be shirking,' said Charlotte, who did not want to go out, and more than half believed what she said. 'Come on. If we must, we must. Necessity doesn't know the law.'

'You write, too, Rupert,' said Charles

kindly. 'Put some Latin in. They'll love that. Or perhaps you'd tell me some to say. I can put it in if you say how I ought to spell it.'

But Rupert said he couldn't be bothered, and took down a book—Jesse's *Anecdotes of Dogs* it was, with alluring pictures and delightful stories; but he did not really read it.

Caroline, looking up in an agony of ignorance as to the way you spelt assafœtida, which the medicine book said was good for 'pains in the head brought about by much ſtudy of the printed book,' saw that Rupert's eyes were fixed in a dismal stare on the portrait above the mantelpiece, the portrait of Dame Eleanour.

He was looking at it as though he did not see it, and yet Charlotte could not help saying, 'Isn't she splendid? *She* knew all about spells and things. It's her books we do it out of—at least, most of it.'

'If she knew all about them, she knew what rotten rot they were,' said Rupert. 'You never try to do anything with your spells except the things that would happen just the same without your spelling.'

'What's that about my spelling?' asked Caroline, who had made a bold dash for what she remembered of the way the word looked in the medicine book, and written, in a violent violet smudge, 'Afferphrodite.'

' I say your magic isn't real.'

'We saw you when you were invisible,' Caroline began, laying down her pen, whose wet nib at once tried to dry, turning from purple to golden green bronze. And then:

'Yes, I know,' said Rupert; 'but if it's really real, why don't you do something with it that can't really happen *in puris natural-atibus?*—that means just naturally. Why don't you bring back Mrs. Wilmington's cat that's lost? Or find my Kohinore pencil. Then there's a thing in that book Mr. Penfold's got. He told me about it. You make a wax image of your enemy and stick pins into it, and every time you stick in a pin your enemy feels a pain in the part you stick the pins into.'

' How awfully wicked!' said Caroline in an awe-struck voice.

'Or you can roast the wax man in front of a fire, and as the wax melts, the man wastes away,' said Rupert hardly.

' Oh, *don't!* ' said Charlotte.

' Yes, do,' said Charles; ' what else? '

' Oh, nothing else. It's better if you get a bit of the enemy's hair, and put that on your wax man's head. Mr. Penfold read me bits out of a piece of poetry about it.'

'Didn't he say it was wicked?' Caroline asked.

'Yes,' said Rupert reluctantly; 'but I know what's wicked without Mr. Penfold telling me, or you either. Just fancy how your enemy would squirm when he felt the pin-pricks; they'd be like sword-thrusts, you know, to him.'

'Don't!' said Caroline; 'don't, Rupert, it's horrid. Please don't. I don't want to know about those sort of spells.'

'Rupert wouldn't do it, of course,' said Charles. 'He's only talking.'

'How do you know I wouldn't?' said Rupert savagely. 'Next time you have a pain in your leg, Caroline, you'll think it's growing pains, but really it'll be me, sticking a long hat-pin into the wax image I've secretly made of you.'

Caroline got up.

'Come, Char,' she said, 'we'll go and sit in the drawing-room if Rupert's going on like this.'

'He doesn't mean it,' said Charles again.

'Of course I don't,' said Rupert, and suddenly smiled. 'I don't know why I said it. Don't be silly. There's lots of things you could try, though, and not hurt any one. Why don't you——?' He looked vaguely round the room, and his eyes lighted once more on the portrait. 'Why don't you make *that* come to life? If she was a witch, her picture ought to be good for that, anyhow.'

'I wish we could,' said all the children together, with deep earnestness.

'Well, do it then,' said Rupert. 'That's the sort of thing to make me believe, not the duffing things you've kept on doing ever since I've been here.'

There was a silence. Then, 'How do you spell "impossible"?' asked Charles, and then nothing more was heard but the scratching of violet pens.

But from that time, and in between all other thoughts and happenings, Charlotte kept on thinking about that idea. If only the picture could be made to come alive!

And Charles's fancy played timidly with the idea of the wax man. Not to hurt the person it was like, of course, but just to see if anything happened. Not pins. But just pinching its foot a very very very little, secretly, with the image in your pocket, when the person it was the image of was there, just to see if the person jumped or called out, as you do if you're suddenly pinched, no matter how gently.

Charlotte's mind busied itself then and later, in and between other thoughts, with the question of what was the matter with Rupert, and

whether something couldn't be done to help
him.

For there was no doubt of it. Rupert
wasn't at all what they had first thought him.
Sometimes, it is true, he would be as jolly as
you need wish a boy to be. He would start
new games and play them in the most amusing
and satisfactory way. But always, sooner or
later, and generally sooner, the light of life
seemed to go out of him, and he would seem
suddenly to be not only tired of the game but
tired of everything else, and not only tired of
everything, but angry with everybody.

'I'm sure he's bewitched,' said Charlotte
more than once in those intimate moments
when Caroline and she 'talked things over' as
they brushed their hair. 'I shouldn't wonder
if somebody's made a wax image of *him*, and
it's when they stick the pins in it that he goes
all savage all in a minute.'

'I do think *that's* nonsense,' Caroline always
said. 'I'm sure it wouldn't be allowed.'

'How would you make an image of a
person's mind?' Charlotte woke Caroline up
to ask, one night; and when Caroline with
sleepy sharpness said, 'You can't; go to
sleep, do,' Charlotte answered, 'I believe you
can; there was something written under somebody's portrait in history, about painting his

mind; and if you can paint a mind, you can make a wax image of it. I believe that's what somebody's done to Rupert, don't you? And stuck knives into it? Oh, well, if you *will* go to sleep!' said Charlotte.

Rupert grew grumpier and grumpier as the days went on, and seemed to care less and less for being with the three C.'s. He would go for long walks by himself, and seemed to prefer to be with William, who 'put up' with him, or even with Mrs. Wilmington, who adored him, to being with the children.

'And we thought it would be so jolly,' sighed Charlotte; 'and the worst of it is Charles tries to imitate him. He speaks quite rudely sometimes, even to you, Caro, and you know he always used to like you best.'

The only thing Rupert seemed truly and constantly to care for was swimming. He went down to the river with Mr. Penfold almost every day, or met him at the bathing-place, and they swam together. With Mr. Penfold, Rupert was nearly always at his best, perhaps because Mr. Penfold never seemed to notice it when he wasn't.

The village was growing more and more busy and excited as the day drew near when Lord Andore's coming of age was to be cele-brated by what the people called a Grangaileranfeat. This was to be held in Lord Andore's park and in certain meadows adjoining ; there were to be roundabouts and cocoanut-shies and shooting-galleries, and a real circus, with a menagerie and performing elephants and edu- cated seals,—all free. The children looked forward longingly to the day. Lord Andore had sent them cards with his mother's name and his on them in print, and the name of each child in writing, requesting the pleasure of their company on the occasion of Lord Andore's twenty-first birthday. And they had joyously, and with much violet ink, accepted. And the day came nearer and nearer. It did not seem worth while to engage in any new magic while there was this real pleasure to look forward to.

And then, the very day before *the* day, when the roundabouts had arrived and been set up, and the menagerie was howling invitingly in its appointed field, the cup of joy was dashed, as Charlotte said, into little bits. Lady Andore slipped on an orange pip and broke her ankle, and the festivities were postponed until September. So said a card brought by the very footman who had not known their names.

'He jolly well knows them now,' said Charles. It was his only comfort.

'There's many a pip 'twixt the cup and the

lip,' said Charlotte; and Caroline said, ' Oh, bother!'

Rupert said nothing. He had been invited too, of course, and had, at moments, seemed pleased. Now he just took his cap and went out, and came home late for tea. The three C.'s learned with feelings of distress, mingled with anger, that Rupert had been to the menagerie by himself, and had seen all the beasts, and that he had also witnessed a performance of the circus people, which they had thought it worth while to give to such of the villagers as cared to pay for their amusements. He had seen everything, from the accomplished elephants to the educated seals.

' You might have told us you were going,' said Charles.

' You could have gone if you'd wanted to,' said Rupert.

' Never mind, Charles,' said Caroline; ' we'll ask the Uncle to take us to-morrow.'

' They're off to-morrow,' said Rupert; ' that's why I went to-day.' He added something bitter and almost unbearable about a parcel of kids.

But the circus, as it turned out, was not off next day. An accident had happened. Something was missing, and the circus could not go on its travels till that something was found.

'I don't know what it is,' said Harriet, when she told them about it at breakfast; 'but they've lost something they set store by. Some says it's an improving seal, and others says it's a boar-conjector-snake, and Poad told my gentleman friend it was the white-eyed Kaffir made a bolt for freedom and India's coral strand, where he was stole from when a babe; but I don't know the rights of it. They sent for Poad. My gentleman friend'll know all about it next time I see him.'

'When shall you see him again?' Charles asked.

'I can see him whenever I've a mind,' said Harriet proudly. 'I'm not one of those as has to run after their gentlemen friends.'

'I do wonder what it is,' Charlotte said. 'Do see your friend as soon as you can and ask him, won't you, Harriet? I do hope it's not snakes or bears. You'll be sure to tell us directly you know, won't you?'

'Sure,' said Harriet.

It was from William, however, that they heard what it was that the circus had really lost.

'It's a tame Le-o-pard,' said William; 'him with the spots that you can't change, and the long tail.'

'I know,' said Charlotte; 'there's a

leopard's skin in the drawing-room. Very
spotty they are. And fierce, too, I believe.
Oh, William! I do hope it won't come this
way.'

'There's something about it in the book,'
said Caroline, who, as usual, had her magic
books under her arm. She found the place
and read, 'Leopard's-bane, its government and
virtues'—quite a long piece. When she had
done, William said:

'Thank you very much; quite pretty, ain't
it?' And Rupert said it was all nonsense.

'But it *won't* come this way, will it?'
Charlotte repeated.

'It's a tame one,' said William, grinning.
'At least that's the character it's got from its
last place. But it won't be any too tame for
Poad, I expect. I hear he's got the job of
catching of it. And serve him right too.'

'Oh, why?' asked Charlotte.

'Because,' said William shortly, and was
told not to be cross about nothing.

''Tain't nothing, then,' he said; ''twas the
way he acted about my dog license, and the
dog only two months over puppy-age, when
no license is taken nor yet asked.'

'I don't fancy Poad much myself,' said
Rupert; 'he needn't have been so keen about
catching me.'

'Now that's where you're wrong,' said William.   Hunting of you, that was no more than Poad's duty; and if he set about it like a jackape, well, some is born silly and can't help it, and why blame the man? But the dog, 'e worn't Poad's duty. He exceeded about the dog, Poad did, and I don't bear malice; but I'll be even with him yet about that dog.'

'How?' asked Rupert.

'Oh, I'll find a way,' said William carelessly. 'No hurry. Acts like that act what Poad did about my Pincher, they always come home to roost—them acts do. Now then, Miss Charlotte, leave that saddle soap alone, and get along into the garden. The gates 'as been locked since eight this morning, and you're to go through the secret way to-day, and not to go outside the garden because of that old speckled Le-o-pard.'

The three C.'s went, but Rupert lingered beside William, fingering the bright buckles of the harness and passing the smooth reins slowly through his fingers.

For some time the three C.'s were very busy in the garden, gathering heart-shaped green leaves and golden fragile daisy-like flowers.

'I never thought,' said Caroline earnestly,

opening the brown book and sitting down on
the terrace steps with a sheaf of green and
yellow beside her, 'that we should need it when
I read about it in the *Language Of*, and in the
medicine book. Look here, it says : " It is
under Apollo, and the flowers and leaves
thereof all leopards and their kind do fear and
abhor. Wherefore if it be ftrewn in the paths
thefe fearful beafts do frequent, they may not
pafs, but fhall turn again and go each to his own
place in all meeknefs and fubmifsion. Indeed,
it hath been held by the ancients, aye and
by philofophers of our own times, that in this
herb lieth a charm to turn to water the hearts
of thefe furious fpotted great cats, and to loofe
the ftrings of their tongues, fo that they fpeak
in the fpeech of men, uttering ftrange things
and very wondrous. But of this the author
cannot fpeak certainly, fince the Leopard is not
native to this land unlefs it be in Northumber-
land and Wales where all wild things might
well be hidden." '

'So, you see,' said Caroline.

But Charlotte said it was all very well, only
how were they to get the bane to the leopard?
'It isn't as if we were allowed free,' she
pointed out. 'I wish they hadn't been so
careful. The leopard would never have hurt
us as long as we carried the bane, and we

could have surrounded it, like snakes, with ash
leaves, and it would have had to surrender.'

'And perhaps it would have talked to us
and followed us like tame fawns,' suggested
Charlotte; 'or Una; only hers was a lion.'

'Nonsense!' said Charles; 'you know you'd
have been afraid.'

'I shouldn't,' said Charlotte.

'You would,' said Charles.

'I shouldn't.'

'You would.'

'I shouldn't.'

'You would.'

'And now you're both exactly like Rupert,'
said Caroline; 'and the leopard wandering
about unbaned while you're wrangling. You're
like Nero and Rome.'

Twenty minutes had passed before peace
was restored, and the leopard's-bane lay drooping in the sun, the delicate gold and green
heaps of it growing flatter and flatter.

'Well, then,' said Charles suddenly, 'if
you're not afraid, let's go. No one's forbidden
us to, except William.'

'I will if you will,' said Charlotte, turning
red.

'So will I, said Caroline, turning pale.

'Rupert said it was nonsense about the
leopard's-bane when you read it this morning.'

'That doesn't make it nonsense,' said Charlotte sharply.

'But suppose you meet it?'

'You can't—if you keep to the road. Leopards get into trees. They never walk about in roads like elephants do. Not even when the circus man is moving. It's serious what we're going to do,' said Caroline; 'and what'll people say about it, depends how it turns out. If we parrylise the leopard and save the village, we shall be heroines like——'

('And heroes,' said Charles.)

'Like Joan of Arc, and Philippa who sucked the poison out of the burgesses' keys at Calais.'

'And if we don't put the stuff in the right place, or the leopard doesn't take any notice of it, they'll just say we were disobedient.'

'And suppose we meet the leopard face to face?'

'It's a *tame* leopard,' said Caroline in a faltering voice.

'Oh, I don't want to go. I really am frightened. I don't mind owning up. I am. I'm so frightened I think we ought to go. I don't want to so dreadfully, that I'm sure it's right for me to go. But I wish you and Charles would stay here. Suppose the leopard came over the wall and there was no one here to cope with it?'

She was very pale and she trembled. And when the others, without hesitation, said, ' Not much, we don't ! ' she certainly breathed more easily.

' Come on, then,' she said. ' We'll strew a little here because of the gardeners. Oh no, of course the roots will make it all safe here. The gate's locked ; we must go through the secret passage and then creep through the stable-yard and out along the garden wall, so that the Wilmington doesn't see us. And then out by the deserted lodge.'

CHAPTER XVIII

THE LEOPARD'S-BANE

THEIR minds once made up, the children collected the fading armfuls of leopard's-bane and made for the arbour that led to the tunnel. Inside the door they lighted the candle, closed and bolted the door as they had been told to, and went carefully down the steps and along the secret passage. And as they went they heard something moving in the darkness that lay thick beyond the little wavering light of their candle.

They stopped and listened. They heard the sound of breathing, and the next moment they saw, vaguely, in the almost darkness, something four-footed, spotted, furry, creeping along the passage towards them. It uttered a low, fierce, snarling growl.

'Throw it down,' said Caroline, casting her flowers from her. 'It can't pass it. It can't.'

A heap of tangled crushed leaves and flowers

Something four-footed, spotted, furry, creeping along the passage.

was all that there was now between the children
and the leopard.

'It can't pass it. It can't,' said Caroline
again, in an agonised whisper. Yet none of
the children dared to turn and fly. Charlotte
had remembered what she had heard of quelling
wild animals by the power of the human eye,
and was trying, almost without knowing that
she tried, to meet the eye of this one. But
she could not. It held its head down close to
the ground and kept quite still. Every one
felt it was impossible to turn their backs on the
creature. Better to face it. If they turned
and ran, well, the door at the end of the passage
was bolted; and if the flower-spell should fail,
then, the moment their backs were turned, the
leopard might—with one spring——

'Oh, I wish we hadn't,' said Charles, and
burst into tears.

'Don't, oh, don't!' said Caroline; and to
the leopard, who had not moved, she said, with
wild courage:

'Down, sir! Lie down!'

The leopard lay down, flat—flatter than you
would think a leopard *could* lie.

'It understands,' said Charlotte.

'Oh yes.' Caroline's voice trembled as
much as the hand that held the candlestick.
'It does. Poor Pussy! Poor Leopard, then.'

A faint rumbling sound came from the crouching heap of spotted fur.

'I believe it's trying to purr,' whispered Caroline. 'Of course leopards' purrs *would* be different.'

'Give a paw, then,' she said very shakily. And the leopard lifted a ragged-looking forefoot. But even Caroline had not the courage to reach out a hand towards it.

'Go to sleep, good dog, then,' she said in a distracted whisper. 'Go to sleep, go by-by, good little leopard, then.'

The leopard curled up and lay quite still.

'It's all right, I tell you,' said Caroline. 'Stop snivelling, Charles. I knew the leopard's-bane would do it. Now let's go back backwards, very slowly, and if it moves, I'll speak to it again.'

Very slowly, still striving to keep their eyes on the leopard, they retreated. They had not gone three steps before they heard it move. They stopped.

'Lie down!' said Caroline. And then, to their mingled horror, wonder, delight, surprise, dismay, and satisfaction, a voice answered them—a curious, choked, husky voice.

'Leopard stay still,' it answered; 'little lady not be frightened. Leopard like flowers Leopard quite good.'

'Is it?' said Caroline, speaking as well as she could through the beating of her heart. 'Is it the leopard speaking?'

'Ess, little missy,' said the choked voice. 'Pretty flowers loose leopard's tonguey, make him talky. Leopard tell a secret. Little ladies sow seeds, pinky seeds, hearty seeds, the right day, the right way, and see what come up. Run way now. Leopard done talky. He go sleepy by-by. So long!'

None of them ever knew how they got to the end of the tunnel, got the bolts undone, got the door shut again, and stood in the dusky arbour looking in each other's paper-white faces.

Charlotte made two steps into the sunlight and threw herself face downwards on the path. Her shoulders heaved. Charles was still weeping without moderation or concealment. Caroline stood shivering in the sunshine.

'But we've got to get back,' she said. 'It's all right this side, because of the leopard's-bane. But if somebody came behind the leopard's-bane, from the house, you know? We must climb the wall and get to the house and warn them. Get up, Char. Charles, if you're ever going to be a man, be one now. There'll be plenty of time to howl when it's all over. We must climb the wall, somehow.'

One leaves the children in the garden, a

locked door between them and the leopard,
trying to find a way of climbing a ten-foot wall.
No gardener was to be found and the gates
were locked.

'We must get over,' Caroline kept saying.
'Oh, we must, we must! The charm worked
perfectly. If we can only get to the other end
of the tunnel and throw in some more bane we
shall have done the great deed. Try again,
Charles. I'll give you a leg up. We *must* get
over. Try again.'

One leaves Charles trying.

. . . . . .

Now although the three C.'s firmly believed
that the magic of the green and yellow flowers
subdued the leopard and caused it to speak—
in a sort of language that somehow recalled the
far-off speech of their ayah in India—I cannot
quite expect you to believe this. And I feel
that I must delay no longer to tell you what it
is you *can* believe. To do this we must go
back to Rupert, whom we left with William in
the harness-room, fingering the bright buckles
and drawing the long smooth reins through his
fingers.

'I say, William,' he said, 'couldn't we play a
little trick on that Poad? There's a leopard
skin in the drawing-room. If I got a couple of
pillows and a needle and thread?'

'Eh?' said William, staring at him. Then
suddenly he smacked his leg and laughed
aloud. 'You've hit it this time, Master
Rupert,' he said; 'blessed if you 'aven't.
You go along in and get the skin. Careful
now, because of Mother Wilmington.'

'The drawing-room's locked,' said Rupert,
'and I don't want to tell the others.'

'The drawing-room windows isn't,' said
William. 'We'll watch our time, and I'll make
a back for you. An' never you mind about
pillows. Straw's good enough stuffing. An'
don't forget the needle and cotton. I expect
you'll find some lady's working-box in the
drawing-room to get *them* out of.'

Rupert, once safely landed in the drawing-
room, found the leopard skin easily enough,
but the needle and cotton were not so easily
found. He found a work-table indeed, made
of satinwood, inlaid with ivory and lined with
faded red velvet, where were reels of silk and
flat ivory winders with thread on them, but
all the needles were red with rust, and fast
embedded in their cushions and cases. He
looked round. None of the cabinets looked
as though they held needles. And besides,
what was the use of finding more rusty
needles? One rusty needle was as useful,
or rather as useless, as fifty could be. He

thought of using the blind-cords instead of cotton, but they were too thick, and one could not push them through the leopard skin without tearing it. Then he saw the golden quiet harp standing in its far corner. Its strings perhaps? But he did not know how to unstring a harp, and when he touched one of its fine wires, just the thing for sewing with without a needle, it gave out the thin sweet ghost of a note of music, faint indeed, but loud enough to warn him of the cry it could and would give if he attempted violence. The harp quivered under his hands as he gently let the string go, and something rattled. It was the lid of a sort of box in the pedestal of the harp.

'Perhaps they kept spare strings there,' Rupert thought, and opened the lid.

'They,' it seemed, had kept spare strings here, and here the spare strings still lay, coiled neatly in little round boxes. Rupert opened several, and choosing the thinner strings, put them in his pocket. One box rattled dryly in his hand, and when he opened it there were no strings, only a number of odd, flat, pinkish heart-shaped seeds. On the box was written, 'Seed of the F. of H.D. Sow only in the way and on the day.'

He put its lid on and thought, then, no

more of the box. But afterwards he remembered it.

And now, with the leopard's skin in his
arms and the wires in his pockets, Rupert
went cautiously to the window. Yes, all was
safe ; so William's signal told him. He
dropped the bright skin into William's hands,
and himself dropped to the ground.

'I've thought of something better than
straw,' he said, when he and William and the
leopard skin were alone together in the
harness-room. And William, when the new
thought was explained to him, slapped his
leg harder, and laughed more thoroughly than
before.

Rupert had only just entered the secret
passage, his first match had just gone out,
when he heard the children at the other end.
He went towards them, fully meaning to
explain what sort of leopard he was, and what
sort of joke—he called it a joke to himself—
he and William had arranged to play upon
Poad. But when he heard them speak, and
saw the showers of leopard's-bane fall on the
flags of the passage, he, as he put it later,
'played up.' And when the children had
gone, he laughed softly to himself and began
to think what would be the best spot in the
tunnel to wait for Poad in. He had noticed,

by the light of that first match, an arched recess, the one, you remember, where the children stored their sacks of wet rose leaves the night they played at Rosicurians and cured Rupert. He would hide in this, and then, when Poad came along, he would jump out at him with that snarl which had sounded so well when he met the children.

He waited till the garden door was locked, and then felt for his matches. He could not find them. He must have dropped them when he was pretending to the children. He felt along the floor, but there were no matches to be found. Never mind, he could feel his way in the dark. He knew exactly where the arch was. To the left, about three-quarters of the way down the passage. He stood up and laid his hand upon the wall, walked forward till he felt the corner of the recess, and stooped to curl himself up in it and wait for Poad. He put his hand out to steady himself as he sat down, and his hand touched, not the stone floor, but soft warm fur. And not dry hard fur like that which he himself wore, sewn tightly round him with harp-strings, but living fur, on a living creature. He drew back his hand, and a cold sweat of horror broke out on his forehead, and the little hairs on the back of his neck seemed

to move by themselves. His hand still felt
the dreadful warm softness of that fur. It
almost seemed to him that he had felt the
spots on it.

'Oh, I wish I hadn't!' said Rupert to
himself, as so many of us have said when it
was too late to say anything. 'Oh, I *wish* I
hadn't!'

He stood perfectly still in the mockery of
his sewn-on leopard skin, waiting for the real
leopard to move, or to settle down. Perhaps
it would settle down? The leopard must
have crept in when the door into the garden
was opened in readiness for the children to
pass through. It must have gone to sleep
there, and perhaps he had not roused it.

'Oh, why didn't I go with the others?'
Rupert thought. And then a good thought
came to him.

'If I had,' he told himself, 'I should have
been out there, and they wouldn't have met
me and turned back, and then they might
have found the real leopard, and it might have
jumped on them. I'm glad it's only me.'

This good thought came to him as he rose
up and steadied himself by the wall. Then
in an instant all thoughts were drowned in
a flood of terror, and Rupert found himself
almost running, feeling his way by the wall

L

towards the house entrance. If he could only get out before the leopard was up and after him! He reached the end of the passage. The door at the foot of the stairs was shut and locked. He was alone there in the dark with a locked door at each end of the passage. He crouched down by the door. In spite of his agony of fear he had enough sense not to beat on the door and scream for help, which was, of course, his first mad impulse.

' Keep quiet,' he kept telling himself, ' some one *must* come soon. If you keep quiet, the leopard will go on sleeping, perhaps. The children will open the garden door when they hear the dinner-bell. Then you can get out. If you make a row, the leopard will wake up and come for you.'

So he crouched and waited. But no one came. Then suddenly he remembered. When the children heard the dinner-bell they would come down the passage. They would find the real leopard. It would certainly wake. His own feelings about the leopard now made him certain that the children, when they were safe in the sunshine, would see that what talked to them, dressed in a leopard's skin, *could* only have been a human being dressed up. Most likely they knew already who it was. So they would come back without fear—

come back to find him, Rupert, and would find *that*!

Then Rupert did what was really an heroic thing. He stood up, and, as quickly as he could, began to feel his way back along the side of the passage farthest from the arched recess. He would go to the garden door, and when the children opened it, he could prevent their coming in. To do this he must pass the leopard.

A warm delicious glow stole through him. This was worth it. Better than crouching like a coward at the far side and letting those children come laughing and talking down the passage to meet *that*, savage from a sudden awakening. He took off his boots, and crept quietly along. No sound broke the black silence. He reached the flight of steps, reached the other door, sat down on the top step and waited.

Nothing had stirred in the silence.

'Anyhow,' said Rupert, 'I feel safer at the top of the stairs than at the bottom.'

Rupert will never know how long he sat there in the darkness. The cracks in the door which showed as pale vertical streaks were his only comfort. He tried to get off the leopard's skin, but the harp-strings were too strong. It seemed to him that he had been there a week.

There were voices, many voices, Charlotte's voice high above the others. Rupert hoped the leopard was too far away to hear, but how could he know where the leopard was? It might have crept quite close to him on its padded noiseless feet, and he would never have known. It might be within a yard of him now.

Rupert understood in that hour what sort of practical joke it was that he had prepared for the policeman.

'Because, of course,' said Rupert, 'I should have been just as dreadful for Poad as *that* is for me. He'd have thought I was It.'

The voices and footsteps came nearer. They were talking outside.

'Best shoot it, when it rushes out at us. I've got a revolver,' said Poad. And a cold shiver ran down Rupert's back. Suppose he had met Poad alone in that dark passage as he had planned?

'Let me get at him with the garden fork,' said another voice—the gardener's.

Then another, a strange voice this time:

'Don't hurt the beast. It's valuable. An' it's tame, don't I tell you? You leave be. Stand back. I'll tackle him.'

Rupert wretchedly wondered how he was to be trapped; also, how near the real

'It's me; it's Rupert,' he shouted.

leopard really was.   He decided that a little
noise more or less couldn't matter now.   He
tapped at the door and cried, 'Let me out.
It's Rupert.'

But his words were drowned in the chorus
of alarm that rose when he knocked at the
door.   And the leopard?   In the midst of the
babel of voices a bolt was drawn, the door
opened.   Rupert sprang out and turned to
shut the door.   But his feet and arms and
head were entangled in strings, and he fell to
the ground.

'It's me; it's Rupert,' he shouted; 'shut
the door!   The real leopard's inside!'

'Why!' said the leopard's owner—he who
had thrown the net over Rupert—'it's a beastly
boy, dressed up.'   He spoke in tones of deep
disgust.

There was a crowd of people.   The three
C.'s had managed to scale the wall by means
of a pear-tree.   They had brought back
William—a prey to secret laughter, and the
leopard's owner, and a dozen other people.   A
score of hands helped to loose Rupert from
the net.

'Oh, I don't know.   I did it for a lark.
To take a rise out of some one.   But I've been
paid out.   The leopard's in there.   I touched
it, in the dark.'

Sensation!

'There,' said William to the policeman, 'I
told you half an hour ago there was a good
chance the beast 'ad taken cover in the
passage, and you would have it you see his
tail up a tree somewhere, and wouldn't go
down.'

'I certainly thought I see 'is tail,' said
Poad, scratching his ear; 'and this gentleman's
pal and half a dozen others is after 'im now,
down by the other lodge. But perhaps it
wasn't really 'is tail. In fact, it couldn't be, if
the animal's in here like what the young
gentleman says it is.'

'I tell you the leopard's in here, now,'
said Rupert. 'Oh, get me out of this beastly
skin somebody.'

William unlaced him, and he stepped out, a
pale boy in shirt and knickerbockers.

'In there now, is he?' said the leopard's
keeper, rudely taking no notice of Poad; 'then
if some one'll get a lantern or two we'll go in
and get him.'

Some one got a lantern or two—it was
William in point of fact; the lanterns happened
to be ready in the summer-house.

The keeper went down the steps.

'On the right-hand side?' he said, quite
unconcernedly.

And Rupert said, 'Yes, to the right.'

William and three other men followed warily, but to most of the party it seemed best to remain by the door. Five people and a net were surely enough to catch one leopard. But every one crowded round the door, and some even went down a few steps, bending over to catch the first sounds of anything that might be happening.

All of a sudden a sound came from the dark passage below, and the listeners started back—a strange sound, the sound of long, loud laughter. It echoed and re-echoed through the vaulted passage, coming nearer and nearer. The crowd drew back.

Out came the leopard keeper, laughing, with his net; out came William, laughing, with his pitchfork; out came Poad, half laughing and half angry.

'What is it? what is it?' said every one outside. And for a moment none of those inside could get breath to answer.

'What is it?' they asked again, and at last William answered:

'Mrs. Wilmington's old cat! Gone in there to have her kittens in peace away from the children. They've caught your little bit all right,' he said to the leopard keeper. 'Look!' He pointed to something white among the trees beyond the wall. 'I told Bill to run up a signal if they found the rest of him where Poad said he'd seen his spotted tail.'

'Did you know that before we went in?' Poad asked sternly.

''Course I did,' said William, his hands on his knees and his ruddy face deeply creased with the joke. 'You wouldn't have catched me going in there without I'd known where my Lord was, him and his spotted tail. I thought it was Master Rupert up to some more of his larks, I did. I wasn't a-going to spoil sport.'

'You 'aven't 'eard the last of this,' said Poad huffily.

'No more ain't you,' said William, 'so don't you think it, James Poad. You that believed one tale when you'd seen the other. You that wouldn't believe the sworn evidence of your own eyes and a spotted tail.'

CHAPTER XIX

F. OF H.D.

You will hardly be able to believe that, owing to the firmness of Uncle Charles's instructions that he was not to be disturbed on any pretence, the whole noisy affair of the two leopards passed entirely unnoticed by him. The three C.'s did not tell, because they feared that Rupert's impersonation of the leopard might not be pleasing to the Uncle. Mrs. Wilmington did not tell, because Rupert was her great favourite. She mended the places where the harp-strings had torn the leopard skin, and put it back in its place and said nothing to any one. William did not tell; he was a man who could keep a joke to himself, was William. Poad did not tell, because he never could be quite sure whether the laugh was on his side or on William's. And Rupert did not tell, for reasons that will be clearer later on. So the Uncle went on writing his book about *Sympathetic Magic*, in complete ignorance of anything leopardish having happened.

When all the fuss and bustle had died down, and Rupert and the children were left face to face, words of reproach rose to every lip. But Rupert, knowing what he had faced in that underground passage for the sake of the children, still had enough of the warm and comforting feeling to be able to say :

' Look here, don't! I'm awfully sorry if I did really frighten you. I didn't know. I'd no *idea* what it would feel like to be frightened by a leopard until I thought I was shut up with one. Don't rub it in ; there's good chaps.'

A frank appeal such as this could not fail with the three C.'s, and if anything had been needed to melt the anger of the girls, being called 'good chaps' would have supplied that need.

' Oh yes,' they said, both together. ' But do let's tell each other all about it,' Charlotte added. ' Let's not say anything till after dinner, and then have a grand palaver in the garden. I do want to understand just exactly what you felt when you felt the leopard, Rupert, to see if it was anything like what we felt when we saw your spots.'

' All right ! ' said Rupert.

Charles had his first swimming lesson.

And Charles said, 'It was the most dreadful thing in the world, but it will give us something to talk about.'

It did.   Rupert's hidden consciousness of having done something 'rather decent,' made him quite like the self that he had seemed to be on the first night.   The children spent a most enjoyable afternoon, and for the first time for many days, Rupert did not seem anxious to get rid of the others.   He even invited them to come down to the river and see him dive.

'Though I'm not a patch on Mr. Penfold,' he said.

They went.   And Charles had his first swimming lesson.

'It would be all right,' he said, sleeking his wet hair as they went home, 'if only you could remember which are your arms and which are your legs.   I never can, in the water, and, anyhow, you seem to have far too many, and they all feel as though they belonged to somebody else.'

As they went over the bridge, Mr. Penfold said :

'I've done that translation, and I've had it typed.   So you can tell your uncle about it and present it to him.   He'll like it awfully, I know.   And I daresay he'll let you have a copy of the translation.   I've had one done expressly for you, with the parts that wouldn't be of any advantage to you left out.   By the way, there's something written in the end about the seventh of July.   That's to-morrow. So you'd better present it then.'

There was a chorus of thanks, and the presentation was arranged for the next day. The children took the old Latin book home with them.   Mr. Penfold was to bring the translation ; 'when I've corrected the spelling and the stops,' he said.   'I'll come, if I may, and see the presentation.   There should be flowers, too, I think, symbolic flowers, suggested by your other book.'

When the children got home they spread the Latin book on the table in the window, to catch the last rosy sunset light, and Charles said with proud affection :

'*Now*, Rupert!   We don't want any old translation when *you're* here.'

Rupert frowned, and the girls shrank as sensitive plants shrink when a finger touches them.   They knew the sort of bitter thing about its not being worth while to do things for kids, which seemed to be trembling on Rupert's lips.   But quite quickly his face changed.   He turned red—or was it only the deepened red of the sunset ?—and said:

'You know, I'm afraid I've kidded you rather about my Latin. I'm not very good at it as a matter of fact. I've only just begun Virgil.'

'But you do know a lot. You're always saying bits of it,' said Charles anxiously.

'That was swank,' said Rupert strongly; 'silly swank. It was all wrong, I expect. There, now it's out!'

The children treated Rupert with added respect.

'How splendid of him to own up about the Latin,' said Caroline over the hair-brushing. And Charlotte reminded her sister that *she* had *always* thought Rupert splendid, which was not true, though she thought it was.

But this was later. At the moment, 'Never mind,' said Charlotte, 'we shall have the translation to-morrow, and we'll try a spell *at once*. I'm sorry the leopard that spoke was only you, Rupert. We did think you'd have to believe in spells after that.'

'There's something written at the end,' said Caroline, who was still examining the book; 'I'd forgotten about that.'

And there was. In very faint brown ink. They had to carry it quite outside the front door (which was, as you know, at the side), to get light enough to be sure that they could not read it because it was written in Latin. And when they did get enough light, they saw that it was in English, and that they could. The writing ran :

'On the seventh day of the seventh month, and at the seventh hour, let the seed be sown. Seven seeds and no more for the one sowing. In the garden of peace let them be sown, which same is the seventh garden of the world. Let him that would sow, take heed to bathe him seven times in fair water, and let him sow with his face set eastward, with silence at the lips and, at the heart, faith in all good things and the love of all things beautiful. After seven weeks the blossom shall appear. Then let him who sowed the seed eat of the flower. The seed of the F. of H.D.'

'What?' cried Rupert.

'That's all,' said Caroline ; 'it stops short like that. There isn't any more.'

There had been more, but some one had scratched the rest out.

'With a knife or scissors,' explained Caroline. 'Oh, what a pity!'

'I say,' Rupert was beginning, but Charles interrupted.

He had stooped to look up under the page that Caroline was fingering. 'There's some more ; look, turn over!'

There was.

'Until it be granted none knoweth his heart's most dear desire. But after it is granted he perceiveth that so and not otherwise was and must ever have been the true Desire of the Heart.'

'That's true, at any rate,' said Charlotte. 'I was just wondering what my heart's desire really was. Suppose you thought it was going to be a new paint-box, but the flower knew better, and it turned out that elephants was what you really wanted?'

'No, but I say,' said Rupert hurriedly, 'look here! You know I don't believe in magic. I'd like to, really I would. But I found something. You've got the key of the drawing-room. I believe I know where those seeds are.'

The drawing-room was almost dark when they got there. Just one last ray of dusky gold lay across the room; it struck the round mirror and was reflected with dazzling brightness on some golden object at the end of the room. 'The harp!' whispered Rupert. 'How queer, because it was exactly there——'

It was still exactly there. And every one was quite sure that this little round box held the seeds of which the book told.

'See,' said Charlotte, holding them in the

ray of yellow light; 'they're shaped like hearts, and they're pink like wishes. I know wishes are pink. They must be some colour, and why not that?'

'But ought we to take them?' was the blighting question of Caroline.

It was settled by a note which Harriet obligingly carried to the Uncle.

DEAREST UNCLE—There are some pinky seeds in the drawing-room. May we have seven to sow?

And the answer was:

Certainly. Seventy if you like.—Your
D.S.T.U.

So, very early next morning they got up. Bathing seven times is no joke, especially when you dry thoroughly between, and this Caroline conscientiously insisted on. 'We must be *quite* sure we get it *quite* right,' she said.

The four children met, by appointment, at the top of the stairs and crept down in silence. They went out by the French window which had once admitted Rupert. When they were outside, he said, 'I bathed seven times too, because Charles did nothing but bother. But it's no good *my* sowing the things, even if it's all true. Because I haven't faith in my heart, or my head either. I think really it's the head's fault.'

'Oh, never mind your head,' said Charlotte; 'we'll all sow one each, and the three over we'll put in all together—all of us.'

The grass was still dewy-wet, but the gardener was at work in the Wonderful Garden. The children went through the ancient formula of 'ena dena dina dus,' to decide who should approach him, and the lot fell on Charlotte.

'Please,' she said, 'may we have a bit of garden for our own?'

'Ay,' said the gardener, pointing to a vacant plot near the arbour.

'Oh, thank you,' said Charlotte, 'but mayn't we have a bit in the garden of peace?'

'Who learned you to call it that?' the gardener asked, looking at her strangely.

'It's the right name, isn't it?' Charlotte asked with sudden anxiety.

'It's the right name right enough,' he admitted.

'We want a bit that won't be disturbed for seven weeks,' Charlotte explained, and he looked at her more strangely than ever.

'Sure you've got the right seed to sow?'

Charlotte opened her hand and he stooped and looked at it. Then he stood up and saluted like a soldier.

'Why——' said Charlotte, 'you—what do you mean?'

'Nothing!' he said, straightening his back; 'only I worked here all my days, and my father afore me, and his father afore him, and so on back. You can see our names on the stones in the churchyard, same as you see Master's people's names on the tombs inside of the church. I'll find a corner for you, my dear, and no one shan't disturb the seed, once you've set it. You know how it's done? No chatter, and which way to look?'

'Yes, I know,' said Charlotte, 'but how do you know?'

'Old man's tales,' he said; 'old man's tales,' and led the way to the terrace.

'Would you like to sow one of them?' said Charlotte eagerly. 'I know the others won't mind if you would. Would you?'

'Not me, my dear,' said the old man, and he sighed. 'Years agone, I don't say. But not now. I'm old, you see. I ain't got no heart's desires nowadays except what I'll get in the way of nature and in the Lord's good time. You go along and set your seeds. I'm glad I seen 'em though. Over yonder, between the lupins and the larkspurs. That'll be your plot, and I'll mark the place.'

Charlotte, very much impressed, beckoned the others. In silence they sowed the seed. The gardener watched them, and when they had planted the seeds and covered them over, he took a pencil and a painted slip-label from his pocket, wrote on it and stuck it in the ground. The children stooped to read what he had written.

'F. of H.D.' it said.

'Well!' said Caroline.

'Least said, soonest mended,' said the gardener. 'I shouldn't wonder if seed leaves was to break ground in seven days. It was allus a wonderful garden, this was,' he said, and turned to his work.

'Well!' said Charlotte again, and they went back through the dewy park.

After breakfast the *Language of Flowers* was earnestly consulted.

'It's no use going on thinking and talking about the F. of H.D.,' said Caroline, when they had talked of nothing else for an hour and a half. 'What we've got to do now, is to find the right flowers for the presentation.'

An hour's earnest study of Miss Peckitt's invaluable present yielded an interesting list. 'Learning' had apparently no floral emblem, so blue salvia, which means 'Wisdom,' was chosen to represent it. It was felt that on an occasion of this sort it was impossible to have too much of a good thing, so twelve flowers were chosen, and all but one, an outsider

called circæa, which means a spell, of which
the gardener had never heard, were found in
the Wonderful Garden.

Rupert prevailed on Mrs. Wilmington to
open the drawing-room on the ground that the
clergyman was coming to tea, and she even
agreed to allow the floral tributes to be arranged
on a large table in that hallowed sanctuary, only
insisting that a linen drugget should be laid
down before so much as a blade of grass was
carried in.

The drugget, white with many a washing,
only seemed to add to the festival air which
the drawing-room soon began to put on.

'Talk of magic,' said Charlotte; 'what is it if
it's not that with Mrs. Wilmington? Rupert
can drive her with a rein of darning cotton.'

Mrs. Wilmington had indeed consented to
'do' the vases on the mantelpiece and cabinets,
'rather than have you children smashing
everything to atoms,' she said, and even, at
Rupert's request, had agreed to put only the
flowers he handed to her. 'Though a shabbier
lot,' she said, 'it was never my lot to beheuld.
More like a passel of weeds, I should say.'

The selected flowers were certainly none
too showy. And the drawing-room decorations
might perhaps have, in the end, looked what
Mrs. Wilmington called 'mingy,' if Charlotte

had not suddenly remembered that the rose, as the flower of secrecy, was entitled to be present, in, as she said, 'the richest profusion.'

The large table was covered with loose pink rose leaves. That was Caroline's idea. 'Yes,' she said, 'I know what it will remind them of. But reminding doesn't matter when all's forgotten and forgiven, and look how soft and fluffy they look, like pink fur.'

This also reminded one of things. But no one said anything, though every one tried so hard not to look at the leopard skin that they might just as well have been staring at it.

'How pretty the flowers look, reflected in the looking-glasses,' said Caroline tactfully; and Charlotte, with less tact but equal good-will, moved an embroidered stool between Rupert and the leopard's spotted hide.

Tea was a meal of masked excitement, of gigglings scarcely suppressed by the children, and of a careful air of there being nothing particular in the wind on the part of Uncle Charles and Mr. Penfold. When the last cup had been emptied, the last piece of cake reduced to crumbs and memory, Charles was at last allowed to say the words which had been arranged for him to say, and which, all through the meal, he had been bursting to repeat.

'Please, uncle, there is a meeting of the

Society of the Secret Rose in the drawing-
room, and the Rosicurians have got a present
for you'—'a presentation,'corrected Charlotte—
'a presentation, and will you please come and
be presented.'

'It's all wrong,' said Charlotte, who had
composed the speech for him and had the
natural vanity of an author. But every one
was getting out of their chairs, and in the noise
they made, nobody heard her.

The drawing - room certainly looked, as
Harriet had said when she peeped into it
before tea, 'a fair treat'—with its white-spread
floor; its vases and jugs and jars of roses;
its rose-leaf-covered table, edged with the
twelve symbolic flowers in jam-pots, white and
elegantly small; and all the splendour of
afternoon sunshine real and reflected. The
Uncle looked at the room over his glasses,
just as though he had never seen it before.

'Beautiful,' he said; 'very beautiful.'

Charlotte took him by the hand and said:

'Dear uncle, this time we make you a
presentation, and it's not to get anything out of
you. But just to show what we think of you.
Caroline will read you what we've written,
like addresses to mayors, you know. We
hadn't time to illuminate it to-day, but we will
afterwards, if you like. And when she has

read it, we will give you the real presentation.
It is under the basin in the middle.   But you
mustn't look at it till we say——'

She stopped.   The others looked at her
meaningly.

'I can't help it,' she said, flushing.   'I've
forgotten the words.   Uncle saying "Beautiful"
put it out of my head.   But it means the same
as the words I settled to say, and Charles didn't
remember his either.'

'Your address was exactly what all addresses
should be,' said the Uncle—'short and to the
point.   I pledge my honour to respect the
secret of the basin until I am permitted to
approach it.'

The basin was a great bowl of blue and
white china that, reversed, occupied the middle
of the table.   On it lay a full-blown rose and
two buds.

Caroline unfolded a large sheet of paper
of the size called demy and the kind which
is used to bake cakes on, line boxes with, and
drain fried fish on.   Caroline had begged it
from the cook, and there was a good deal of
violet ink on it.

'Hem!' said Caroline, turning the large
pages.   'Oh yes, it begins here.'

'To the noblest of known Uncles, Charlotte,
Charles, and Caroline present their compli-

ments and thanks. We have culled in your wonderful garden the blossoms we think express all the things we want to say. These dainty floral pets' (can you tell which part of this address came out of the *Language of Flowers*, and which was Caroline's own invention?)— 'these dainty floral pets represent the most delicate and appropriate sentiments, and, offered to the beloved object, cannot fail to convey the deepest secrets of the enamoured heart. All our hearts are yours, dear uncle, because you are such a brick. The flowers are'—she pointed to the first pot on the left—'branch of currants. It means "you please us all." Because you do. Next pot—yellow acacia. We only got leaves, because it flowers a different time, but it means "secret love." Our uncle is in a secret society with us and we love him being in it.

'"Clematis indicates that beauty of the mind without which the fairest bodily endowments are but fleeting shows." Uncle is clever, so we got clematis. And white pinks mean "talent," so we got them. Sorrel we got, partly because it means affection, and partly because it is pretty and there is lots of it. And plane-tree looks dull, but in reality "it indicates to the discerning recipient that the giver considers himself privileged to offer the tribute of its agreeable foliage to the hands of Genius." That means the Uncle, because he writes books. Pythagoras says a lot about plane-trees. "Laurel needs no words to inform the reader of its meaning. It is too well known as the ornament of the foreheads of the great. It also signifies success," and we hope your book will be a great success. Red clover means industry, because uncle works so hard every day and not to be disturbed on any pretence. And "nightshade whose dark leaves and mysterious purple blossoms denote witchcraft and magic." We have mixed roses with that, because they mean love, and uncle loves witchcraft. So do we. And so we have put the double daisy. "This innocent little flower in its double state has, humble as it is, a deep meaning to the student of the language of our floral darlings. It signifies 'I share your sentiments,'" so we put it last, because we share uncle's about magic and things, and we hope he will share ours about the presentation when he sees it. That's all,' said Caroline, very much out of breath.

'Hear, hear!' said Mr. Penfold; and the Uncle said:

'Thank you; thank you very much. The most learned and delightful address I have

ever listened to. And the flowers are beautiful
in themselves as well as in their symbolism.'

'We're so glad you like it,' said Charles, 'but
wait till you see the presentation. He may
look now, mayn't he, Caro?'

'Lift up the basin,' said Charlotte; 'be careful not to drop it, uncle, it's awfully heavy.'

Uncle Charles raised the great bowl in his
hands and set it down among the rose leaves.
Under it was a white cloth covering something
and on the cloth another red rose, full blown,
and two buds.

'This is the real inside heart of the presentation,' said Caroline. 'Don't look for a minute.
We found them inside Pope's *Iliad* and
Thessalonians. And we are almost sure they
are. And we hope you'll be pleased.'

'I can hardly believe that I could be more
pleased than I am already,' said the grateful
uncle, and with that he lifted the white cloth
(one of Caroline's best handkerchiefs) and laid
bare the books.

There was a breathless silence. The Uncle
lifted the books and looked at them.

'You know,' he said presently in almost
a broken voice, 'I believe they are. I am
almost sure they are.' Then he said nothing
for a minute and then, 'Thank you,' he said;
'thank you,' and opened the book again. 'It'll

make all the difference,' he said to Mr. Penfold ;
' absolutely all the difference.'

' We found them,' Charles was beginning,
when Mr. Penfold made him a sign to be
silent, and made another sign towards the
door. Then he led the way from the room.
The children followed, and when they were all
out he closed the door softly.

' When people are very happy or very
unhappy, they like to be left alone. I think
that just now your uncle is very happy.'

' How glorious ! ' said Caroline.

' So am I,' said Mr. Penfold. ' An angel
in human form, called Mr. James Hodgkinson,
has sent me five pounds towards restoring the
church. I have blued the lot on tiles for the
roof of the porch. If you like to come down
you can help put them on. Like to ? '

' Rather ! ' was the enthusiastic answer of
the three C.'s.

Rupert did not answer. And when they
looked round to see why he did not answer,
they saw that it was because he was not
there.

CHAPTER XX

THE WAXEN MAN

'You know what Rupert was saying that day,' said Charles one day when Rupert as usual was down at Mr. Penfold's, 'about doing something real with our magic?'

'Like making her come alive,' said Charlotte, looking up at the picture of Dame Eleanour.

'No, like making wax images of people and sticking pins in them. I should like to do that. I feel as if the *Language Of* was bust up, somehow.'

'Oh, don't say that,' said Caroline, pained.

'Well, not for always, perhaps,' said Charles kindly; 'but we did give the Uncle such a tremendous blow-out for his presentation, and we did the leopard, and we sowed the F. of H.D., and anything else seems rather piffling after that. I wish we could make a wax image of some one.'

340

'Not to stick pins in,' said Caroline firmly.
'That would be ink-black magic, I'm certain.
And very very wrong and unkind besides.'

'No pins, I don't mean,' said Charles, 'but
just make one. We could decide what to
stick into it after we'd made it.'

'Caro and I wouldn't agree to sticking anything into it,' said Charlotte; 'and, anyhow,
you haven't got any wax.'

'Yes, I have,' said Charles triumphantly;
'so there! I've been saving it up ever since
he said that.'

'Where from?' asked the girls together.

'The sticking-out bits of candles,' said
Charles, 'and one or two ends out of candlesticks in the morning when they are put on
the boot-shelf in the scullery to be cleaned.
It's a good big lump now. Shall I get it?'

'It would be fun to model something,'
Caroline admitted, and Charles, falling flat on
his front, felt behind the big books on the
bottom shelf and produced a large ball of a
grey semi-transparent nature.

'Here it is,' he said. 'Now I'll tell you
what I've thought. Only don't tell Rupert.
We'll do it first and tell Rupert afterwards.
And then he'll have to believe.'

'Well, what is it?'

'We'll make,' said Charles slowly and

M

seriously, 'a wax image of the Murdstone man, and we'll make him hollow, his legs and arms needn't be, nor his head, but just his chest. And make his heart separate, and put it in. And take out his heart and melt it every day. That would soften his heart, and he would say he was sorry and Rupert would forgive him.'

' " When hollow hearts shall wear a mask," ' said Charlotte.

'That's only song-nonsense. People die if you take their hearts out,' said Caroline with conviction.

'Well, then, don't let's make him hollow. Let's make him solid and then think what to do.'

'I know,' said Charlotte; 'but if he's a pig, he's a pig, however solid you make him. What's bred in the bone will come out in the wash. And if we're not to stick pins in him, what's the good?'

'Oh,' said Caroline, 'I think I know. Look here! We'll make the wax image and then be kind to it. You can tame wild beasts with kindness.'

'It kills cats,' said Charlotte.

'No, it was Care killed the cat,' Caroline reminded her, 'and, anyway, this won't be a cat, even if it did. We'll think of nice things to do to it. Let's make it now.'

'Bags I!' said Charles hastily. 'It was my idea, and I collected the wax.'

'Like an old bee,' said Charlotte. 'All right, fire ahead.'

Charles had been warming the wax between his hands, and now, hardly waiting for Caroline to fetch and spread a newspaper, he began to divide the wax into six pieces.

'One head, two arms, two legs, one body,' he explained.

The girls watched with breathless interest. Charles rolled the smallest piece of wax round in his hands till it was like a marble, and the biggest piece till it was like a fives ball; the remaining four he rolled lengthwise till they were like thick tobacco-pipes. Then he stuck the four pipey bits and the round marble on to the fives ball and held the whole thing out triumphantly.

'I think it's awfully like,' he said, 'especially the right arm that he hit Rupert with. I *should* like to stick just one pin in that.'

'You mustn't,' said Caroline. 'Yes, it's awfully nice, but it hasn't any clothes. I know statues of Greek heroes don't have any clothes. But he's not a Greek hero. And nowadays people have to have clothes even in their statues. Look at Mr. Gladstone. And it

would be more like real if it had a nose and
ears, wouldn't it?'

'I say,' said Charlotte, 'let's get bits of
bent twigs and pretend they're him, and then
make wax clothes. Do let us help, Charles.
It does look so interesting to do. You shall do
the first kind thing for him if you'll let us help
make him.'

'*I* think he's all right,' said Charles, looking
at the blobby thing he had made, which was
more like an imperfect octopus than a man;
'but if you promise me to do the first thing, I
don't mind.'

'Right O! I'll get the sticks.'

When the sticks had been found, the three
children began to model parts of the Murdstone man, but Caroline and Charles soon
stopped and were content to watch Charlotte.
She really seemed to know what she was
about, which the others felt could not be said
of them. She chose suitable twigs, fastened
them together with bits of wax, and then
began to clothe them with wax. She produced
an arrangement not at all unlike a jacket and
waistcoat. The trousers were a failure. The
most accomplished sculptors have admitted that
trousers are difficult to treat artistically. But
they remembered that, last time they had seen
him, the Murdstone man had worn knicker-

bockers, and in these, revealing the shape of the stockinged human leg, Charlotte was considered to have surpassed herself. The head was very difficult, but even this was managed, the hair question being settled by a large flat cap with a peak. The new model had a nose and mouth, ears large, but still ears, and hands each with four fingers and a thumb. And when Charlotte rolled up the tiniest bits of wax, flattened them and stuck them on the coat and waistcoat for buttons, Caroline shouted, 'Bravo! You're as good as Praxi— what's-his-name!' and even Charles said it wasn't half bad.

'Now,' said Charlotte, 'the first nice thing to do for him is to put him in a bed of rose leaves. That's what they say when they mean a life without a sorrow or care.'

'And then burn incense. We can make the incense out of the proper flowers,' Caroline said.

'Rose leaves are dull,' Charles said, 'and perhaps the Murdstone man doesn't like incense.'

'The real one mayn't. This one's got to like what we want it to like,' said Charlotte. 'We made him and *we* know what he's got to like.'

'Then we might make it so that he'd like

having pins stuck into him,' Charles suggested hopefully.

'We might; only we shouldn't be so silly. Come on, bring the *Language Of* and the Murdstone man. I'll get a box and Caro can get the rose leaves. We'll go out and find a secret place in the wood.'

A cardboard box that had held Charlotte's best shoes was filled with sweet pink petals and the waxen image put in it. It looked better standing up, but you don't stand up in a bed, even of rose leaves. A sort of pedestal was built of old bricks brought with some toil from the ruins of the deserted lodge's pig-stye. A flat stone, which took all three to lift, was placed on top. And on this the box. But the box, which said 'Smarm and Simple's Hygienic Footwear' in blue letters outside, troubled the girls because it was ugly, and Charles because it was untruthful.

'Whatever he is, he isn't footwear,' said Charles. 'We could make it true by trampling on him, but you won't agree to that.'

'No,' said Caroline, 'but look here. Let's paste a bit of my green sash on it, and then put moss round. That'll make it more woodland-like.'

Cook provided the paste, and Caroline cut the sash. She paste-wetted the first piece of

silk so that it came out in wet spots, very messy
looking, as Charles did not fail to point out.

'Never mind,' said Caroline, 'I'll cut
another bit—it's much too long—and use
less paste.'

'More paste less speed,' said Charlotte.
'I'll cut mine. Then they'll be alike, just as
they were before.'

This time the box certainly looked very
rich, and the moss round it looked very fresh
and beautiful.

A smaller pile of bricks supported the lid of
a cocoa-tin for incense.

The Language of Flowers, hurriedly consulted, informed them that jasmine stood for
amiability, St. John's wort for animosity,
Indian pink for aversion, the pimpernel for
change, sage for esteem, and the hazel for
reconciliation. Further, that the tamarisk
stood for crime and the potato for benevolence.

All these were found in the Wonderful
Garden except the potato, and none of the
children knew what a potato looks like when
it is growing, and they did not like to ask
any one, for fear they in turn should be asked
what they wanted it for.

'Never mind,' said Charles, 'we can save
one from dinner. I don't suppose it will matter
its being cooked.'

That the potatoes that day should happen to be mashed, seemed to all a mishap yet not a calamity. A quantity, deemed sufficient to influence Mr. Murdstone through his waxen image, was secreted in the envelope of a letter from Aunt Emmeline, and not more than an eighth of the potato escaped into Charles's pocket through the square hole where the Italian stamp had been cut out for his collection.

'We'll arrange the things we want him to be round the box,' said Caroline, 'and the things we want him not to be we'll burn and call it incense.'

Charles owned that he had been wondering what sort of incense you could make out of mashed potato.

Jasmine, with its white stars, bright Indian pinks, gay tufts of sage, and the oval-ringed leaves of the hazel, arranged round the box, made a charming tangle. 'The silk wasn't wanted, really,' said Charles. 'The hygienic boots would never have shown through the flowers.' But the girls agreed that it was nice to know it was there.

The mashed potato and the rather faded pimpernel were carefully concealed under the more attractive offerings.

'It looks fine,' Charles said, and what he said they all thought.

Nothing much happened except smoke.

It is very hard to make small pieces of green things burn in a cocoa-tin lid in the open air by means of a box of matches, and the fragments of a potato-dampened envelope from an aunt in Italy. Nothing much happened except smoke, and the head of a match burnt Charles's finger.

'There's no more paper,' said he, 'except the bit we've written his name on.'

'There's the match-box,' said Caroline; 'let's make a little bonfire with twigs and then put the incense things on when it's burnt up.' This they did; and the starry gold of St. John's wort, the gay brightness of Indian pinks, and the feathery greenness of the tamarisks twisted and writhed amid flames and smoke.

'Now we'll leave it. Please, Murdstone man, let your crimes and your animosity and your aversion be burnt away, and may you lie on beds of roses really as soon as you are changed and amiable. Then when you are truly benevolent, Rupert and us will esteem you, and the hazel is for reconciliation. Now let's go away and leave the incense to do its healing work, and to-morrow we'll come and put a fresh rose-bed and burn new incense.' Thus Caroline. The others agreed, and after having put on the box the label with the Murdstone man's name, so that Destiny could not pretend to make any mistake as to who the witchcraft was meant for, they went away through green coverts, in Indian file, to build a wigwam in another part of the wood with three hop poles, three red blankets, and their three mackintoshes.

'I hope Rupert won't ask a lot of questions about what we've been doing to-day,' said Charles. But Rupert did not ask any. He came home singularly silent, and went to bed early, announcing that he was going to spend the following day, also, with Mr. Penfold.

'So we needn't tell him,' said Charlotte, 'till the good work is done. I'm glad of that.'

Next day, with a fresh armful of suitable flowers and some more potatoes, fried this time and bearing heavy traces of their close intimacy with the breakfast bacon, the children sought the secret spot where they had laid the waxen image of Mr. Murdstone on its bed of roses. The ashes of the incense bonfire were there, the pedestal was there, the green-covered box was there, half filled with half-faded rose leaves; but the waxen image was gone!

'He must have fetched it away himself,' said Charlotte, breaking an awe-struck pause; 'he must have felt what we were doing and made up his mind to be benevolent. And he fetched it away so that we shouldn't waste any more good potatoes on him.'

' I wish he'd do something to show that he's changed into a Real Good and what sort of Good he's changed into,' said Charles.   And it certainly is tiresome to work magic and then not to know exactly how it has acted.   That their magic had acted, the children were of course quite certain.   They had done magic too many times, as you know, to entertain a moment's doubt as to whether their spells were going to work or not.   And the fact that the spell they had worked was not worked exactly as the book said, did not trouble them.   For, as Caroline said, ' If you can do harm to wax people, you can do good to them.   More really, I should think.   Because one's wrong and the other's right.'

But it was a rather disappointed party that took its way through the greenwood, leaving the secret spot with its trampled flowers and scattered ashes.   They came across their wigwam and spent the rest of the morning there, and, when the dinner-bell rang, loaded themselves with the mackintoshes and blankets which had been forgotten yesterday.

As they trailed out of the wood into the drive, Charles, who was first, dropped his blanket and stopped short, blocking the view of the others, who were following him down the narrow path.

'What is it? what is it?' they asked.

'Shish!' said Charles and backed into the hazel bushes, and the girls pressed forward to see what there was to shish about. Then they in turn backed into the green covert, and the bushes closed over them as they stood there holding their breath as footsteps went by them along the drive. When the footsteps had passed far enough away for the children to dare to move, they backed with one consent into the wood, not stopping till they came to an open glade where they could comfortably look at each other and exclaim, 'Well!' They were past all other words. For what they had seen was Rupert coming up the drive, looking pale but not unhappy. And beside him, with his hand on Rupert's shoulder, and talking to him in the friendliest way, was—the Murdstone man!

'Rupert will *have* to believe now!' was the first thing any one found breath to say. It was Caroline who said it. The others still had not breath enough for more than 'Rather!'

CHAPTER XXI

THE ATONEMENT OF RUPERT

'I DO wonder what has happened,' Charlotte whispered. 'I suppose the Murdstone man was coming to tell Rupert he had been spell-changed into being nice now. And he must have met Rupert on the way.'

'But he could have said that in the road and then gone home. There must be some reason for his coming home with Rupert. He can't,' said Charles hopefully, 'be going to tell *us* that he's changed? That would be ripping.'

'I expect he's telling the Uncle,' said Caroline. 'When the wicked Magician takes off his spell and the wicked Prince turns good, he always tells everybody at once.'

'Then he'll come and tell *us*,' said Charles. 'We're part of everybody, the same as grown-up people are.'

355

The three C.'s had come slowly back to the house, and, seeing no sign of Rupert and the changed Murdstone man, had, with great tact, chiefly Caroline's, refrained from going in search of Rupert or of information.

They had just shut themselves into the dining-room, and waited. For it was quite plain that something more must happen. The once-hated Murdstone man could not just come to the house and go away again and the matter end there. But waiting is tiresome work, however proud you may be feeling of your tact and delicacy, and you are so interested and anxious that it is idle even to pretend to read. The three C.'s were very glad indeed when at last they heard footsteps in the hall, and voices.

'Now!' said Caroline. 'Now they're coming. We'll be most awfully nice to him, won't we. Now he's sorry and he's owned up.'

'Of course,' said Charles. 'Do you think I could ask him to let me have the wax image of him to keep in memorio?'

'No,' said Caroline, 'of course you couldn't. Hush! for goodness' sake, hush!'

But there seemed to be no urgent need for hushing. The footsteps and the voices went past the dining-room towards the front door, which was at the side, as you know. No one listened, yet no one could help hearing, through the open window, the parting words of Rupert and the Murdstone man :

'I'll do it now. That'll be the last. Thank you, sir. Good-bye!'

Then came the sound of retreating boots on gravel. The front door banged, and next moment Rupert came in. His eyes were very bright and his face very pale. He came in, shut the door, leaned against it, and seemed to swallow nothing, twice. Then he said, looking straight in front of him, and Charlotte noticed that his hands were clenched :

'Look here, I've got something to tell you. I don't suppose you'll want to speak to me again after it.'

'Yes, we shall,' said Charles, 'whatever it is.'

Rupert took no notice. He went on, after a moment's silence:

'I told a lie about Mr. Macpherson, a beastly lie. He didn't hit me like I said he did. I didn't mean to say it, I just said it, and then I couldn't take it back. I've been most awfully wretched. That's all.'

'But you've owned up now,' was the only comforting thing even Caroline could think of in that terrible moment. Charles, as pale as Rupert, with his eyes quite round, said :

' You *couldn't* have ! '

Charlotte said nothing.

' I'd like you to understand.' said Rupert miserably, ' before I go away.'

' Go away ? ' said Charlotte quite as miserably. ' Where ? '

' Back to Mr. Macpherson, of course. Your uncle won't keep me after this.'

' Did he say so ?

' No, he said I was to come back to him when I'd taken Mr. Macpherson to the door. But I feel I must tell you first, in case he sends me off right away.'

' Oh, Rupert,' said Caroline, ' I *am* so sorry ! ' And then she did something rather heroic. She saw that Rupert wanted to say more, wanted it desperately, and that he could not possibly say it to all three of them together, though he could have told it to one of them, either to her or to Charlotte, if they had been alone. So Caroline got up and said :

' Charles, come outside. I want to say something ' ; and when she got him outside the door, ' come out,' she said earnestly. ' Yes, you shall. Rupert doesn't want the lot of us. Let him talk to Charlotte. He can't stand a crowd.'

' Isn't it dreadful,' said Charles in very

shocked tones, ' Rupert turning out a liar like this ? '

' Oh, *don't,*' said Caroline hotly; ' it must have been awful for him, all this time. And now he's sorry and he's owned up. We've got to try and forget about it. Let's talk about something else.'

But it was very difficult to talk about something else.

Rupert, left with Charlotte, saw the others go past the window.

' I wanted to tell you before,' he said ; ' that day when you talked about being disagreeable. Only I couldn't.'

' Dear old Rupert ! ' said Charlotte. ' I'm so jolly glad you've got rid of it. *That* was the black dog. I knew there was something. Do tell me, old chap, unless you'd rather not. The others are off down the avenue.'

Rupert left the door and came to the table, and, half-sitting on it, with his face turned away, and twisting the table-cloth into pleats, he said :

' You know I always thought I was going to be an extra honourable sort of chap. Father used to say things. I never did anything like it before. You see I was awfully sick at having to go with Mr. Macpherson at all. He treated me as if I was a baby. At least that's what I thought. He says now he meant to be kind and he thought I was younger than I am. And the bread and milk. Everything else I told you was true except hitting me. And he did say there were ways of dealing with sulky boys. And I decided I would run away. And I hurt my hand on a gate. And I was so angry, it seemed the only thing to do.'

'I know,' said Charlotte.

'And then, when I was explaining to you, somehow I couldn't find the proper words to explain how hateful it was, and I thought you'd think I'd run away just for nothing. And then my hand hurt, and I thought you thought something more ought to have happened. And then I said that. Mean beast!'

'I do *wish* you hadn't,' said Charlotte.

'It didn't seem to matter just at first. I can't think why. I thought he meant to hit me next day, and, anyhow, you didn't know him. And then I got ill and nothing mattered. But when I got better, it kept on getting worse and worse and worse, like a corkscrew worming into you harder and harder and harder all the time.'

'But why didn't you own up before?' Charlotte asked.

'I couldn't. I never should have if it hadn't been for this.'

He pulled his handkerchief with some difficulty from his pocket. Something was wrapped in it. Rupert, his face still turned away, unfolded and held out the waxen man.

'I came back through the woods yesterday, and then I saw you'd been trying that beastly spell I told you with the pins.'

'Oh!' said Charlotte.

'And I knew it was because I'd told that beastly lie.'

'Oh, it *wasn't*,' said Charlotte. 'We did everything nice for him, to make him sorry he was hateful and to make him friends with you. And oh, Rupert, the spell *did* work! We did it to make him friends with you. *And he is.*'

'He's been jolly decent about it, anyhow,' said Rupert. 'I found the wax thing as I came home from Mr. Penfold's last night, and I took it away and put it at the back of my collar-drawer. And this morning I took it down to Mr. Penfold's. It made it easier to tell, somehow. And *he* was jolly decent too. He took me over to Tonbridge to tell Mr. Macpherson. And he said a lot of things. He said he'd known all along I'd got something I wanted to get off my chest. And he said things about repentance and things. I do like him.'

' I'm glad we made the image,' said Charlotte, because it seemed unkind to say nothing, and she could think of nothing else to say.

' And I'm going to stick it, whatever it is. Mr. Macpherson is all right, but it will be hateful leaving here. Only I suppose you'll all be glad I'm going.'

' Rupert ! '

' Well, then, I know *you* won't really. I say, Charlotte, you might tell the others. And tell them I know I've been a grumpy brute, but it was *that* going on all the time inside me like a beastly Spartan fox. It's been like waiting at the dentist's all the time, and this is like having all your teeth out at once, twenty times over.'

He tried to laugh, but he did not succeed very well. Charlotte also tried, and burst into tears.

' Don't ! ' said Rupert awkwardly. Charlotte came close to him and rubbed her wet face against his coat sleeve.

' You're sorry,' she said, ' and you've owned up and you'll never do it again.'

' You bet I won't,' said Rupert. ' I say, don't ! It makes it ever so much worse. Now I've got to go back to your uncle and get the kick-out. And I jolly well deserve it.'

' Just wait a minute,' said Charlotte. ' I'm

going to get something I want to give you before you go. Wait here, won't you?'

'Don't be long then,' said Rupert in calm wretchedness.

Charlotte dried her eyes and went out, went to her own room and got her favourite *Lays of the Scottish Cavaliers*. She wrote Rupert's name in it and then marched straight to her uncle's room, opened the door, and went in.

Uncle Charles, for once, was not reading or writing. He was sitting by his table drumming on it with his fingers and looking both sad and angry.

'Uncle!' said Charlotte.

'Where is Rupert?' said the Uncle, frowning.

'He doesn't know I'm here,' said Charlotte, answering her uncle's thoughts rather than his words. 'I asked him to wait while I got something to give him. Uncle, you aren't going to send him away, are you?'

'I feel it only due to Mr. Macpherson to send Rupert back,' said the Uncle, 'to show that we regret the aspersions'—the Uncle spoke as to a grown-up equal—'the aspersions cast on him by my abetting Rupert in his flight and removing him from Mr. Macpherson's care. If it is a punishment to Rupert, it is not an undeserved one.'

'Yes,' said Charlotte, who hadn't thought of this, 'but Rupert's been punished—all the time he has. No one else knows but me. He's been perfectly miserable. Only he just *couldn't* tell. And now he has, has told everybody, honourably everybody. Oh, dear uncle, don't; I *am* so mizzy!'

'Come here,' said the Uncle, and Charlotte found a thin black-coated shoulder a very good place to cry on.

'But you see,' he said, 'it's only fair to Mr. Macpherson to send Rupert back. I am willing to believe that he has been punished enough.'

'You don't know,' said Charlotte; 'he's been simply as unbearable as a bear, he's been so unhappy.'

'I didn't know that,' said the Uncle slowly; 'but no, it's not fair to that man. Rupert must go.'

Then Charlotte had one of her bright ideas, and its brightness dried her tears.

'Look here, uncle,' she said, 'I've got it— I really have. Wouldn't it make up to Mr. Macpherson and show your confidence just the same if you asked him to come here on a visit?'

'I *couldn't*,' said the Uncle, and it was plain he spoke from the heart; 'my work would all

Charlotte found a thin black-coated shoulder a very good place to cry on.

go—to pieces. I simply *can't* have visitors, grown-up ones, I mean. The books you've found, they've revolutionised the whole scheme of my work. Yet,' he added thoughtfully, ' I owe you something for that.'

' Then pay us with Rupert,' said Charlotte eagerly. ' Couldn't you bear Mr. Macpherson just for one week-end? Then everybody would know you were friends with him. Oh, uncle, poor Rupert, he is so sorry. And he did own up.'

' What was this about a waxen image?' asked the Uncle. Charlotte told him, and he nodded now and then and said, 'Yes, yes!' and 'Exactly!' And at the end he said :

' Well, you have attained your end. You have reconciled them. The charm seemed to have worked.'

' They've all worked,' said Charlotte, 'every single charm we've tried. Have yours, uncle?'

' I wish they had,' he answered, sighing. ' Charlotte, I wish I could do what you wish. Don't try spells to make me, because I can't. Rupert must go back to-morrow, for a fortnight at least. But he shall come back then till the end of the holidays. Will that do? And I'll explain to him that it's not punishment, but

just the *consequences* of what he did. If he
hadn't told that lie he wouldn't have had to
go back.'

'But would you have kept him at first, if he
hadn't told it?' Charlotte asked.

'He was unhappy there. That would have
been enough,' said the Uncle—'that and your
spells.'

.   .   .   .

'It's all right,' said Rupert to Charlotte
later. 'Your uncle's forgiven me and I'm to
come back. And he explained why I must go.
And I see it. And I can stick it all right.
And I'd rather suffer it up and start fair. I'd
rather pay something. I shall have to write
and tell my father. That's worse than anything.'

'And when you come back,' said Charlotte,
'we shall think it was all a bad dream.'

He went next day. The three C.'s saw
him off at the station, all wearing arbor vitæ
in their button-holes to signify 'unchanging
friendship,' and Charlotte at the last moment
pressed the *Scottish Cavaliers* into his hand.

'I say, though, wasn't it *dreadful*, him telling that lie,' said Charles as they turned away
from the platform. It was a public place, but
one of his sisters shook him, then and there,
and the other said, ' Look here, Charles, if you

ever say another word about it, we'll never speak to you again.   See?'

And Charles saw.   ' I don't mean I don't like him and all that,' he tried to explain, ' but you wouldn't like me not to think lying was wrong, would you?'

Then the girls saw.

' You needn't think we think *anything*,' said Caroline.   ' You just shut up, Charles.   We're two to one.'

CHAPTER XXII

THE PORTRAIT

THERE were now two things for the three C.'s
to look forward to : the return of Rupert and
Lord Andore's coming-of-age party. The
magic of the waxen man had ended so seriously
that no one liked to suggest the trying of any
new spells, though Charlotte still cherished
the hope that it might some day seem possible
to try a spell for bringing the picture to life.
There were no directions for such a spell in
any of the books.

'But,' she thought, 'considering all the
experience we've had, we ought to be able to
invent something.'

But the banishment of Rupert had left a
kind of dull blankness which made it difficult
to start new ideas. There was a sort of feeling
like a very wet Sunday when there is some one
ill in the house and you can't go to church.
In Caroline and Charlotte there was a deep

unacknowledged feeling that they ought to be very good in order to make up for 'poor Rupert.' And Charles cared little for anything but swimming, in which art he was progressing so far that he sometimes knew, even in the water, which were his arms and which were his legs, and could at least imagine that he was making the correct movements with all four.

Uncle Charles was less frequently visible even than at first, though when he did appear he was more like an uncle and less like a polite acquaintance. The books the children had discovered had meant a very great deal to him. He told them so more than once. He went away now, almost every other day, to London to the British Museum, to Canterbury to its Library, and once, for two days, to look up some old parchments in the Bodleian Library, which, as of course you know, meant going to Oxford. Mr. Penfold was very kind, and the children did quite a lot of building under his directions, but altogether it was a flattish time.

Then suddenly things began to grow interesting again. What began it was the visit of a tall gentleman in spectacles. He had a long nose and a thin face with a slow, pleasant smile. He called when the Uncle was out and left a card. Caroline heard Harriet explaining that the Master was out, and rushed after the caller in hospitable eagerness.

'I'm sure uncle wouldn't like you to go away without resting,' she said breathlessly, when he stopped at the sound of her pattering feet on the gravel, and she caught up with him, 'after you've come such a long way and such a hot day, too.'

'After you've brought me out so far and made me trot so quick,' he answered. And after that of course one could no longer regard him as a stranger. Charlotte and Charles, in the meantime, had hastily examined the gentleman's card in the Russian bowl on the hall table.

'Mr. Alfred Appleby,' it said, and added, as Charlotte said, 'most of the alphabet, beginning with F.R.S., F.S.A., and this mingled with his name so that when Caroline privately asked them what was on the card, they could only think of Mr. Alphabet.

Mr. Appleby accepted Caroline's invitation and turned back with her.

'I'm sorry,' she said, 'that I can't take you straight into the drawing-room, but if you don't mind waiting in the dining-room a minute, I'll get the drawing-room key and take you in there, only I'm afraid the dining-room's rather awful, because we've been thinking of playing

Red Indians, and the gum is drying on the scalps on most of the chairs.'

Mr. Appleby declined the drawing-room at any price, and was able to tell them several things they did not know about Red Indians, wampum, moccasins, and war-paint. He was felt to be quite the nicest thing that had happened since what Caroline and Charlotte in private conversation always spoke of as 'that awful image day.' When Mrs. Wilmington came in to see what those children were up to, Mr. Appleby won her heart by addressing her as Mrs. Davenant. 'Took me for the lady of the house at once,' she told Harriet. And Mrs. Wilmington drew Caroline aside and said:

'If you'd like to ask the gentleman to lunch, Miss Caroline, please yourself. There's fowls, as it happens, and a Paradise pudding, and peas. Perhaps your uncle would wish it.'

So the gentleman stayed to luncheon, and very good company they found him. He told the most amusing stories, all new to the hearers. He carved the fowls in a masterly way and had two goes of pudding. And all the time he looked with exactly the right admiration and wonder at the portrait of Dame Eleanour in her ruff, with her strange magic philtres and her two wonderful books.

'We found those books, Mr. Alphabet,' said

N

Charlotte. And then the whole story had to be told. Mr. Alphabet—for so we may call him now—was deeply interested, and nodded understandingly as the tale of the different spells unfolded itself to his intelligent questioning.

'And do you propose to continue your experiments?' he asked, when he had heard the tale of the leopard, the last of the adventures which *could* be told, for the affair of the wax man was of course a thing that could never be disclosed.

'There's nothing particular that we want to do a spell about, just now,' said Caroline. 'I did think of trying to do one to get father and mother home, but it might be very inconvenient to them to leave India just now. You never know, and we shouldn't like to work a spell that would only be a worry to them.'

Mr. Alphabet said, 'Quite so!'

'What *I* keep on wanting to try,' said Charlotte, 'is to make *her* come alive,' she nodded towards the picture; 'only there doesn't seem to be any spell for that in any of the books. She looks such a dear, doesn't she? Suppose she made a spell herself and did something magic to that picture, so that it should come alive if some one in nowadays-times got hold of the other end of the spell; you know what I mean?'

'Quite so,' said the visitor; 'why not?'

'It wouldn't be the real her, I suppose?' said Charlotte, 'but it might be like a cinematograph and a phonograph mixed up. I want to see her move and hear her speak, like she did when she was alive.'

And again the gentleman said, 'Why not?'

'If only we could find out the proper spell,' said Charles. 'You see, everything came right that we've done, from the fern-seed on. Only we can't.'

'I must think it over,' said Mr. Alphabet; 'and now I think as I've stayed so long, I'll take the liberty of inviting myself to stay till your uncle returns. I should very much like to see this Wonderful Garden. And perhaps you'll permit me to smoke an after-dinner pipe there?'

The afternoon passed delightfully. Mr. Alphabet was one of those people with whom you feel comfortable from the first. He understood what you said, which is one of the two feet on which comfortable companionship stands; and he said nothing that you could not understand if you really used your brains, and that is the other foot. He told them the names of many flowers which had been

strangers to them, and he talked of magic—
Indian magic and Chinese magic, the magic
of Egypt and of Ceylon, of Australia and of
Mexico; and they listened and longed for more,
and got more to listen to.   When, after tea, the
Uncle returned, and having warmly greeted
Mr. Alphabet took him away to his study, the
children agreed that their new friend was the
'right sort,' and that they hoped they would
see him again often.

'Once a week, at least,' said Caroline.

'Once a day,' said Charles.

They saw him once again, and once only.

And that was when, he and the Uncle
having come out of the study together, the
Uncle went to see William about putting the
horse in to drive Mr. Alphabet to the station,
and Mr. Alphabet came into the dining-room
to say good-bye to the children.

'I've been thinking over what you said
about Dame Eleanour,' he said to Charlotte,
'and I'll tell you what. You ask your uncle
to allow you to hang a green curtain over her,
frame and all, and then make garlands of
suitable flowers. Then hang the garlands
across the picture and wait. You must never
lift the curtain, of course, and the curtain
must be green. And you must wish very
much to see her move and to hear her speak.

And I shall be very much surprised if you don't in—let me see—in about three weeks. The curtain must be green, mind. Nothing else will do. Don't let your housekeeper fob you off with a red moreen or an old blue damask. Green's the colour.'

'And do you really think?' asked Charlotte with gleaming eyes.

'Well, with any one else I shouldn't dare to think anything. But you've been so exceptionally fortunate hitherto, haven't you? With *you* I should think there could be no doubt of success. I don't say you'll see her *here*, mind you. I don't say how or when you will see her. These things are among the great mysteries. Perhaps one day when you're at breakfast, you'll see the curtain move slightly, and at first you'll think it is the air from the open window, and then you'll see a bulge in the green curtain—don't forget it's to be green—and then a white hand will draw it back, and she will come stepping down out of her frame on to the nearest chair, with her rustling silk petticoat and her scarlet high-heeled shoes. Perhaps that's how she'll come. I only say "perhaps," mind. Because, of course, you might meet her in the wood, or in some scene of gay revelry, or in the Wonderful Garden itself—her garden, which is kept just as she planted it. There's an old document your uncle's been showing me—she leaves her blessing to the family so long as the garden's kept as it was in her time—with a long list of the flowers and a plan of the garden with the proper places for the flowers all marked. Did you know that? No? I must get your uncle to show you. I should think she would be very likely to appear in the garden.'

'You're not kidding us?' Charles asked suddenly.

'Could you think it of me? No, I see you couldn't. You try my spell, and write and tell me how it works. All right, Davenant —coming. Where's my hat?—oh, outside, yes—and my umbrella, right. Good-bye, all of you. Thank you very much for a most delightful day.'

'Thank you,' said Caroline, and they all said, 'Good-bye, and come again soon!'

'Don't forget green!' were this amiable gentleman's parting words as he climbed into the dogcart beside William and waved a cheery farewell with his umbrella to the party at the front door (at the side).

Uncle Charles, when the matter was laid before him, raised no objection to the curtaining of the picture. He even drove with them to

'Take your last look,' he said.

Maidstone and bought a special curtain for the purpose, soft, wide, green woollen stuff it was, very soft, very wide, very green. Mrs. Wilmington hemmed the curtain, and the Uncle himself, tottering on the housemaid's steps, hung the curtain in place.

'Take your last look,' he said, coming down the steps and holding the green curtain aside so that Dame Eleanour looked out of the dusk of the curtain almost as if she were alive. 'Take a good look at her, so that you will know her again if you do see her.'

'"If"?' said Charlotte.

'I mean when,' said the Uncle, letting the long straight folds of the curtain fall into place.

The question of garlands now occupied all thoughts, even those of the Uncle's.

'Arbor vitæ,' said he, 'means tree of life.'

'Then we'll have that,' said Caroline, 'especially as it means "unchanging friendship," too.' She thought of Rupert. 'I hope Rupert's back before she appears,' she added; '*that* would make him believe in magic, wouldn't it?'

The Uncle, for the first time, was introduced to the *Language Of*, and he seemed much struck by the literary style of that remarkable work.

'"Never did the florographist select from

cunning Nature's wondrous field a more
appropriate interpreter of man's innermost
passions than when he chose the arbor vitæ
to formulate the significance, 'Live for me.'"
I was not aware that human beings *could*
write like that,' he said, 'and I thought you
said arbor vitæ meant something quite
different.'

'They often do,' said Caroline. 'We used
to think the book didn't know its own mind,
but we think now it put in new meanings when
it found them out. It's rather confusing at
first. But "live for me" is fine. It's just
what we want the picture to do, isn't it?
What else?'

'I leave it to you,' said the Uncle, laying
down the book. 'Your author's style is too
attractive. I could waste all the rest of the
daylight on him. Farewell. If I can be
of any assistance in hanging the garlands,
let me know.'

They thanked him warmly and hesitated.
Then Charles said, 'It was us that she was to
come alive to, so I expect it had better be us to
hang the garlands.'

'We,' said the Uncle gently, 'not us.'

'But I meant us,' said Charles. 'Not we
with you in it.'

'I was trying to correct your grammar, not

your statement,' said the Uncle; 'but never mind. Good-bye.'

Nobody was quite sure what a garland was, because in books people sometimes wore garlands on their heads, when of course they would be wreaths, and sometimes twined them round pillars, in which case they would be like Christmas decorations.

'We had better have both kinds,' said Caroline, 'to be quite sure.'

On a foundation of twigs of the arbor vitae, twined round with Jaeger wool originally bought for Caroline to knit a vest for her Aunt Emmeline ('but I know I shall never finish it,' she said), symbolic flowers were tied, some in circlets or wreaths, others on long straight lengths. 'Rye grass which means a changeable disposition,' was suggested by Charlotte, 'because we do want her to change : from paint to alive,' she said; 'and pink verbena means "family reunion," and she is a relation, after all. Besides pink's such a pretty colour.'

Caroline ascertained that yew meant life; but Charles was considered to have made the hit of the afternoon by his discovery that Jacob's ladder meant 'come down,' which was, of course, exactly what they wanted the lady to do.

The gardener knew what Jacob's ladder was,

though the children did not; and their fear that it might be a dull shrub with invisible flowers was dispelled when they beheld its blue brightness.

'We ought to wear coronilla ourselves,' said Caroline—'a new piece every day. It means "success attend your wishes."' But the gardener had not heard of coronilla. 'The book says it's "a flowering shrub of the pea family,"' Caroline read from the *Language Of*, which, as usual, she had been carrying under her arm, '"with small pinnate leaves"—whatever they are. "An elegant bush with reddish-brown blossoms when first expanded, varying to yellow at a later period of their graceful existence."'

'Oh, that!' said the gardener, 'that'll be scorpion's senna. That's what that be. Something to do with the shape of the stars in the sky. Old women sells it for a charm for shy sweethearts.'

'In our book it says, "Success crown your wishes."'

'Just so,' said the gardener, 'and she names the day. That's it, along there.'

The garlands looked very handsome and the wreaths very beautiful. It was Caroline who made this distinction. And their dark foliage and the bright pink and blue and yellow of

their flowers showed charmingly against the
green curtain.

'And now,' said Caroline, 'we've just got
to wait, and Charlotte and I must stick to our
glove and handkerchief cases if they're going
to be ready to go in time for mother's birthday.
And, Charles, if I were you, I should get Mr.
Penfold to show you chip-carving like he
offered to, and do a box for her. And we
mustn't forget that we're not to look behind the
curtain.'

'I shan't forget that,' said Charlotte.
'What I should like to forget's my head. It
feels twice its proper size.'

'I've got a headache too,' said Caroline.
'I expect it's the sun.'

'If it was the sun, mine would ache too,'
said Charles, 'but with me it's the nose. I've
had four hankies since breakfast; and one of
those was the Wilmington's.'

'Well, let's go and get on with our em-
broidery. All my silks are frightfully tangled.'

They were not disentangled that day. The
headaches were worse. I will not dwell on the
development of the catastrophe. The doctor
put it in a few brief, well-chosen words the
next day :

'The girls have got measles right enough,
and the boy hasn't yet.'

CHAPTER XXIII

THE END

You see the tragedy? Measles, with Lord Andore's party and Rupert's return both fixed for the week after next. No words of mine could do justice to the feelings of the three C.'s. I think, perhaps, on the whole, it was worse for Charles, who was suspected throughout of impending measles, of which he was wholly innocent, his cold being only a rather violent example of the everyday kind. He was kept out of draughts and taken for walks by Mrs. Wilmington and not allowed to bathe, and he became bored beyond description. Really the girls were better off in bed, with a brightening vista of jelly, beef tea, fish, chicken, leading to natural beef and pudding and getting up to breakfast.

When the three were reunited it was the very day of Lord Andore's party, and of course they were not allowed to go, 'for fear of chills.'

Charles, after tea had been taken away, shut the dining-room door carefully and said:

'I've got something to confess.'

'Well?' said the others, as he stopped short, and displayed no intention of ever going on.

'I don't suppose you'll ever care to speak to me again when I've told you.'

'Don't be a copy-cat,' said Charlotte sharply. 'If you've done anything really, say so. You know we'll stand by you,' she added more kindly.

'Well, then,' said Charles, 'I'm very sorry; and I do hope it hasn't spoiled the whole show; but you don't know how fed up I was with being alone, and the Wilmington fussing, and the Uncle never out of his books for more than a minute at a time. And I did it one day when I felt I couldn't bear anything another minute.'

'Did what, dear?' said Caroline, trying to be patient.

'Looked behind the curtain,' said Charles miserably.

'I *knew* you would,' said Charlotte; 'at least I mean I should have known if I'd thought of it. It's exactly like you, and I'll never do any magic with you again.'

'Oh yes,' said Charles, 'rub it in.'

'I expect it *has* spoiled it all,' said Caroline. 'Oh, Charles, how could you?'

'I'm much more sorry than you are,' said Charles wretchedly, 'because the magic had begun. She'd gone out of the frame.'

'Gone!' said the girls together.

'Quite gone. It was all black behind the curtain. She wasn't there.'

'Are you sure?'

'Certain sure.'

Both girls sprang towards the curtain, and both stopped short as Charles hastily grabbed an arm of each.

'Don't!' he said; 'you wait. I've thought about it a lot. I haven't had anything else to do, you know.'

'Poor old Charles!' said Charlotte. 'I'm sorry I scratched, but it is aggravating, now isn't it?'

'Not for you it isn't,' said Charles. 'You haven't looked behind the curtain. You haven't broken *your* part of the magic. It's all right for *you*. You'll see her right enough. It's me that won't. You're all right.'

'But I expect your looking broke the spell and she's back again,' said Caroline, reaching out a hand to the curtain.

'Don't!' shrieked Charles, 'the spell didn't break. It went on. Because I looked again to see if it had. And she wasn't there.'

'How often have you looked?' Caroline asked severely.

'Every day since,' said Charles in a low voice.

'And when did you look first?'

'The day you went to bed,' said Charles in a still lower voice. 'She wasn't there then, and she isn't there now. Oh, don't rag me about it. I shan't see her. That's jolly well enough, *I* should think, without you going on at me.'

'We won't,' said Caroline heroically, and turned her back on the picture. 'But you won't look again, will you, Charles?'

'I shan't want to, now you've come back,' he said. And this compliment quite melted the hearts of his sisters. Nothing more was said of Charles's unjustifiable indiscretion.

The next day the Uncle asked Caroline if she and Charlotte would care to dust the drawing-room.

'Mrs. Wilmington's going to Lord Andore's fête,' he said, 'and she is very busy.'

Mrs. Wilmington gave them the key and they dusted with earnest care and thoroughness. Charles tried to help, but he was not an expert performer with the duster. More to his mind was the watching of the mandarin's old slow nod, his painted smile, his crossed china hands.

'Oh, to think that the Wilmington's going, and the Mineral woman, and Rupert, and everybody but us,' wailed Charlotte.

'Never mind,' said Caroline; 'there's the Flower of Heart's Desire to look forward to, and Rupert coming back. And think of all the grapes Lord Andore sent us, and the chocks from Mr. Alphabet.'

She began to move the old silk handkerchief—Mrs. Wilmington considered the drawing-room too sacred for anything but silk—across the marble of a big console table, when she saw that something lay on it which was not usually there. It was a square thing like a letter, fastened with a sort of plaited ribbon of green and white silk and sealed; and on the end of the ribbon, which hung down about three inches, was another large green seal.

'Look here, Char, how funny!' said Caroline. 'It looks awfully old. Written on vellum or something, and the seal's uncle's coat of arms.'

'Let's take it to uncle,' Charlotte suggested. 'Why, what's up?'

Caroline was holding the letter out to her in a hand that shook.

'Look!' she said, and her voice shook too. 'Look! the thing's *got our names on it*.'

It had. On the square parchment face were the three names written in a strange yet

readable handwriting, in ink that was faded as
with the slow fading of many many years.

To
Caroline,
Charlotte, and
Charles.

'You open it, Caro,' said Charlotte ; and
Charles, who had come across from his favourite
mandarin, said, 'Yes, Caro ; you open it.'

It seemed a pity to break the green seals,
and they were glad that the plaited silk slipped
off easily when the letter was folded a little.
But the second green seal had to be broken.
The parchment, crackling in Caroline's un-
certain hands, was unfolded, and within was
writing—lines in that same strange but clear
hand, that same dim, faded ink.

At eight of the clock, lean on this marble table
and gaze in the mirror and you shall see and speak
with me. But look only in the mirror, uttering no
word, and wear the pink verbena stuck behind your
ears and the roses on your hearts.—Your kinswoman,

ELEANOUR.

'Then I didn't spoil it,' Charles spoke first ;
'not even for myself. Because it's addressed
to me the same as to you.'

'Yes,' said Caroline ; 'you'd better be

between us two, though, Charles, and you *must not* look round.'

'As if I should think of doing such a thing,' said Charles indignantly.

.   .   .   .   .   .

At five minutes to eight that evening the three C.'s stood in front of the console table with pink verbena behind their ears and red roses over their hearts. Mrs. Wilmington had 'done' the vases in the dining-room that very morning, and curiously enough, roses and pink verbena were the flowers she had chosen.

'It must be a strong magic to have made her do *that*,' said Charlotte; 'secrecy and family reunion.'

The room was not dark, of course, at that time in the evening, but then it was not quite light either.

The three C.'s, Charles occupying a guarded position in the middle, stood quite still and waited.

And presently, quite surely and certainly, with no nonsense about it, they saw in the looking-glass the door open that led to the Uncle's secret staircase. And through it, in trailing velvet, came a lady—the lady of the picture. Her ruff, her coif, her darkly flashing jewels, her softly flashing eyes,—the children knew them well. Had they not seen them every day for weeks, framed in the old carved frame in the dining-room.

I am sorry to say that Charles at once tried to look round, but his sisters' arms round his neck restrained him.

The lady glided to a spot from which she could look straight into the mirror and into the children's eyes.

'I am here,' she said, in what Charlotte said afterwards was a starry voice. 'Do not move or speak. I have come to you because you have believed in the old and beautiful things. You sought for my books and found them; also you have tried to use the magic spells to help the poor and needy, and to reconcile them who are at strife. Therefore you see what you desired to see, and when the flowering time is here, you shall have your heart's desire. Do not speak or move lest you break the spell. I will sing to you. And when the last note dies away, close your eyes and count very slowly twenty-seven—the number of the years on earth of your kinswoman Eleanour.'

The beautiful presence moved along the room to the harp, that too was in the field of vision bounded by the tarnished gold of the mirror's frame. She seated herself on a chair of faded needlework and drew the golden harp towards her. Then she sang softly in the starry voice that was hers in speaking. The song was in a language that none of them knew (Charles said afterwards that it was Latin), but it was not like any Latin the girls had ever heard. And the music was starry too. And the meaning of the song seemed to be love and parting and hope and noble dreams and the desire of great and good things; a song that made one very happy and yet made one feel as though one must cry. Softer and softer the voice grew, softer and softer the gentle, resonant tones of the harp. The song ended.

'Now,' said the lady, 'farewell!'

The children closed their eyes, Caroline put her hand over Charles's to 'make sure,' and so moved was he by the singing and the beautiful mystery of the whole adventure, that he hardly wriggled at all. There was a soft rustling sound behind them. Very slowly they all counted from one to twenty-seven. Caroline's hand was clasping Charlotte's, and at the end of the count a long pressure, returned, told each that the other had finished her counting.

They opened their eyes, turned round. The drawing-room was empty. It seemed impossible. Yet it was true.

'It's all over,' said Charles.

'But we've seen Her,' said Caroline.

'We've heard Her,' said Charlotte.

'Yes,' said Charles, 'I intend to be perfectly good every minute, as long as I live. I wish Rupert had been here. He would never have done anything wrong again either, like he did when——'

'It's very wrong,' Charlotte interrupted, 'to remember things other people have done wrong. Come on, let's go back to the dining-room. It's lonely here without Her.'

They went back to the dining-room and sat talking the great mystery over, almost in whispers, till it was time to go to bed.

'And to-morrow we're to go out,' were Charlotte's last words. 'And the F. of H.D. ought to be flowering. It's just seven weeks since we sowed it.'

'Of course it is,' said Caroline; 'don't talk as if you were the only one who remembered it. I say, if you had to say what your heart's desire would be, what would it?'

'To see Her again,' said Charlotte, 'and hear her starry voice.'

Next morning there was a discussion about the curtain the moment the three entered the dining-room. Ought they, or ought they not to remove the curtain. The girls were for leaving it, and putting up fresh garlands every day as long as they stayed in the Manor House.

But Charles, who had faithfully put fresh flowers, not always garlanded, it is true, but always flowers, every day during the measle interval, had had enough of it, and said so.

'And she's had enough of it too,' he said; 'it was to make her come and she came. She won't come again if you go on garlanding for ever.'

The Uncle, for a wonder, breakfasted with them. Charles appealed to him.

'We saw her; she did come, her real self,' he said; 'yesterday. So the charm's worked, and we oughtn't to go on garlanding, ought we?'

'You really saw her?' the Uncle asked. And was told many things.

'Then,' he said, when he had listened to it all, 'I think we might draw back the curtain. The magic has been wrought, and now all should be restored to its old state.'

'I told you so,' said Charles.

'Shall I take down the curtain?' said the Uncle. And the three C.'s said 'Yes!'

He pulled at the green folds, and the curtain and drooping soft flowers of yesterday fell in a mingled heap on the floor. And from the frame, now disclosed, the lady's lips almost smiled on them as her beautiful eyes gazed down on them with a new meaning.

'But she'll never speak to us again,' said Caroline, almost in tears.

'Or sing to us,' said Charlotte, not very steadily.

'Or tell us to count twenty-seven slowly,' said Charles, sniffing a very little.

'But it's something, isn't it,' said the Uncle, 'to have seen her, even if only for once?'

.   .   .   .   .

You will understand that anything Mrs. Wilmington might say was powerless to break the charm of so wonderful an adventure. Hollow tales she told of the portrait's having been borrowed for a show of pictures of celebrities who had lived in the neighbourhood, and of the picture being brought back very late the night before, after the servants had gone to bed; also of a gentleman who told her that Mr. Alphabet sent his love; also of a lady, a great actress from London, who had taken part in the Pageant which was one of the features of Lord Andore's coming-of-age party—'a very nice lady she was, too, dressed up to look the part of the picture, and put down as Dame Eleanour in the programme, which I can show you printed in silver on satin paper.'

'I daresay it's true what the Wilmington

says,' said Caroline when they were alone, 'but it doesn't make any difference. *Our* Lady wasn't dressed up to look the part. She *was* the picture. Perhaps our heart's desire *will* turn out to be seeing her again. Let's go and see if the seed has flowered.'

It had. In that plot of the terraced garden which the old gardener had marked with the pencilled slip-label, seven tall straight stems had shot up, perfect and even in each leaf and stalk, as every plant was which grew in that wonderful soil. And each stem bore one only flower, white and star-shaped, and with a strange sweet scent.

'I wish Rupert were here,' said Charlotte. 'We ought to wait for Rupert.'

And as she spoke, there was Rupert, coming to them through the flowers of the lower garden.

'So they've flowered,' he said, without any other greeting.

'Yes, and now we're going to eat them and get our heart's desire. Oh, Rupert, I do wish you believed in it all.'

'Perhaps I do,' said Rupert. 'The decent way old Macpherson has behaved while I've been there makes you ready to believe in *anything*.'

'Then let's eat them,' said Caroline; 'one

each, and the other three we'll divide as well
as we can.'

Each plucked a white starry blossom. The
stalks snapped off clean and fresh like primrose
stalks. Then the four put each a hand on the
stalk of the fifth flower and broke it between
them. And so with the sixth and the seventh.
Caroline divided the three flowers with extreme
care and accuracy and handed its share to each
child. Then, standing in a ring in the sunny
garden, the four ate the white flowers. The
taste of them was pleasant but strange, something like pineapple and something like flower-
artichokes (which have the most mysterious
taste in the world)—something like spice and
something like the fruit you eat in dreams.

And as they finished eating they heard a
foot on the steps of the terrace and turned,
and it was the Uncle, coming towards them
with pale-coloured papers in one hand and a
bunch of waxy white flowers in the other.

Fond as all were of Uncle Charles, no one
could feel that the moment was fortunately
chosen, and I am sorry to say that Charles
voiced to some extent the general feeling
when he said almost audibly, 'Oh, bother!'

The Uncle came towards them smiling
kindly.

'I have come,' he said, 'to make a presentation to you.' He gave to each a white flower. 'I have again consulted that entrancing volume of yours, *The Language of Flowers*, and it tells me that this is the appropriate flower to convey the sentiments with which I approach you.'

Every one said, 'Thank you very much.' And Caroline added, ' But what does it mean, Uncle?'

'What? Has your book taught you so little?' he asked.

'You see,' Caroline kindly explained, ' I don't even know what the name of the flower is, but it's most awfully kind of you, uncle, all the same.'

'Oh, the name of the flower?' said the Uncle. 'It's stephanotis.'

'But that means, "Will you accompany me to the East?"' said Caroline.

'Well,' said the Uncle, 'and will you?'

'To the East?'

'Yes,' said the Uncle; 'let us sit down on the steps and talk over the idea.'

They sat down and the Uncle explained.

'Your finding those books,' he said, 'has so completely revolutionised my ideas of magic that I cannot complete my book. I must throw it into the melting-pot, rewrite it entirely. And to do that I need more know-ledge than I have. And I intend to travel, to examine the magic of other lands. The first country I shall visit is India, and it occurred to me that you might like to go with me and visit your parents. I have been corresponding with them by cable,' he added, waving the pale-coloured papers, 'and your parents are delighted with the idea of the family reunion (pink verbena). We start, if the idea smiles to you, next week.'

'Oh, uncle!' was all that any one could find to say, till Charlotte added, 'But what about Rupert?'

'Rupert is to go too,' said the Uncle, 'as far as Suez, where his father will meet him.'

'Is father coming home, then?' Rupert asked breathlessly.

'For a year's leave,' said the Uncle. 'But you haven't any of you answered the stephanotis question yet, Will you accompany me to the East?'

Caroline ran to a flower-bed and came back with some leaves and flowers which she thrust into the Uncle's hand.

'Small white bell - flower, wood sorrel, aquilegia,' she said; 'they mean perfect joy; we love you beyond measure; and Yes. Yes! Yes!'

.   .   .   .   .   .

As they turned to go to the house they saw

the seven stems on which the white starry flowers had grown, and suddenly and surely each child saw that the Uncle, when he brought them the bunch of pale papers in one hand and the bunch of stephanotis in the other, was really bringing to each child its Heart's Desire.

THE END

Printed in Great Britain by
NEILL & CO. LTD., EDINBURGH